Making It Real
Henderson Family Book 3

SYNITHIA WILLIAMS

I0638225

ACKNOWLEDGEMENTS

There were several people who helped me fine-tune Kareem Henderson's *Happily Ever After*. Thanks to my fantastic beta readers, Liv and Tia, for your helpful comments and insights as I worked on this draft. Thanks to the guys I harassed about life in a barbershop and the backstories of their female barbers. Of course, I have to thank my awesome editor, Jess Verdi! Yet again your comments helped me dig deeper and fine-tune the story. Thank you to my nephew, Jayden, for coming up with the name of Kareem's barbershop. You rock, little man! For the readers who begged me for Kareem's story, I hope you fall in love with him and Neecie. And finally, yet again, thank you to my own personal hero, my hubby, for all your continued love and support.

CHAPTER 1

Kareem Henderson shifted in the hard as concrete chair in a useless attempt to find a more comfortable position. Clenching his teeth, he fought the scowl struggling to take over his face. His steady gaze remained trained on the red, sweaty face of the bank manager—Mr. Tim Small, based on the gold nameplate on the shiny desk—sitting across from him in the fancy office of First Legions bank. Mr. Small's watery eyes shifted to Kareem every five seconds. If Kareem didn't need his loan approved, he would have yelled "Boo" just to see the man jump. He had no intention of robbing the place, but the manger's overactive sweat glands said Mr. Small wasn't so sure.

"Can you help me?" Kareem asked, his voice sharp with annoyance. The name fitted the guy. The longer Kareem stared, the more Mr. Small seemed to shrivel up into his seat.

Kareem got the man's hesitation. As a tall guy dressed in all black with dreads, Kareem didn't give off the warm and fuzzy vibe, but he'd tried extra hard to be pleasant, and his business plan was on point.

Mr. Small wiped a shaky hand across his brow, plastering a few thin brown hairs to his forehead. "You have a very ... interesting plan. I can tell you worked hard on drafting your proposal and researching similar businesses."

"I worked with Business Connections to put everything together."

The first real smile popped up on Mr. Small's face. "Ah, yes, Sandra Brevard is the director over there. She's a great person.

First Legions partners with her organization on many of our philanthropic activities."

Kareem considered dropping the fact that Sandra, his future sister-in-law, had sent him. Revealing his family connection would clear up the suspicion on Mr. Small's face better than Proactiv on an acne-prone teen. But Kareem had lost the privilege of using his family name to open doors for him over a decade ago.

"She is a great lady," he said.

Mr. Small nodded. "Though I would love to approve a loan for your ... salon..."

"I'm calling it a gentlemen's lounge."

Mr. Small's eyebrows rose, and he gave Kareem a weak smile. "Right. Still, Mr. Henderson, your idea is risky. I couldn't, with a clear conscience, approve the loan."

"I have most of what I need already saved." Kareem's voice became as hard as the damn chair he sat in.

Sweat sprouted across Mr. Small's brow. "Right. You do, and that is good for you, but still. I think it would be best if you ... saved a little more."

Kareem gripped the arms of the chair. His nostrils flared, and he tried not to breathe like an angry bull. He could save the rest of the money in a year or two, but a loan would get him to his dream sooner.

"Is there anyone else I can talk to?" he bit out.

"I'm afraid not. I am the branch manager, you see." Mr. Small's voice wavered.

Kareem pried his fingers from around the arms of the chair. "Thank you for your time." He jumped out of his chair.

Mr. Small pushed back from the desk so fast his chair nearly rolled into the wall. If Kareem's body weren't so tight, he might find the entire situation funny. The entire meeting had been doomed from the moment he shook Mr. Small's limp hand.

Mr. Small jumped from his chair and held his hand toward the door. "You do understand my position?"

He understood the man was eager for him to leave. "I understand the argument you're trying to make. I can't say that I agree with you."

Kareem leaned over to pick up the folder with his business plan, the folder Mr. Small had cracked open for all of two minutes. The manager jumped, and the corner of Kareem's mouth quirked.

Kareem lifted his chin and straightened. "Have a nice day." He turned and walked out of the office.

His body pulsed with the need to lash out. He sucked in a breath and twisted his head from side to side. Getting angry and acting on that anger had screwed up his life back when he was twenty-two and considered himself invincible. Five years in prison for carjacking proved otherwise. There were other outlets he could take for this anger, but none as satisfying as shaking some sense into the branch manager.

Kareem made his way across the thin, blue carpet in the bank lobby. An old lady took one look at him and shuffled out of the way. It reminded him of his gang days. Back then he enjoyed people getting out of his way. Now the unnecessary fear annoyed him. He needed this loan, needed to reinvent himself. He smiled at the old lady and tipped his head.

The door to the bank opened. Once glance at Sandra Brevard striding in and Kareem's feet stuck to the floor. He'd never looked up the word classy in the dictionary but was pretty damn sure all he'd find was a reference to Sandra. Sexy sophistication in a tall, curvy package. Just the type of woman he wanted but wouldn't know what to do with if he were lucky enough to land her. Sandra belonged to his brother, David, something he'd had a hard time coming to terms with a few months back. His feelings had dimmed, but he couldn't shake his admiration for the way she'd helped with his business plan or pretend she wasn't attractive.

Sandra spotted him, and a smile spread across her beautiful features. Some of the tension in Kareem's neck eased.

Sandra crossed the room to him looking like perfection in a fitted cream suit. "Kareem, what are you doing here?" Her husky voice filled with hope.

"I came to talk to Mr. Small about a business loan."

Sandra's eyes glanced toward Mr. Small's office. "How did it go?"

Kareem shrugged. "It didn't go at all. He denied me."

Sandra's arched brows drew together. "I don't understand. Your business plan is perfect, and you have most of your capital already saved."

"Apparently I'm too risky."

Sandra scoffed. "That's crazy. Just because your idea is different doesn't make you too risky."

The corner of Kareem's mouth lifted. Sandra hadn't laughed at his idea to open a high-end gentlemen's salon when he brought it to her. Instead, she used the resources of her organization, which helped small businesses make connections and grow, to solidify his plan. Not many people supported him the way she had. That was something he could only blame himself for, but still, having someone on his side was nice.

"Don't worry," Kareem said. "I'll try someplace else."

"I'm sorry, Kareem. I wouldn't have sent you over here if I didn't think they'd approve your loan."

"It isn't your fault. You've helped me enough already."

Footsteps preceded Mr. Small's appearance. "Ms. Brevard, how nice it is to see you this morning." The guy was all smiles and sweat-free when he took Sandra's hand.

"Hello, Mr. Small," she said then pulled her hand away. "I was just talking to Kareem, and he mentioned things didn't go so well today."

Mr. Small's beady eyes darted Kareem's way. "Why yes, unfortunately, he's too much of a risk."

"Kareem or Kareem's idea?" Sandra asked in a no-nonsense voice.

Mr. Small cleared his throat. "His idea, of course."

Sandra turned back to Kareem. "Talk with David; maybe he can give you an idea of where to go next."

Kareem's shoulders tightened at the mention of his brother. "I'll think about it."

Her frown slowly softened into a look of concern. "He's your brother, Kareem. I know he wants to help make your idea a reality." Her voice filled with adoration when she talked about David. Jealousy struck his chest. Jealousy was a bitch that way, a slit your tires and key your car kind of bitch when Kareem compared his life to the perfect model of David's. Never would he have expected that one day he'd envy his baby brother.

Mr. Small perked up. "David Henderson?" He looked at Kareem. "David Henderson is your brother?"

"Yes," Kareem said.

"And Roger Henderson, of Henderson Automotive..."

"My father," Kareem said, his voice going ice cold.

"Well." A grin spread across Mr. Small's pudgy face. "Knowing that, we might be able to work something out."

Kareem's grip on his business plan tightened. "No thank you, Mr. Small. I wouldn't want you to *take a risk* just because I'm a Henderson. I'll find another way."

Sandra placed a hand on his arm. "Call David, okay?"

Kareem pulled away from her touch. "I'll handle this myself. Rehearsal dinner tonight, right?" He knew damn well his baby sister's rehearsal dinner was that night. Just needed to change the subject.

Sandra sighed and nodded. "I'll see you at seven."

"Seven it is." He stalked away and burst out the door to the bright sunshine of a fall afternoon.

He sucked in cool, crisp air, but his stomach heaved. He didn't deserve his family's help, after his screwed up past, the pain he caused, and the way he once lusted for Sandra. Yeah, he'd be in the running for asshole of the century if he went to David for help.

• • •

Kareem pulled his red and black Honda CVR 1000 motorcycle into one of the pothole free parking spaces in the strip mall where his barbershop was located. After the disappointing bank scene, he'd gone home, hopped on his bike, and zoomed around town to get rid of his frustration. The ride hadn't worked. Hours later, tight shoulders, a clenched stomach, and a headache still lingered.

He slid off the bike and stared at the fourth unit in the strip mall, the words *Fresh Cutz* painted in black across the window. A sense of pride washed over him. He'd opened the place against all odds. His sole purpose after five years in prison was to open up his own shop. Thanks to a $50,000 winning lottery ticket two days after he got out, Kareem had his own place in the world.

Hitching his book bag further up on his back, Kareem crossed the parking lot toward his shop, the sky darkening in the late afternoon. No one had booked an appointment with him today. Better for them anyway; the mood hovering around him would not have played nice with cutting hair.

Two teenage boys who normally got their hair cut in his shop stood near the door trying to holla at a young girl Kareem didn't recognize. Not unusual—trying to get in a female's pants was pretty much the priority of teenage boys.

"Come on, girl," one of the boys, dressed in tight red skinny jeans and a black and gold t-shirt, said. "You know you want us."

The girl flipped long braids over her shoulder. "No, I don't. Now move." She pushed the boy out of the way.

The other boy, in grey sweatpants that tapered at the ankle and a white t-shirt, grabbed her arm.

"Quit playin," the boy said with a sly grin. "We saw you checking us out. Just take a ride."

She jerked her arm away. "I said no." Her voice wobbled. She tried passing, and again they blocked her way.

Kareem's hand tightened on the strap of his book bag. Scowling, he marched over to the trio. "What's going on over here?"

The girl jumped and stared at him warily. The boys only shrugged and grinned.

"Nothing, Kareem," red pants said. "We just talking."

"Looks to me she wants to be left alone." Kareem walked over and stared at the girl. "Am I right?"

"Yes," she said, crossing her arms tightly over her chest.

"Where are you going?" Kareem asked.

She pointed toward the parking lot. "My car's over there."

"Go to it," he said in a hard voice. She scurried around the two boys to an older model green Toyota Camry.

"Come on, Kareem, why you had to scare her off like that?" grey sweats asked.

Kareem glared at both boys. Anger boiled in his stomach. "When a woman says no, leave her the hell alone."

Red pants swallowed hard, then tried to blow out his chest. "We were just playing."

Kareem pointed to the departing Camry. "The look on her face said she wasn't having fun. If the only way you two can get some ass is by dragging an unwilling female to your car then you're sorrier than I thought. Get the hell away from my shop."

Grey sweats ran a hand over the thick curls on his head. "We're already running late and haven't gotten our haircuts yet."

"Yeah, and we got a party tonight. C'mon, man," red pants said. "We weren't going to hurt the girl."

"I don't give a damn if you're entertaining the president. No haircut in my shop tonight. Get the hell on, and don't come back until you learn some respect. Maybe next time you'll understand no means no."

He turned his back on the two boys. His frustration from earlier was now up another notch thanks to two idiotic teens.

He swung open the door to Fresh Cutz. Warm air, the smell of oil sheen, and the sounds of hip hop music greeted him. He clenched his teeth and gazed across the room.

Two of his male barbers were at their station. Lee, a tall, dark-skinned guy with a sharp fade, swept hair around his station while Al, a short stocky guy with a tapered fro, sat in his barber chair. Kareem's gaze swept to the station to the right of the door and his only female barber. Neecie Baldwin gave him one of her sweet smiles. Her hands worked furiously while she re-twisted the roots of her client's dreads.

"Thank you for stopping those boys," she said, gold bangles clanging at her wrist.

He didn't answer. His eyes did a quick scan of her body, something he couldn't stop where Neecie was concerned—short, cute, and thick. Her fitted black shirt clung to large, full tits, and a long, flowing, flowered skirt hinted at hips and an ass made for grabbing.

Heat spread through his balls. If Neecie weren't so damn sweet, he'd think she purposefully came to work dressed to drive him crazy, which in turn made him want to do really naughty things and turn her clean smile dirty.

He jerked his gaze away from Neecie to glare at Lee and Al. "Who changed my music?"

Al cringed and shrugged his shoulders. "My bad, Kareem. We thought you weren't coming back."

"That doesn't mean you can turn this place into a club." Kareem strode to the back of the shop and flipped the satellite radio from the hip hop station to reggae.

Once the mellow beats of Mighty Diamonds filled his place, he stomped back out to the main shop. "Where are Joe and Rico?" He pointed to the two empty chairs next to Al and Lee.

"They both left a few minutes ago," Lee said, leaning on the top of the broomstick. He looked at his big, gold watch. "You mentioned closing up early tonight because of your family thing, so they left. We were only hanging out until Neecie finished."

Neecie's bangles clinked together as she placed a hand on her hip. "Please," she said, exasperation heavy in her voice. "I'm okay to stay here by myself. I told you both you can go."

Kareem spun to face her. "We're not leaving you here alone."

"But—"

"No buts." Kareem took off his book bag and tossed it into the chair at his station. "Al, Lee, you can leave if you want. I'll stay here with Neecie."

"I'll be done in twenty minutes," Neecie said.

"You're good. The world won't end if I'm late to Janiyah's rehearsal dinner." He'd stop and buy a bouquet of flowers for Janiyah if he was late, however. He didn't want to upset her on her wedding weekend. Kareem glanced at Al and Lee. "Take off, fellas. I'm good."

"Cool," Lee said. "I've got a lady waiting on me now."

Some of Kareem's frustration went away at the guys' willingness to wait for Neecie. The woman swore she could take care of herself. He didn't doubt her, but that didn't mean he would leave her in the shop alone with night approaching.

He locked the door after Al and Lee, then grabbed his book bag out of his chair and left Neecie to her client.

He pushed aside the burgundy curtain that separated the main area from the back of the shop. Shelves that held product, towels, and supplies filled the space, along with a fridge in the left corner. He went through another door to his office—small and crowded by a large oak desk, but all his. A place he could escape to when he got tired of the conversations in the shop or kick other people out of when he didn't want to be bothered.

He'd get a bigger one. He glanced at the yellow walls. In a better place and a bigger city. He needed to follow Sandra's recommendation to open his place in Charlotte, North Carolina. The city had two major league teams and plenty of professionals from the banking community who would be willing to try a high-end barber shop. He had no connections there, but maybe the banks would consider his idea less of a risk.

Eventually all his dreams would become a reality—a sophisticated place, where men could come and relax and get taken care of, not the rented space he had in a strip mall, with sketchy heat in the winter and barely there air conditioning in the summer. A place to help him shed the mistakes of the past and the filth that clung from the gang ties he once coveted. No matter how *risky* Mr. Small of First Legions bank thought the idea, Kareem would realize his vision.

Neecie knocked on the door and stuck her head in his office exactly twenty minutes later. Kareem glanced up from reviewing his business plan—again. The plan was tight, but still he searched for what could be revised to make it appear less *risky* for the next bank manager.

"I'm done with my client." Neecie stepped further into the office. She didn't make eye contact. Instead her gaze darted between the wall and his desk.

Yeah, she hadn't made eye contact with him in his office since catching him in there with his ex-girl bent over the desk.

That night Neecie's dark eyes had grown wide with shock after she'd burst in, but she'd stayed a second longer than necessary before spinning on her heels and hauling ass.

"Did you lock the door behind him?" Kareem asked.

"Not yet. I'm going to clean up my area then go."

Kareem frowned and slowly stood. Locking the door at night was the first thing he stressed when she'd started working for him. He didn't need some strange guy, high on desire after seeing Neecie and her perfect tits through the glass, coming in and harassing her.

"Lock the door."

"I am, but first can you change the music for me?" Her gaze met his, and she quickly looked away again.

The shy routine only heated his blood. Neecie liked what she'd seen that night, and damn if he didn't want to give it to her. But she wasn't that type of girl—not like his ex who loved sex the only way Kareem knew how to give it.

Kareem came around his desk. "Why would I change my music?"

Neecie instantly stepped back and out of his office. The way she scurried to avoid being alone with him in that place was almost funny. Her embarrassment also turned him on, making him wonder what bending her over his desk would be like as he followed her out.

"I found this hot new artist over the weekend on satellite radio," Neecie said in a light, smooth voice, with just enough of an edge to scrape along the desire he tried to ignore.

Neecie waved her cell phone, a smile—more relaxed now that they were out of his office—on her face. "Of course I downloaded his album. Maybe we can listen to it." One of her feet twisted back and forth. "Since none of the guys are here and won't give you a hard time."

He narrowed his eyes on her, but her smile only turned into a mischievous grin. His annoyance from earlier slowly melted away. Indulging Neecie's taste in music when they were the only two in the shop was their secret. Otherwise, he controlled the music.

"What is it this time?" Kareem strolled over to the radio and speaker system. "Some dude wailing about being in love, or another pop album that's going to make me want to rip out my dreads?"

"Love is a beautiful thing, Kareem," she said, completely ignoring the sarcasm in his voice. She scrolled across the screen of her smartphone. "And this guy ... you can tell he's been in love before. It's in the way he says the words. It's like poetry. If only I could meet a man who put words together like that."

The corner of Kareem's lip twitched. "You're hanging out in the wrong place, honey. The men that come through here don't know a thing about poetry. Except the vulgar kind."

"Maybe so," she said, handing over her phone. "But one day I hope to fall in love. Get married. All that stuff."

"You seem the type. Ready to be the perfect housewife."

"Hold up." Neecie placed a hand on her hip. "I never said I wanted to be a housewife. I just said I want to get married one day. I'm not trying to submit to some guy and sit around waiting for him to hand out an allowance."

Kareem raised a brow. The housewife jab had worked to bring out her spark. Seeing the spitfire beneath the sweetness always made him want to fire her up.

"Submitting to a guy isn't always bad. In the right circumstances." His gaze traveled across her thick curves before returning to her eyes.

Neecie inhaled quickly and broke eye contact. "Love is a partnership. Mutual trust, mutual love, mutual understanding. Give and take. That's all I'm saying."

Kareem let her avoid his meaning. Neecie was too good to get what he wanted to give.

Glancing down at the screen of the cell phone he cringed at the picture of the album she'd downloaded. The guy on the cover looked like the kind of lame dude she'd fall for—tall, lanky, wearing too tight pants, a fedora, and glasses with a guitar in his hands. Kareem read the title, *Love Poems*, and snorted.

Neecie laughed and playfully pushed his shoulder. "Stop, and hurry up while I clean up."

"You know this guy is just like every other guy." Kareem used the AC adaptor cord coming from the speakers to plug into her phone. "All this love crap he's spitting is just a front to get in a woman's pants."

"All men aren't like that."

He switched the stereo to the AUX mode. "Yes, they are. All men are thinking about what angle to work so they can hit."

She waved her hand, bringing over a whiff of some new fruity body spray he wasn't familiar with. Every week she came in smelling like some new, tempting thing—another weapon to add to the smile and too many curves that distracted all the men in his shop.

"Whatever, Kareem, just play the damn music." She pushed past the curtain to go back to the main part of the shop.

The corner of his mouth lifted. Neecie was so sweet and sentimental, even her curses were cute. "You just lock the damn door."

"Music, Kareem," Neecie yelled back.

He shook his head and hit play on the phone. Not many people ordered him around. He would have put her in her place long ago—if she weren't so damn cute.

The sappy sounds of a guy in love filled the air. Kareem groaned. *Back to the office where I don't have to listen to this crap.* Plus, he didn't need to watch Neecie swaying her hips back and forth to the music. Not in his frustrated state.

Back in the office, he picked up his business plan then tossed the papers back on the desk. Tension swept through his body, and he glared at the paperwork. Kareem wasn't stupid. He knew what Mr. Small meaning of the word risky really meant—a former thug trying to cater to a high-end clientele. The guy probably had a good laugh with the rest of the bank employees after Kareem left.

To hell with all of them. Today was a setback, but he'd be damned if his story ended here.

The next song came through his open office door. One completely dedicated to holding a woman's hand. Kareem groaned. There wasn't a single man Kareem knew only interested in holding a woman's hand. Not when there were soft hips, thick thighs, and full breasts to enjoy. A picture of Neecie in her fitted black shirt and flowing skirt filled his brain. He closed his eyes and shook his head. Normally, he wouldn't hesitate to get with a woman he desired, but Neecie was the type who wanted cuddling, hand holding, and eventually love. All things that made Kareem uncomfortable. His previous relationships—if he dared called them that—had been with gang ladies before prison and women only interested in a few wild nights in bed after.

The thought didn't eliminate the vision of Neecie's shy gazes or his fantasy of bending her over the desk. Kareem spun on his heels and marched out of his office.

"That's the last song, Neecie. I can't take any more of this nonsense."

Voices from the other side of the curtain stopped him in his tracks. Angry voices. Damn, this is why he told her to lock the door. Frowning, he jerked one side of the curtain back. Neecie and a guy Kareem had never seen before were so busy glaring at each other they didn't notice Kareem.

Kareem's head tilted to the side. He hadn't seen this man before. The last guy sniffing around Neecie was some idiot who resembled the singer on the album she'd bought—soft, skinny, and sentimental. This guy, average height, clean cut, with a suit so sharp he could slice a tomato, did not appear to be Neecie's type.

Instantly, Kareem disliked him. Neecie was a nice chick, and this guy looked like he would run game all over her romantic heart.

"You need to leave, Chad." Neecie pushed the guy in the chest.

Kareem smiled. The spitfire was out. She tried to push pass him, but the guy grabbed Neecie's arm.

Blood rushed in Kareem's ears. His heart revved up, and he saw red. He stomped from behind the curtain, pushed Neecie behind him, and got in the guy's face.

"You can't keep your hands to yourself?" Kareem's pulse pounded. He wanted the pretty boy to make the wrong move. He'd happily put a dent in the punk's face for grabbing Neecie.

"How about you mind your business," the guy said with a sneer mastered by those used to looking down on people. "This has nothing to do with you."

Kareem took a step forward and cracked his knuckles. "When you're manhandling my people, it has everything to do with me."

The guy scoffed then glared around Kareem at Neecie. "Really, Patrice, you're hanging out with thugs now. I expected better of you."

Kareem balled his hands into fists. *Who the hell is Patrice?* "I've got your thug, pretty boy."

Neecie rushed between them. Her small hands had little effect as she tried to push him back. The girl was five foot one, if that.

"Kareem, stop, I've got this," she said.

"This asshole put his hands on you." He didn't look away from the smug smirk on the other guy's face.

"Listen here, young man, why don't you go back inside and worry about cutting hair instead of me and Patrice." He waved a hand toward the back of the shop, his voice bored.

Neecie spun and put her hands on her hips. "That's enough, Chad. You have no right showing up here."

Chad narrowed his eyes. "I have every right. You're coming home next weekend, or else I'm dragging you there."

Neecie crossed her arms. "I'm not going anywhere."

Kareem took a step closer to Neecie and placed his hand on her shoulder. She jumped, then stiffened beneath his touch. Not surprising—he wasn't one to initiate personal contact. But he felt the need to back her up.

"Doesn't sound like she wants to go anywhere with you, pretty boy. So get the hell out of my shop."

Chad glared at Neecie. "Patrice, the time for playing games is over. You went away, had your little fun," he flicked a nasty scowl Kareem's way, "but it's time to grow up. Look at you, you deserve better than this. Come home. Roland still asks about you."

Neecie ... Patrice held up a hand. "Shut up, Chad!"

Kareem's grip on Patrice's shoulder tightened. "Who the hell are you anyway?" Kareem asked.

The guy lifted his chin, looked at Kareem's hand on Neecie's shoulder, and sneered. "I'm her brother, which means I have more of a right to this conversation than you do. So, again, *partner*, why don't you go back into your little office and leave this to me and my sister."

Sister! Neecie didn't look like she belonged in the same room with this jackass, much less the same family. He loosened his grip on her shoulder. If this guy really was her brother, then Kareem should step away. The idea caused his stomach to tighten.

"Is he really your brother, Neecie?" he asked.

Chad scoffed and shook his head. "*Neecie?*" He said her name as if it were funny. "Really, Patrice?"

She stiffened beneath Kareem's touch and moved back. The back of her brushed against the front of him, and damn if his mind didn't take note of the softness of her ass in that brief second.

"Yes," she said. "Kareem, meet my brother, Chad Baldwin."

Chad raised a brow and tugged on the front of his suit like he'd won a victory. Kareem wanted to knock the smug look off his face, but he knew when to step out of other people's family crap. He lifted his hand, but Neecie's snapped up to grip his wrist. She took a step back, pressing her soft, warm curves against him.

"Chad, meet, Kareem, my f ... fiancé."

Kareem's fingers dug into her shoulder. *Fiancé!* There were a lot of things he wanted to do to Neecie, but marriage wasn't on the list. To throw that out meant she was desperate. His need to back her up intensified.

Neecie sucked in a breath. "And ... if I'm coming home for Mother and Father's anniversary party ... he'll be there with me." She turned her head and looked at him with soft, pleading, brown eyes. "Won't you, baby?"

CHAPTER 2

Kareem's strong fingers were ironclad on Patrice's shoulder, and she fought not to flinch. Telling Chad that Kareem was her fiancé wasn't the best plan, but the idea was the only thing she could think of—the only thing that would get her obtrusive older brother off her back. She turned to look up into Kareem's eyes. They were dark brown, almost black. Flat, hard, rarely alive with humor, but when they were her heart trembled.

Covering his tense hand with hers, Patrice gently squeezed. *Please, please, please go along with this.* He couldn't hear her thoughts, but hopefully he'd read the desperation in her eyes. His grip on her shoulder immediately loosened, but remained firm.

Her heart pounded as she waited for him to prove her a fool in front of her brother.

Chad's disbelieving laughter broke the moment. "Fiancé? You expect me to believe that."

Kareem's hard gaze zeroed in on her brother. "You have a problem with that?" Patrice relaxed, and gratitude swept through her.

"If it were true, yes, I'd have a problem with it." Chad crossed his arms in an oh so superior fashion. "But I know you're lying. The investigator never mentioned a fiancé."

Patrice's eyes widened. "Investigator. You had someone following me?"

"What do you expect when you run off? We've kept up with you for years."

"There was no need. I kept in contact with Beth." And Patrice almost always asked her younger sister to keep her infrequent calls a secret. "Thanks for reminding me why I left."

Kareem pulled her to his side. "It doesn't matter what your investigator said. The two of us are together."

Chad's lips pinched together. "Then where's the ring?"

"I asked last night," Kareem said. "Spur of the moment."

Chad scoffed. "Convenient excuse." He looked to Patrice. "This isn't necessary. Just leave your ... friend out of this, and let's have dinner and talk. Patrice, we miss you. *I* miss you. Come home."

Tightness wrapped around Patrice's heart, and she lowered her eyes. She missed him too. Her overprotective, arrogant snob of a brother who always did whatever he could to look out for her but never really saw her. A part of her would always miss her family, but ordering her home, the investigator, only proved nothing had changed. She ran a hand across the wide hips she'd spent years hurting herself to make smaller.

Kareem looked from her to her brother. "Why are you so hard up for her to come home?"

Patrice knew the answer to that question. "It's our parents' thirtieth anniversary," she said.

Chad nodded. "They're having a celebration and want the entire family to attend." Chad's anger melted away and concern filled his brown eyes. "Patrice, we are your family, and we love you. Let's sit down tonight over dinner and talk. You can't honestly say you don't want to see us again."

No, she couldn't, but she wasn't ready to go home—wasn't ready to see if five years of trying to deprogram the Baldwin Family wiring in her brain had actually worked.

"I have plans tonight," she said. "Kareem and I have plans."

Chad crossed his arms and raised a brow. "What plans?"

Kareem wrapped a muscled arm around Patrice's shoulders. "My sister's rehearsal dinner. She's getting married tomorrow."

Patrice bit her lower lip. She'd forgotten his sister's wedding was this weekend. He didn't talk much about his family, but she overheard enough to know he was the son of Roger Henderson, who owned several very successful automotive dealerships. His sister's wedding would be a big event with everyone who was anyone in the area attending.

"Then tomorrow," Chad said. "We can have breakfast or lunch."

She shook her head. "The wedding. I'll be there all day." Kareem's arm around her stiffened. Her insides quivered. Using his family event as an excuse to escape her family was kind of shady.

"Sunday, and that's it. I have to be back in Charlotte on Monday. You are not going to ignore us anymore, Patrice," Chad said in a voice so much like their father's that both homesickness and anger placed a heaviness in Patrice's chest. "I'll be at your home at noon to pick you up."

Patrice stepped forward. Kareem's arm fell from her shoulders and she missed his strength. "Chad—"

"No arguments, Patrice," Chad snapped. Then the tension left his shoulders and for a second concern filled his eyes. "Just talk to me. You owe everyone that much."

She wrestled back the guilt his words tried to stir up. When she'd left she didn't think she owed the family anything. Going away preserved her sanity along with her health. She opened her mouth to deny him. Chad watched her, his eyes wide with hope. The argument died on her lips.

"Fine. Lunch on Sunday."

Chad nodded, his hope quickly morphing to a self-satisfied look before his eyes flicked to Kareem. "I'll see you *alone* on Sunday."

She lifted and lowered her chin. Chad took a deep breath and swiftly turned and strode out the door. His black Maserati was parked along the curb in front of the shop.

After he drove off, Kareem cleared his throat behind her. Her stomach buzzed like a pair of hair clippers.

She turned to face him. "Thank you for not ratting me out."

The frown on his face should scare her. Instead his dark, flat eyes increased the buzzing in her midsection. Not with fear. Kareem was a beacon to the female sex drive. One hundred percent of handsome sex appeal flavored with danger—absolutely nothing like the guys who she was normally attracted to. She shouldn't want him. If only her body would listen to her brain.

"In my office, now," he said. He smoothly spun away from her and marched to the curtain separating the front from the back.

The sounds of the love poem album played softly in the background—the only song on the album dedicated to making love. Her mind jumped back to catching him in his office with his ex. She closed her eyes and sighed. *That* was not making love. *That* was pure sex. Raw, hot, unfiltered sex. Warmth started at the pulse between her thighs.

Dammit, brain, I want love, not sex.

Opening her eyes she took another deep breath then followed him to the back of the shop. Kareem waited at the door of his office. She hesitated, and he placed a hand on the small of her back and nudged her forward. Heavy footfalls came behind her, and the door closed with a solid thud. She sucked in a breath and twisted her foot back and forth. She looked everywhere but the desk. Kareem slid past her; the smell of the shea butter oil he used on his dreadlocks and Irish Spring soap sent a thrill across her skin. She sucked her lower lip between her teeth.

We're just in here to talk.

She finally made contact with his dark gaze, and her teeth dug into her lip. The corner of his mouth quirked up, and a hint of amusement filled his eyes. He knew she was thinking about that embarrassing moment and found her discomfort funny.

Heat flashed up her cheeks; still, she lifted her chin. "Thanks again for backing up my lie." Several more seconds passed with his gaze drilling into her. She crossed her arms over her chest. "Well, are you going to curse me out or something?" she said, irritated.

He hooked his thumbs into the back of his black slacks and leaned back on his heels. "You want to tell me what's going on, *Patrice*?"

Patrice cringed. "You can call me Neecie." He frowned, clearly not satisfied. "It's a nickname. I never technically lied about my name."

"Pat is short for Patrice."

"My baby sister couldn't say Patrice when she was a toddler. She tried for Treecie, I think, but it always sounded like Neecie to me."

Kareem shook his head and cut his hand through the air. "Fine. Why did your brother burst into my shop tonight?"

"Isn't it obvious? I left my family five years ago and haven't talked to them since."

"Why don't you want to go back?"

Oh, she had many reasons. The pressure to be the perfect daughter in one of North Carolina's most distinguished political families. Her crazy way to stay thin by eating then purging. A fiancé at the time who loved her but ignored the bulimia. Yeah, she wasn't ready to face that, nor was she ready to admit everything to Kareem or see the disgust on his face when she admitted her old weaknesses.

"I'm not like my family. I don't want what they want for me." She met his eyes. "You can understand that."

"I feel that." He took a deep breath. "So I'm your fiancé. What kind of trouble is that going to bring?"

She relaxed her arms until they crossed in front of her midsection. At least he wasn't glaring anymore. "Nothing really."

Kareem scoffed and pushed aside a folder on his desk before sitting on the edge. Patrice stared at the folder then raised her eyebrows, an idea striking. "Maybe this could work for both of us."

"How?" This time he crossed his arms, drawing her attention to biceps bulging beneath his black shirt.

She dragged her gaze away from his arms. "If, and that's a big if, I go home next weekend you can come with me."

"Why?"

"Because I know one of the reasons they want me back is to shove some suitable guy under my nose and try to convince me to stay." More like shove her ex fiancé beneath her nose, based on Chad's reference to Roland. "If you're there, they won't do that."

"How does that help me?"

She glanced at the folder on his desk. "I have connections in Charlotte. You need connections there. I'd introduce you."

He stood and stepped into her personal space so quickly she barely had time to blink. "How do you know about my plans?"

The steel in his voice sent a shiver down her spine and tightened her nipples. "You left the folder open at your station last night." She pointed to the folder. "I took a look."

Kareem narrowed his eyes. "Snooping."

"It's not snooping when it's wide open." She tried to sound sure, but the guilt crept in anyway. "Just do me this favor, and I'll help you."

"What connections could you possibly have?"

She snorted. If only he knew. "Believe me, I do. And if you go, I'll help you."

He stared at her for a several seconds. "Whatever, Neecie." He stepped back and went around his desk.

She let out a breath, both happy and remiss without him so close. "We can talk about it tonight after the rehearsal dinner."

Kareem's brows clashed over black eyes, his lips pressed together, and tension radiated from his body. "What?"

The image of prodding an angry bull came to mind. "Do you honestly think my brother is going to take what we said at face value? He's going to follow me this weekend just to prove we're not together."

"So now I've got to take you to the dinner and the wedding tomorrow?"

"Were you taking someone else?" She thought of his ex. Patrice hadn't seen her since that evening in his office about two months ago, but that didn't mean Kareem wasn't seeing the woman again.

His head jerked back. "No, I'm not taking a date."

Patrice rushed forward and leaned her hands on his desk. "Then take me and tell them I'm just a friend."

He actually gave part of a smile with that. It twitched the scar above his lip and made her yearn to see a real smile on his face.

"My family won't see you coming with me as a just a friend thing. I'll have to tell them we're dating, which means they're going to be all in my business. And, Neecie..." He placed his hands on his desk and leaned forward, bringing his face within inches of hers. "I don't like my family in my business."

She forced herself to stand her ground. "Hello! I ran away from my family five years ago and came up with a fake fiancé just to keep them out of my business." She stood straight. "I understand, and I promise you, if you do this for me I'll call on all the old favors I have and help you with your plan."

"I still don't think you can help me."

She tilted her head to the side and grinned. "Google the name Milton Baldwin the third, then tell me you don't want my help."

He straightened and scowled. "Who the hell is that?"

"My father," she said. "Look him up, along with my mother and brother, and you'll know that by helping me if I go home, I can give you access to the connections you're seeking."

CHAPTER 3

The cake was cut, the bouquet thrown, and now everyone danced like teens at prom to celebrate Kareem's baby sister's wedding. He watched Fredrick spin Janiyah then pull her into his arms. His sister's laughter carried across the room to where Kareem sat at an abandoned table. He smiled then sipped champagne from one of the crystal flutes. Janiyah seemed happy. Fredrick looked ecstatic. Good for them. Doubtful he'd ever know that level of contentment.

A knot formed in his stomach. Clutching the champagne flute, he downed the contents then checked his watch. Time to grab Neecie and get out of here before all the happiness had him spiraling down the *if only I had done this* trail of regrets.

He glanced around the crowded ballroom of the country club. Hundreds of people laughed and mingled beneath bunches of silver and white balloons hanging from the ceiling. The place resembled a winter wonderland. Neecie talked with David on the other side of the dance floor. David pointed toward the door, and she headed in that direction. Kareem didn't worry about her leaving since she came with him.

David watched Neecie walk away, then made his way to Kareem, a grin on his face. Kareem groaned. Surprisingly, his family hadn't given him the third degree when Kareem brought Neecie to the rehearsal dinner the night before—only a hopeful look from his mom, a raised eyebrow from David, and an excited grin from Janiyah. But after bringing her to the wedding, he'd have more luck winning the Publisher's Clearinghouse than escaping without experiencing one hundred questions.

David pulled out one of the silver chairs wrapped in white tulle two spots over from Kareem and sat, a sly grin on his face. "Rehearsal dinner last night and wedding today. Are you trying to get Mom's hopes up?"

The corner of Kareem's mouth tilted up. "Mom can't wait to marry us off."

"I think it's part of a mother's DNA or something—seeing their kids happily married. I bet Neecie's mom is the same way."

"Don't go there."

After researching Milton Baldwin, III, Kareem was pretty damn sure Neecie's family would go ballistic if he were really marrying her. He still couldn't believe his Neecie, with her riot of natural curls, colorful personality, and fascination with love was the same cotillion-attending, perfect socialite daughter of one of North Carolina's most influential state Supreme Court judges.

David twisted in his seat to face Janiyah and Fredrick on the dance floor. "I wonder if the mom gene will develop in Janiyah."

Kareem frowned and shook his head. "I can't imagine her as a mother."

"She's married now. Before long, there will be babies." David chuckled and plucked one of the petals off the white rose and lily flower arrangement on the table. "We'll be uncles."

First Janiyah married, then David soon after. Envy created a tight knot in Kareem's chest. He shifted in his seat and ran a hand over his face.

"Where'd you send Neecie?" Kareem asked.

"She was looking for the bathroom. She'll be back in a second." David unbuttoned the jacket of his tuxedo and leaned his forearms on the table. Dark eyes studied Kareem. "So what's up with you two? I thought you didn't notice her?"

Kareem sat back in his chair. He'd already ditched the tie to his tuxedo, but his throat constricted. Time for the barrage of questions. "I noticed her. We're together, if anyone asks." He wasn't sure if he was accepting her offer or not, but for the weekend he'd go along with her lie—at least to keep her brother off her back.

David scratched his beard. "Why would anyone ask?"

"Just in case they do," Kareem said with a shrug.

"Is this serious?"

Kareem picked up the champagne flute and brought it to his lips. Empty, damn. He drummed his fingers along the stem. "For now."

"You know I love your cryptic answers." David shook his head.

Kareem smirked. One of the few joys Kareem had in life was annoying his younger brother. "That's why I give them."

"You know you can talk to us."

"In case you hadn't noticed, we're talking now."

David didn't take the bait. Instead he shifted in his seat and stared at Kareem. "I mean really talk. You're not the black sheep of the family anymore."

"But I used to be?"

"Stop trying to avoid a serious conversation. If you need anything, any help ... all you have to do is ask."

Kareem gripped the champagne glass. "I'm good, David."

"But if you—"

Kareem glared at David. "I'm good."

David's lips pinched, and he returned Kareem's glare. Finally, David lifted his chin. "Fine. We'll do things your way. But remember, we're your family. We want to help."

"Good to know." Kareem glanced back at Janiyah and Fredrick on the dance floor. David didn't get it. His family didn't get it. They'd worked the Henderson magic to lessen his sentence after the carjacking and to cover up his problems while in jail. Kareem wouldn't call in any more favors.

Neecie came back into the reception hall. She stood in the doorway and glanced around the room. When she spotted them, she smiled and headed their way. Kareem sat forward to rest his elbow on the table. He ran his finger over the scar above his lip and watched the subtle sway of her wide hips. Instead of the flowing skirts and colorful scarves she wore in the shop, she looked every bit the socialite with a cream-colored silk top, black pencil skirt with matching blazer, and *bend me over the table* black pumps. She'd pulled her hair back into a simple bun, leaving nothing to distract from her cute features.

The front of his tuxedo pants tightened as his cock swelled. He'd love to bend her over the table. But the daughter of a judge, and sister of a state representative, didn't deserve to be manhandled by a former convict. He frowned and watched her. Why the hell was she cutting hair in his shop? And why had she run away from her family?

She came over and leaned her forearms on the back of the chair next to him. "You're scowling," she said with a smile. A fresh coat of a berry-colored lipstick enhanced the fullness of her lower lip.

David chuckled. "He always scowls."

"It's part of my charm," Kareem said without any humor. "Are you ready to go?"

Neecie frowned and glanced at her watch. "I guess so."

The music changed—one of the sappy songs from the *Love Poems* album she'd made him listen to the day before. Her eyes lit up, and a hopeful smile spread across her face.

"I love this song," she said and held out her hand. "You can dance with me at least once before we go."

Kareem raised an eyebrow and looked at her hand. "I don't dance."

"Oh, come on, Kareem. Just one dance."

She bounced just a little then bit her bottom lip. Her enthusiasm nearly made him smile—the eternal romantic. For a split second he wished he were a guy who wrote sappy love poems and knew how to be romantic.

David rose from his chair. "Don't waste your time, Neecie. Kareem would rather cut off his feet than dance." David held out a hand. "Why don't you take a turn with the more charming member of the family?"

Neecie smiled at David, but disappointment hovered in her eyes. She peered at Kareem. "Do you mind?"

Kareem shook his head. "Go ahead."

David led her out to the dance floor, pulled her into his arms, and swayed to the song. David kept a respectable distance between their bodies, still Kareem scowled. Neecie didn't look right in David's arms. If David wore dirty jeans and raggedy t-shirts he would still appear polished, whereas Neecie was bright, happy, full of sunshine—kind of like a daisy.

Kareem ran his hand over his face. *I'm losing my damn mind.* Comparing a woman to a flower. A waiter with a tray of champagne passed his table. "Hold up," Kareem called and waved the guy over. "I need another."

"You know they're only dancing." Sandra came from behind and sat in the chair next to him.

Kareem pushed away the champagne and sat up in his chair. The off shoulder cream dress all the bridesmaids wore stopped above the knee of her long legs. If Neecie was a daisy, then Sandra was a rose—classy, poised, sophisticated. Kareem's desire for her had faded, but he still noticed her go-on-forever legs when she crossed them and turned his way.

Kareem cleared his throat. "I'm not worried. David knows better than to screw up what he has."

Sandra chuckled, and the husky sound brought smile to his lips. "I think David and I have played that game enough." She reached over to softly hit his shoulder. "Look, I know yesterday with Legions Bank was a setback. I hope you're not going to give up on your idea."

Kareem shook his head. "Not going to happen." He glanced at Neecie and David. "I think I found a contact in Charlotte who can help me expand."

"That's great, Kareem. I wish you luck."

The smile on Sandra's face gave him hope. "I appreciate that. Not many people understand what I'm trying to do."

"Maybe you should tell the rest of your family." Sandra used her chin to motion toward David. "I know David is eager to find out more."

Not going to happen. If he failed, he didn't need his family to know about another of his fuck ups. "I'll think about it."

She smiled and nodded as if she understood he wasn't going to say anything to David. If his family knew about the deal Neecie had offered they'd be disappointed. Keeping her brother at bay by pretending to be her man for a weekend was one thing.

Going home with her was another. Gaining support for his idea would take weeks—weeks trying and ultimately failing to suppress the urge to completely debauch Neecie. Kareem grabbed the flute and sipped the champagne. What kind of screwed up was he?

Guys with blood on their hands tend to be fucked up.

Kareem's throat tightened. The sights and sounds of the banquet all slowly faded, and the dank smell of a jail cell filled his nostrils. He ran a sweaty palm over the white tablecloth.

"Hey!" Sandra said.

Kareem flinched and glanced her way. His heart drummed. She smiled and waved at someone across the room. Kareem's shoulders relaxed. His screwed up response to a bad memory passed without being noticed.

"You and David set a date yet?" he asked. The music and conversation in the room masked the slight tremor in his voice.

"Soon, I think." A small grin graced her lips, and she swept the bangs out of her face before looking at David on the dance floor. "Sooner than we thought."

The love in her eyes was like a punch in the gut. He wanted a good woman to look at him like that. "Why so soon?"

Her hazel eyes slid his way. "You got your secrets, so I'll keep some of David's."

The love song ended and the Luther Vandross song "If Only for One Night" came next.

"I love this song," Sandra said and grinned at him. "Come on and dance with me."

He hated dancing, but the whisper of old feelings combined with his gratitude for all of her help polishing his business plan had him putting the champagne flute down and holding out a hand. "If you want your feet smashed, I'm your guy."

They rose, and David and Neecie came back over. David grinned at Sandra before going around the table and pulling her into his arms for a kiss.

"Isn't this your favorite song?" David asked.

Sandra wrapped her arms around David's neck. "You remember."

"I never forgot." David kissed her again. "Come on, dance with me."

Sandra grinned, then turned to Kareem. "Looks like you don't have to dance." David swept her onto the floor. Where Neecie didn't fit in his brother's arms, Sandra looked perfect.

"You were going to dance with her?" Neecie asked.

Kareem shrugged. "Yeah, she asked, so I figured what the hell."

"Oh."

He looked away from his brother and Sandra to Neecie. She pressed her lips tight and toyed with one of the napkins on the table. Ah, hell, he'd done that—taken the smile off her face. He didn't know how to explain his willingness to oblige Sandra. Guilt twisted his midsection. Like he really was her man and she'd caught him doing wrong.

"Let's get out of here." Before this feeling that they were real took hold.

She nodded. "Sure."

"I'll go tell my family I'm out," he said.

"I'll wait for you by the door."

He considered asking her with him to say goodbye to his family. They were supposed to be together. If he agreed to her plan, and her family came snooping around his, Kareem didn't want his family to contradict anything. Neecie held his stare for a few seconds before she smiled and walked away. His eyes dropped to her hips, roamed down her legs, then made their way back up. The need to possess her stirred his cock.

Candlelight and soft music. That's what she deserved. Not his style. He needed to remember that.

Dragging his gaze away from Neecie, Kareem made his way to his parents. They hovered along the edge of the dance floor, watching everyone have a good time. Kareem doubted a queen would look more regal than Loretta Henderson in her silver, off shoulder gown. Roger Henderson, always dressed to impress, complemented his wife's good looks in the same black tuxedo worn by the wedding party. Another couple that looked perfect together.

Kareem leaned over to kiss his mother's cheek. "I'm leaving." He stepped back before she could pull him into a hug.

"So soon?" his mom asked, in a voice that begged him to stay longer.

"Yeah, I've got to get Neecie back home." The excuse sounded lame to his ears. But better to say that than admit he felt suffocated by all the in love couples.

Loretta placed a hand on his forearm and squeezed. "She's a nice girl. It took you long enough to bring her around. I guess Aaron wasn't far off when he teased you about her."

His youngest brother insisted Kareem liked Neecie from the second she'd started working in his shop. To keep his matchmaking mother at bay, Kareem always denied his interest. "We just hooked up. Don't get too excited" he said, unwilling to offer any more.

There was a tap on his shoulder, and he turned to the exuberant face of his baby sister. Janiyah jumped up and wrapped her arms around his neck. He was momentarily smothered by silk and lace before she pulled away with a grin.

"I know you're leaving. I can tell by the disappointed frown on Mom's face. I had to hug you before you snuck out."

"I was coming to say goodbye."

"I wish you'd stay longer. I know Neecie would like to dance, and that's something I'd love to see," Janiyah said teasingly.

Fredrick strolled over, his wire-framed glasses askew from all the dancing, and wrapped his arm around Janiyah's waist, pulling her against his chest. "Leave your brother alone, and let him go home with his woman."

Janiyah tried to pout, but it was gone as soon as Fredrick kissed her cheek. His parents chuckled at the display. The love between the two tightened the envy knot in his chest.

Kareem reached over and squeezed Janiyah's shoulder. "I'm happy for you."

She got that doe-eyed expression, which meant she was about to cry or hug him. "Enjoy the honeymoon." He hurried away before she sucked him back into her tight embrace.

David and Sandra were still on the dance floor wrapped in each other's arms. No need to say his goodbyes to them. His youngest brother, Aaron, stood in a corner with Janiyah's best friend Liz. The redhead tugged on one of the kinky twists on his brother's head, and Aaron ran a finger down her arm. Kareem shook his head. Nothing good would come of that.

"Aaron, I'm out."

Aaron looked up then threw up his hand. "Have a good night." He winked then pointed toward Neecie waiting at the door.

Kareem waved him off, and Aaron went back to flirting with Liz. Kareem glanced at Neecie. A pull went through his midsection. The rest of his family all had someone to go home with that night. None of them were plagued with memories of the wrong they'd done in the world. If he'd made better decisions, maybe a sweet chick like Neecie would be waiting for him, her cute smile and romantic vibe ready to wrap around him as they made love and fell asleep in each other's arms.

Kareem snorted. "I've got to get away from all this happiness," he mumbled.

He wanted to take her hand, wrap his arm around her shoulders, pull her close to him and breathe in some of the fresh air that surrounded her.

"You ready?" she asked, still smiling, still tempting him to yearn for things he lost one night years ago with a gun in his hand.

His shoulders tightened. Resentment boiled in his stomach. "Let's get the hell out of here." He brushed around her and rushed out the door.

CHAPTER 4

Patrice entered DiPrato's Delicatessen on Sunday morning and immediately spotted her brother sitting at one of the tables toward the back of the crowded restaurant. The place boasted a New York-style deli with a southern flair. Patrice stopped at the back of the long line to place her order. Chad saw her, stood, and waved her over. Her brother seemed out of place with the casual brunch crowd in his Coppley suit.

"I'm glad you finally made room for me in your busy schedule," Chad said. He placed a hand on her elbow and leaned in to touch her cheek with his. Patrice jumped. She'd gone five years without the cheek-touching her family preferred over kissing.

Chad's eyes filled with disappointment. "I take it you don't want to touch me now?"

Patrice looked away. "Not when you have me followed."

She reached for her chair, but Chad pulled it out for her. After she sat, he took his seat. "What was I supposed to do?" He draped a napkin over his lap.

"Trust me."

"That became rather hard to do when you disappeared without a word. To Africa of all places." Chad raised his palms and shrugged. "What made you go there?"

"I wanted to go there."

"We would have taken you."

"I wanted to go alone."

A waiter arrived and placed a platter of DiPrato's popular pimento cheese with flat bread in the center of the table, as well as a plate of Eggs Charleston before Chad and smoked salmon with a toasted bagel for Patrice.

Patrice stared at her favorite brunch menu item and balled her hands into fists on her lap. "Do you know my favorite dish at every restaurant?"

"I would prefer to have learned because you were home with us. Not based off an investigator's report." Chad clasped his hands together, closed his eyes, and lowered his head.

Patrice gritted her teeth and mirrored his movement.

"We thank you for this food today. And for the blessing of reconnecting with my sister. Amen," Chad murmured.

"Amen." Patrice grabbed her napkin and snapped it open before covering her lap. "I just needed some time to myself."

Chad picked up his fork and held it over his food as if searching for the perfect place to dig in. "Time is taking a summer away. Five years is running away."

"Time is however long I need to clear my head." She cut a small piece of her salmon. Her shoulders relaxed after the first delectable bite. Annoyance with her brother wasn't enough to overcome five years learning to be okay with enjoying good food.

"Roland asked about you," Chad said without looking away from his food.

Patrice flinched and closed her eyes. "How is he?" She opened her eyes to Chad's knowing expression.

"He's well. Still cares about you."

"I'm glad to hear he's doing well. I know it was a shock to him when I broke off our engagement."

Chad sat back in his seat. "A shock to him. It was a shock to all of us. We thought the two of you were in love."

"Roland didn't understand me."

"How is that possible?" Chad shook his head, his voice filled with disbelief. "You two were together since high school."

"That's true." Patrice took a deep breath then met her brother's eye. "He also looked the other way every time I forced myself to throw up after meals and complimented my slim figure constantly."

Chad dropped his fork, which hit his plate with a clang. He leaned forward, rubbing a hand across his brow then jaw. "Don't joke like that, Patrice."

"It's not a joke. I had some real issues going on, and I needed some time." Patrice sighed and took a sip of water. "I did love Roland, but if I had married him I would have continued hurting myself while he looked the other way. One day I realized couldn't live like that."

"Why didn't you talk to us?" Chad rested his forearm on the table. "We would have gotten you the help you needed."

Her family's idea of help was exactly why she needed to go alone. A few weeks with a therapist and they would have assumed she would be cured. "I needed to work some things out for myself, and I needed to do it away from everyone else."

Chad's lips pressed together. "Did you stop to think about us? Your family? We worried about you."

Guilt churned the salmon in her stomach. "Surprising, since you had an investigator following my every move."

"That's not the same, Patrice, and you know it. When you went to Africa we figured you were on some journey for enlightenment. But when you came back stateside and started working in beauty salons and barber shops, we wondered if you'd lost your mind."

"I haven't lost my mind. I enjoy making other people look good." After years of forced perfection by her family, helping others find their own beauty, even if it was through a hairstyle or makeup, made her feel better.

"Even still, you shouldn't be working in a corner barber shop. Dressing like some," he waved at her flowing red skirt and matching scarf she'd used to tie back her hair, "gypsy, and dating a thug."

"Kareem is not a thug."

"Really, is there another word for a man that went to jail for carjacking then got into numerous fights behind bars?"

Patrice gripped her napkin; she'd overheard the talk in the shop and knew Kareem used to be a member of a gang and had gone to prison for carjacking, but not the details. "I see you've snooped into his past."

"As I should. I'll admit, his family is decent," Chad said as if even that concession pained him. "But he isn't good enough for you."

"You don't know anything about him."

"And what do you know about him, Patrice? This guy you're claiming to marry. Do you know his favorite color?"

Easy. "Black."

Chad's lips twisted. "Favorite song."

"He loves reggae and Bob Marley."

"His goals," Chad said, narrowing his eyes.

Patrice smiled and leaned back in her chair. "To grow his shop."

Chad's annoyance gave way to a smirk. "Who came to his house last night *after* he dropped you off?"

Her heart rate sped up. Of course her brother would follow Kareem as well.

"His friend Omar." In her mind a picture of Kareem's ex-lover Misty waltzing into his apartment flashed.

Chad glared for several seconds before letting out a breath and looking away. Patrice relaxed. She'd guessed right; otherwise, Chad would gloat.

"I don't like you with him. He's bad news."

"If you want me home next weekend then you're going to have to get over that. He's coming with me."

Once she convinced him. Though he'd been her alibi this weekend, Kareem hadn't given her a definite answer.

"Why?"

She'd asked herself the same question from the moment the words flew out of her mouth. The same lie wouldn't have sprung up if it had been Al or Lee in the shop when Chad arrived. Kareem had a way of looking out for the people in his circle. She only hoped after working with him for a year he would be willing to look out for her.

Yeah, he's really the kind of guy happy to sacrifice his time and pretend to be your man.

"Don't worry about the why," Patrice said. She picked up her fork and cut her salmon again. "Just accept that the Patrice who left five years ago isn't the Patrice who's coming home. If you want to get to know that Patrice, you've got to get to know the man in my life as well."

• • •

Kareem sat on the balcony of his spacious two bedroom apartment, a cigar in one hand, a pencil in the other. He exhaled a line of smoke then re-worked the shading on the sketch in his notebook. All weekend long the joy in Janiyah's and Fredrick's eyes had inspired Kareem to draw them. The picture would make a nice wedding present, but he didn't share his sketches. Plus, Janiyah would get teary eyed and hug the life out of him. Kareem smiled. His sister didn't do anything halfway.

His cell phone rang on the plastic table next to his chair. Dropping the cigar in an ashtray, Kareem put the notebook on the table.

An unfamiliar number lit the screen. He frowned and answered. "Yeah?"

"What's up K-rock?" The gravelly voice of Tim Brown, his old cellmate from prison, greeted him.

Kareem pinched the bridge of his nose and leaned the chair back on two legs. Hearing from Tim brought a mixture of wariness and pleasure. "Got a new phone, huh?"

Tim's rough laughter echoed through the phone. "I had to get rid of the old one. The guard brought in a new shipment of contraband this week."

"Anything good?"

"Just phones and cigarettes. They're cracking down after those guys released that video on the web a few months back. Made it hard to get anything." Tim sounded like someone complaining about the service at a five-star restaurant instead of prison contraband.

Kareem grinned and shook his head. "That's why you haven't called in a while."

"Exactly. So what's going on? You keeping your nose clean?"

"Every day," Kareem said solemnly. If not for Tim stepping in and ending a fight—and the life—of the guy trying to make Kareem's life in prison a living hell, Kareem would still be sharing that jail cell.

"What's happening with the shop?" Satisfaction filled Tim's voice. "You got any further on your fancy plans?"

Tim's comments weren't mocking. Tim had actually liked Kareem's idea from the second Kareem confided in him around the third year in.

"Got turned down at the bank yesterday because my idea is too *risky*."

"What?" Tim didn't talk loud, but his disbelief was evident. "You got most of your cash."

"Apparently that isn't enough."

"Bullshit. What are you going to do?"

Kareem dropped his chair back on four legs and leaned forward. He rested one elbow on his knees and rubbed his forehead with his free hand. "Not sure. I think I found a way."

"What's the deal?"

Kareem quickly ran through what happened with Patrice and her offer.

"You're going to do it, right?" Tim asked when Kareem finished.

"I don't really know. I doubt her family will be thrilled she's back to support the dream of her bad boy fiancé."

Tim cackled on the other end. "That's probably what she wants. Think about it. Pampered daughter of a judge runs away for five years. Bringing home a guy like you is bound to drive her folks crazy."

Kareem scowled. "I don't want to be her ticket to revenge or something."

"So what, as long as you get the contacts you need. Besides, it sounds like fate to me. You said yourself opening the business in Charlotte made the most sense. She's giving you a way."

"I get that, but still. I can barely handle my own family's demands, much less one like hers."

"Means to an end, K-rock. Besides, hobnobbing with these folks will make it easier to draw them in as clients. You know this, so why are you really hesitating?"

That was easy to answer. It would take longer than a weekend to make any real connections that would help his plan. Weeks pretending to be Neecie's fiancé meant he would eventually do everything in his power to thoroughly seduce her. Sleep with her every damn way he could imagine. No need pretending enough decency resided in him not to try.

"I don't want to take advantage of her. She's a good woman. Romantic and sweet."

"If she's grown enough to run away and lie to her brother, she's big enough to handle whatever happens. This is about your business, not her sentimental nature."

The same thought that kept creeping into Kareem's mind. "I've got to let her know soon. I'll fill you in after I do."

"Yeah, do that." Tim took a heavy breath. "Look, you're not a criminal. I am. You were a young man that made a bad choice and later was put in an impossible situation. You're out; don't waste your freedom."

Kareem's neck and shoulders tightened. Guilt shrouded him like the darkening sky. "That's the thing; I shouldn't be out. I shouldn't have let you kill Cide."

"You didn't *let* me kill anyone," Tim said in a scornful voice. "I did what needed to be done. That crazy would have eventually offed you. I'm already in here for life. No need for you to have that same sentence. What's done is done, K-rock. Live, you deserve to be happy."

Kareem's guilt didn't lift. He stood, grabbed his notebook and cigar, and went through the sliding glass door back into his apartment. "I hear you," Kareem said, more to brush Tim off than to agree. "I need to get out of here. You need me to send you anything?"

"Not now. But I'll let you know after the next shipment the guard sneaks in."

"Fine. Watch your back in there."

"Always. You watch your back out there."

Kareem ended the call and slid the phone in the back pocket of his jeans. His hands shook. Instead of the smell of the grilled cheese sandwich he'd made before going on the balcony his brain recalled the rank scent of the jail cell.

Crack! He slapped the side of his face, unwilling to succumb to the memories, the regrets that came whenever he spoke with Tim. He grabbed the keys to his bike off the bar overlooking the kitchen and marched out of his apartment and away from unpleasant memories.

CHAPTER 5

The soulful sounds of Kem played through the speakers in Patrice's rented bungalow. She bit her lower lip and stared at the tower of wooden Jenga blocks on the coffee table in front of her. Playing Jenga calmed her nerves and gave her something to focus on other than going home and facing her family again. Holding her breath, she slowly pulled a rectangular wooden block from the middle of the tower. The blocks shook but remained upright. She exhaled and smiled.

The doorbell chimed. She glanced at the clock in the shape of the sun above her television. Not quite nine, but too late for anyone to come visiting. In the year she'd lived in Columbia she made few friends outside of the shop, and the guys didn't visit.

Letting out a frustrated breath, she placed the Jenga piece on the coffee table then used the table to push up from her sitting position on the floor. She ran a hand over the multitude of two-strand twists on her head and considered not answering the door.

Screw that. Whoever decided to pop in can see my twisted hair. Maybe her hair would remind the person how impolite showing up unannounced was.

One glance through the peephole and buzzing started in her midsection. Kareem stood on the other side, encased in shadows and resembling a dangerous temptation the throbbing sensation between her legs didn't want to resist.

"Um ... just a second, okay?"

She couldn't make out his muffled response before she hurried down the hall to the bedroom. Flinging open the drawer that contained her scarves she found nothing but a few socks and empty space.

"Damn!" They were all in the wash. Her heart tripled the crazy dance in her chest. She lifted a hand to one of the rollers at the end of her twists. Of course he would come when she looked like her Grandmother Mabel.

She took a deep breath and trudged back to the front door. Her sweaty palm slipped on the doorknob. *It's not like he's interested, and you do need to talk to him.* Her heart still hammered.

Patrice swung open the door before she could freak herself out more. "Hey, what's up?" She aimed for nonchalant, but didn't quite stick the landing.

Kareem's flat black eyes roamed over her, pausing for a second on her hips in the red pajama bottoms. *Shit, the hole at the hip.*

"Umm ... hey?" Kareem crossed the threshold, completely filling the door with wide black leather encased shoulders.

Patrice sucked in a breath, but her lungs refused to accept the oxygen. The enticing mixture of cold air, leather, and Kareem made her body hum.

She met his direct gaze. The scar above his lip danced, and the corners of his mouth twitched. Dark, thick brows drew in then out.

Patrice narrowed her eyes and placed a hand on her hip. "Don't you dare laugh."

"I'm not," he said, his mouth trembling. "I swear. I just ... I mean ... interesting hair."

"I swear I'll kick you out if you laugh."

"Nah, you look very cute. Kind of like my grandmother." Then he grinned—full-fledged, teeth showing grin—something Patrice had never seen and hadn't been sure he could actually do. Her heart constricted then vibrated. His hard features were transformed, taking ten years off and giving a glimpse of the carefree young man he might have been, before mistakes sandpapered his smooth edges.

"What every girl wants to hear." She shook her head and chuckled. "Are you going to tell me why you're here?"

"I don't know. I think I'd rather figure out what's going on with these orange rollers." He took one of her rolled twists between his fingers. The movement brought him closer, and the inviting scent of his soap turned her insides into putty.

She playfully slapped his hand away. "One more word and you're out."

His grin turned into a half smile, which made her want to find her way around his body. "You're the one who answered like that."

"And you're the one who popped up unannounced. What you see is what you get." Though to see the smile in his face again, Patrice would gladly always answer the door in rollers.

She turned and made her way to the living area. "Come on in."

Kareem's heavy footsteps pounded on her hardwood floors. "What's up with the music?"

Patrice waved a hand over her shoulder. "No, sir, my place, my music. Again, if you don't want to hear love songs you shouldn't have popped up."

"Believe me, I'll call first next time. Give you a chance to put on some real music."

In her living room, she spun to face him. Kareem stood only a few steps behind her. His dark eyes seemed to pierce through her defenses and see everything going on in her head. Heat crept up her face. She cleared her throat and looked away.

"Will you be popping in more?"

"For the entire time we're doing this."

Patrice twisted her foot on the floor. "Soooo ... you're coming with me."

"Still considering the offer." He took another step closer. Not in her personal space, but that didn't matter. Kareem's presence filled the entire room. "Why did you ask me to do this for you? You could have gotten any of the other guys in the shop to help."

Patrice sighed and sat back on the floor next to the cheap oak coffee table that came with the furnished house. "Because you helped me when you didn't have to." She pulled another Jenga piece.

"How?" Kareem stood on the other side of the table and stared down at her.

"You gave me the job when I had no references or proof I even knew how to cut hair." She shrugged and studied the Jenga tower. "I appreciate that."

After a few seconds Kareem sat on the floor on the opposite of the coffee table. The scar on his face crinkled as he frowned. Then he took another piece out of the side of Jenga tower. "It was your look. I could tell you needed a place to land."

"That's what you do. You're a keeper of misfits. You give us a place to land. That's how I know you're a decent guy."

Using her pointer finger, Patrice pushed a middle piece out of the tower then pulled it away. She grinned when it remained standing.

"I'm not a decent guy." Regret filled his voice.

Patrice glanced up from the game. He scowled at the pieces, then chose a block too close to the one she'd previously removed. The wooden tower crashed into a pile on the coffee table.

"Guess I lose," he said.

Patrice pulled the pile together then began to rebuild the tower. "We can play again." She raised a brow, and he gave a *why not* shrug.

They didn't talk while she set up the game. Then she removed the first piece. "Is your past the reason you say you're not decent?" Kareem's hand paused halfway to the tower, and she rushed on. "I disagree. You made a mistake that nearly screwed up your life. But you didn't let it. You started a business. You give people a second chance. Then even though you pretend like you're not, you're always looking out for me and everyone else. Despite what you say, I see the good in you."

A line came between his brows—almost a frown, but more a look of disbelief. The idea struck that he didn't see what she saw. Didn't realize that he was a decent guy. She wanted to know why. Not surprising; she'd been fascinated by Kareem from the second she'd met him.

As if sensing her examination of him, he leaned forward. "Why do you need me there with you?"

She focused back on the game. "Your turn." His attention went back to the blocks and she relaxed.

"I do miss my family," she said after they both removed pieces. "Seeing Chad made me realize I miss them a lot. I'm afraid that if I go ... I'll forget the person I tried too hard to find."

"Who?"

"Myself."

She didn't meet his stare but felt his gaze boring into her, speculating on the reasons why she was afraid to return. She didn't dare tell him why she left in the first place. Kareem didn't tolerate weakness, and throwing up because she thought she wasn't thin enough was a weakness.

"There's something else." He narrowed his eyes. "What else is there, Neecie?"

She bit her lower lip. "I was engaged and broke it off before leaving," she said in a rush. "Chad has . . . implied that my ex is still around."

Kareem leaned back onto the couch. He bent one leg and rested a sinewy arm on the knee. "You want me to keep him off."

"Kind of. It would be easier to convince him there's no chance of a reconnection if I'm with another guy."

Kareem's dark, unreadable gaze focused on her. "That I believe. You're too damn stubborn to let your family change you."

"I'm glad you feel that way." She tried to run a hand through her hair but instead got a fistful of twists and rollers.

Kareem's rare but heart-stopping smile popped up. "Do you realize that *if* I agree, we'll have to pretend to be together for longer than a weekend?"

Patrice swallowed hard. "Why is that?"

"To make this work. For you to really help your *fiancé* get the connections needed, we'll have to be seen together. Attend events and network together. I can't do this in a weekend. We'll have to pretend for several weeks."

An enticing situation she'd also realized earlier in the day. "Oh, really?" The idea of pretending to be Kareem's fiancée for several weeks sent anticipation across her body. "How long were you thinking?"

"However long it takes." His voice became a decadent invitation.

Patrice's eyes shot to his. She couldn't read a thing from his facial expression, but the heat in his eyes made her lightheaded.

"Plus, I believe you miss your family." He broke the moment. "Staying longer will give you more time to be around them."

"Is there anyone else who'll be upset if we pretend to be together for a while?"

"No," he said, sounding as if her question was ridiculous.

She raised a brow. "Are you sure? A few months ago you told the guys you were done with Misty and then I ..." The vision of Kareem and his ex-played in her mind. She averted her gaze and hastily removed a piece. The blocks leaned; she sucked in a breath. Thankfully, they didn't fall.

He gave a sound that was sort of like a chuckle. "I've been meaning to talk to you about that."

She held up her hands and leaned back. "No need."

He rested a hand, palm up, on the table. "I didn't mean for you to catch us."

She scoffed, tried to sound as if the entire episode was no big deal. "Well I didn't want to catch you. I didn't want to see that."

"But you did," he said in a low voice.

And now, like a fool yearning for a walk on the wild side, she wanted to experience what she saw. Her breasts became heavy, and heat spread between her thighs. Patrice cleared her throat and scratched the back of her neck. "You know, I really don't understand men. One day you're through with a woman, but the next day you're sleeping with her."

"I promise I'm not sleeping with Misty."

That sent satisfaction through her. "Well you can't be sleeping with other women if we pretend to be together. It makes everything look bad."

Kareem's hand jerked while removing a block, sending the tower crashing again. Wide dark eyes met hers across the table.

She swallowed hard. "You know I'm right. How can we be engaged if you're bending someone over a desk?"

The surprise left his features, and a tempting smirk came across his face. He leaned forward. "Then who am I supposed to bend over a desk? Or a table. Or a chair."

The room became ten times hotter and her blood burned like lava in her veins. "I ... I'm not offering myself." Her voice was tight and breathless.

"Are you sure?"

Hell no she wasn't sure. She wanted him. Even after leaving her family she'd only dated nice guys. Kareem tempted her to do something wild, raw, and just for pleasure. But a guy like Kareem would leave skid marks over her heart when he moved on without a second glance.

Patrice nodded. "For now."

Raw hunger made his flat eyes come alive—alive with hunger, but no tenderness. She'd never believed Kareem capable of tenderness until she witnessed the way he looked at his brother's fiancée.

"Are you in love with Sandra?"

A shadow came across his face, and his eyes went flat. "What?"

"You didn't want to dance with me, but were going to dance with her. When you looked at her, it was different. Do you love her?"

He abruptly stood. "No."

Tension pulsed through his body. She should drop the subject. She got off the floor.

"Do you want her?"

"What would that make me to want my brother's woman?"

"I don't know. You tell me."

Kareem's nostrils flared, and he sucked in a deep breath. He stared at the floor then back at her. "I don't. I care about Sandra because she helped me with my business plan. But that's all."

"Okay." She nodded. "I believe you."

Kareem's shoulder's relaxed. He glanced at the sun clock. The corners of his mouth softened. "That's so you."

She glanced at the clock and shrugged. "It came with the house."

"Still, it's you." He glanced back at her. "I'll give you my answer by the end of the week."

Kareem walked over, this time invading her personal space. "Keeper of misfits, huh?"

She shrugged. "What would you call it?"

He lifted a hand to her cheek but didn't touch. Still, her body hummed as if he did. Something flickered in his eyes, and his brows drew together. He dropped his hand. "I'm just a business owner. I'll see you at work tomorrow." He checked out her hair, and the corner of his lip lifted. "Wear the rollers. They're cute."

Patrice rolled her eyes and swatted at him, but he swiftly avoided the hit. "Get out."

His chuckle warmed her long after he left.

CHAPTER 6

Patrice didn't know how she managed to cut hair the rest of the week without leaving patches of bald spots. Every day Kareem watched her with flat, unreadable eyes, like he did now from where he sat at his barber station next to hers, peeling an orange and studying her harder than a pre-med student during finals.

"All done," she said to the guy in her chair. He was one of her regulars, a good tipper, and used to accidentally brush into her booty every time she swung his chair around until Kareem called him on it.

Her client sat forward and checked out his crisp fade in the mirror, then gave her a smile. "Looks good, Neecie. Thanks, girl."

He pulled out a wad of cash and slapped it in her hand like a street dealer. When she tried to pull back, he held on. "When you gonna let me take you out?"

She smiled and pulled her hand until it slid out of his. "Have a good afternoon, all right?"

He took her usual answer with a shrug then waved to the rest of the guys before leaving. She didn't have anyone waiting for her, so she sorted the cash he'd plopped in her hand and grinned at the ten-dollar tip.

Lee snickered from the other side of the room. "Dang, Neecie, when you gonna give that guy a chance?"

She raised a brow. "Not gonna happen," she said, sliding her money in the pocket of her apron. "You think I'm going to give any of my clients some play, just so they can come back and tell you guys all the details?"

Al stopped cutting his client's hair and raised his hands. "Well, hell, that's why we want you to go out with them." His client agreed, and they dapped each other up.

Patrice tossed a towel at Al and hit him in the face. "Aww, Al, are you so hard up for some play that you got to get it second hand from Mr. Wayne?"

Rico let loose the grin that, combined with his nicely faded curly hair, made most women melt, smirked at Lee. "You just want to hear Neecie's story because you don't have any stories of your own."

Al pulled on the collar of his shirt. "Man, I have to beat the ladies off."

Lee shook his head. "What ladies, because I sure haven't seen any ladies."

Patrice grabbed a broom and swept around her station. "All his ladies are on his computer's hard drive."

The guys in the shop laughed, and Lee and Rico took over with the taunts to Al. Al's teasing didn't offend her. Once she'd proved she could give just as good as they could, the fellas opened the floodgates and just let the conversation flow, including her in any jokes, discussions, or debates. The easy camaraderie in the shop was the reason she preferred cutting men's hair to working in a beauty salon with women. Less pressure to always be on point when she hung with a bunch of men.

She glanced around at each of the guys. Al, Lee, Rico, and Kareem. She didn't know every one of their stories, but in the past year she'd gathered they all were former members of the Runners. And once they walked away they came to work for Kareem. That was as far as the revelations went. Whatever they'd done in the gang they didn't discuss in the shop. Not in front of her at least.

"What's got you so quiet?" Kareem asked.

Patrice increased her previously lazy efforts to sweep the floor. "Nothing. Hungry. I'm going to go next door and get something for lunch."

She finished cleaning her area and untied her apron. She slid a few of the bills into the front pocket of her sweater and reached for her white leather jacket on the rack.

Kareem stood. "I'll go with you."

She lifted her shoulder as if it were no big deal and smiled, even though her heart thudded. Guess he was ready to give her an answer. "Sure."

Outside, the drizzling rain from earlier left a wet cold in the late October afternoon. They walked in silence to the soul food restaurant next door. Inside the warm space, the aromatic fragrance of good food filled the place. They placed a take out order then sat in the two small chairs near the door.

Kareem shifted in the seat to face her and examined her from head to toe. She didn't want to squirm, but the heat in his gaze made her feel as if she were dancing barefoot on a hot plate. Fantasizing about Kareem giving her hot looks was one thing—quite another thing to actually have him do just that.

"You really want to use your family's connections to help me with my business plan?"

"Yes."

"Why?"

"Because I like your idea." When he frowned she grinned. "I think you can make it work."

More long seconds of Kareem examination. "You really think that, don't you?"

Patrice relaxed and nodded. "I do. Look at how hard you work to make Fresh Cutz successful. You're there first thing in the morning every day. You try to pretend like the kids who come in get on your nerves, but you always give them good advice. You gave every one of us that work for you a second chance. And you're always looking out for me and everyone else in the shop."

"I'm not a good guy," he said again, with enough seriousness to make her want to reach out and hug him. Something that would surely have Kareem pulling away.

"Hey, you bought my lunch. That's a good guy in my book," she said with a grin.

The corner of his mouth quirked, and he turned away from her. "It'll take more than me buying you a fish sandwich to make me a good guy."

"Okay, how about playing my loving fiancé for a while?"

That earned her the semblance of a smile—enough to turn his handsome face into a serious threat to the stability of her knees.

Kareem shook his head. "I don't know about loving." His dark eyes slid her way, and a seductive twist softened the hard line of his lips. "But I can convince them you're mine."

Patrice's heart did a fluttery jig in her chest. "That should work." Her voice quivered, and she cleared her throat. "Any other questions?"

"Have you considered what's going to happen when your family learns about my past?"

"I did." She couldn't help but think of that after Chad threw Kareem's past in her face.

"Is that going to make things harder? I mean, I imagine they'll be pissed we're together. Do you really think they'll help?"

"I left five years ago for my own reasons; it doesn't change the fact that the Baldwins are loyal. If I ask, they'll help."

He nodded and leaned back in his chair. "You sure?"

"I am." She ran her hands over her pants and glanced at him from the corner of her eye. "Do you want to tell me more about your past?"

Kareem's body tightened, and he stared forward. "All you need to know is I was in the Runners. We ran guns up and down the East Coast. I was twenty-two when I went to prison for carjacking. Spent five years there and been out another five."

"That's a Cliff's Notes version," she said, frowning.

"This is a Cliff's Notes engagement. Just an overview of what a relationship should look like, none of the specifics."

She'd do well to remember that. Unfortunately her fascination with him made her want to know more. "So, is that a yes?"

The lady at the counter called out that their food was ready. "It's a yes." Kareem stood and walked with his sexy swagger to grab the bag. Patrice's eyes strayed to his wonderfully curved backside then jumped to his face when he turned around.

Kareem cocked his head in a silent motion for her to get up. She stood, and his dark, tantalizing stare stole her breath away. *I can convince them you're mine.* Heaven help her, because she wanted to be his.

• • •

That weekend, Kareem's eyes slid to Neecie in the passenger seat of his Nissan Maxima as they made their way to Charlotte for the "big charade." Her natural curls framed her face like a halo, and she tapped her hands to the beat of the song. Torn jeans clung to her curvy hips, and an oversized tan sweater draped her tits to perfection.

Kareem gripped the steering wheel. *I'm going to sleep with her.*

Despite her confession that she saw the good in him, he decided to ignore the good part that said leave her alone and keep their ruse up only in public. Privately, he was going to make Neecie every bit his woman.

Neecie slid her seat back and put her bare feet on the dashboard, revealing pink toenails and a cross tattoo on the top of her right foot. A chain of roses weaved from the top of the cross around her ankle.

"Your feet on my dash, for real?" Kareem said.

She turned to him with a bright smile. "Yes, for real. I promise not to put toeprints on your windshield."

Kareem leaned on the armrest between them. "You'll be cleaning the windshield if you do."

Her chuckle sent various levels of pleasure through his body.

"Can we change the music now?"

"My car my music," he said.

"Aha, throwing my words back at me. It's like that now."

He glanced her way. The cute smile on her face brought up the corner of his mouth. "It's like that. Besides, how can you get tired of reggae?"

"How can you not like love songs?"

"Love songs are just a flowery way of telling a woman you want to have sex. I'd rather just come out and let her know what I'm after."

He rubbed his chin and stole a glimpse her way. Patrice's right foot shook back and forth on the dash.

"All men don't think that way.

"All men don't tell you they think that way."

Admitting he wanted to have lots of sex with her sat on the tip of his tongue. "Tell me about your family," he said instead.

She blew out a heavy breath and pressed her right hand to her forehead. "My family is perfect." A tinge of disappointment clouded her voice.

"You sound like that's a bad thing."

"It's not. It's great ... for them. My dad, Milton, comes from a long line of politicians and lawyers going back to Reconstruction. During the civil rights movement my great-grandfather made a name for himself in politics, and my grandfather made his way to the state senate, but my dad chose to pursue law. He believes he can make more of a difference sitting on the bench. He was known for giving teens who'd made a mistake the chance to right their wrongs. But if they showed up in his courtroom again, he didn't hold back."

Kareem pursed his lips and nodded. Wonder what Milton Baldwin, III, would have said if Kareem had shown up in his courtroom. Hanging with a gang of gun runners and participating in a carjacking. Kareem's body tensed. The guy would've thrown the book at him.

"My brother took over my grandfather's senate seat right before I left. He's ten years older than me. He and his wife,

Melanie, have an adopted son. Joshua. He's—" She paused and pursed her lips. "Fifteen now. Wow. I've been gone a long time."

"What about the rest of the family?"

"My mom, Janice, is the youngest daughter of the Corley family. Made their money through a home healthcare business they started in the seventies that is now Journey's Healthcare. Melanie's family made their money in agriculture."

A family of moneybags. He sat up and gripped the wheel with both hands. "That's all?"

"No. Then there's my baby sister Elizabeth. We call her Beth." She stopped talking. Kareem's gaze shifted her way. She wasn't quite smiling, nor was she frowning. Her lips were pursed like she was holding in her thoughts.

"You and Beth aren't cool."

She waved a hand and shook her head. "No ... I mean, yes, we are cool. It's hard not to be cool with Beth. She's perfect. Polite, sweet, talented. She plays the violin and speaks fluent French and Spanish ... all by the time she graduated from high school. And beautiful." A heavy sigh escaped her lips. "Beth could be a model if she wanted, but she doesn't let it go to her head."

Kareem frowned. "If your family is so perfect, why did you leave them behind?"

She wiggled her toes, coming dangerously close to putting prints on his windshield, and pulled on one of the frayed edges on her jeans. "You've heard the square peg, round hole analogy before." She looked at him, and he nodded. "I'm that square peg. I tried, really tried, to be the wonderful, ladylike, graceful daughter they deserved." Her brows came together. "Too hard. I didn't want to do that anymore. I had to just be me."

Kareem's heart thudded. "Did they make you feel bad for who you were?" How could anyone not see how perfect Neecie was already? Overly romantic maybe. But he'd yet to witness the woman have a bad day.

"No, they never intentionally did. It's just part of living the high-profile life that comes with being well known in the community. I put more pressure on myself than they ever did."

He half grunted, half laughed.

"What?" she asked.

"Nothing really. Just, I kind of know what you mean."

Her brown-eyed stare zeroed in, an obvious sign she wanted to know more about him.

Kareem pointed to the radio. "Go ahead and change the music."

She did, and soon Miguel's "Adorn" filled the car. He hated that song.

"Are you going to elaborate now?" Neecie asked.

"Elaborate how?"

"You know. The putting more pressure on yourself thing."

He'd walked right into the *hey, let's talk* situation. "Nothing to elaborate on."

Her bright chuckle accompanied the happy love song playing. "Usually when people say I know what you mean, they follow the phrase with a story. You know, a way to open up a bit and demonstrate how we're relatable."

"We're relatable?" he said.

Neecie's foot leaned closer to his windshield. "I swear I'll leave toeprints for days if you don't answer."

"Neecie."

A millimeter of space separated her foot from the glass. His heart rate accelerated—not because of fear of toeprints on his windshield, but from the discomfort of knowing he'd opened himself up to some sort of explanation.

"Get your foot away from my windshield, woman. There's nothing much to explain. I want to make sure I get things right with my lounge. Fix some of the BS I smeared on my family's good name."

She didn't immediately respond. He couldn't look her direction. Slowly, her foot eased back until she rested it on the dashboard.

"I'm confused. Your family name will get you almost anything you want in Columbia. Why not use it?"

"Because I don't deserve to use it." His gaze slid toward Neecie, haloed by the bright sun filtering through the windows. "I don't deserve to use your family name either."

"You're not using their name; you're using our connections. Besides, you're coming to do me a favor." Neecie sighed and leaned her head against the headrest.

Miguel sang about letting his love adorn a woman. Code for let me in your pants. Kareem's eyes drifted to Neecie. Hell, Kareem could almost relate to the song because his hands itched to touch Neecie's soft skin.

Her head turned and her eyes met his. "And even if you don't think you deserve to use your family's name, you do deserve to use every resource you have to make your dream a reality. There's nothing wrong with that. Succeeding despite your history will only prove you're just as smart and determined as your father and brother."

She closed her eyes and hummed along to the music. Kareem leaned back in his seat. Here he was thinking about getting his hands on her, and she contemplated all of the reasons why a *decent* guy like him should use all resources available to succeed. The true definition of a decent woman, she was smart, supportive, probably more down for her man's needs than any female he'd dealt with since getting out five years ago.

Neecie sang along with the song, holding her hands out and waving her head from side to side, her eyes closed and a sexy smile on her face.

Kareem smiled. A real, long-term thing wouldn't work, but he would make the most of the short time he got to have a good woman on his side.

CHAPTER 7

When the large, two-story, white colonial home came into view down the long drive, Kareem let out a low whistle. He knew that Neecie's family was rich. He just hadn't expected to feel like the Fresh Prince of Bel Air coming here. He would be the out of place guy thrown in the middle of a lifestyle he didn't quite understand.

"Just park next to the fountain for now," Neecie said.

She pointed to a line of cars next to the fountain in the circular drive. Maserati, BMW, Jaguar. The place looked like a high-end car lot.

"Your parents expecting company?"

"No, they belong to my family."

Kareem turned off the car and twisted in his seat to face Neecie. For the first time since agreeing to come, he second-guessed his decision. If he didn't feel comfortable with his own family there was no way he'd feel comfortable with hers, much less convince them that he was, as she said, the loving fiancé.

He cleared his throat and twisted his head from side to side. If he was going to get the connections he needed to expand his business he'd have to make this work.

"Nice house."

"Thanks." Her normally light voice was tight, and she ran her hands across her torn jeans. With her lower lip pulled between her teeth, she didn't appear to be breathing.

"Are you okay?"

She cleared her throat. "Yeah, sure, I'm great." Her hands rubbed faster.

That didn't look like great. He held out his hand, hesitated, and then finally placed his over hers. Her fingers were like ice.

"Are you scared?"

"Nervous. Which is silly, I know. It's just … I haven't seen them in so long. I'm not the same person I was when I left. I don't know if I'm walking into a house with the same people I left behind."

"Five years is a long time. Believe me, I know."

She cringed. "I'm sorry. I'm sitting here freaking out about being away for five years after traveling around *finding* myself. You left for five years for a completely different reason."

The words were like a punch to the gut. He didn't talk to people about his time in prison. Except for the occasional unwanted memory attack he tried not to relive the time he spent there. But he understood the scary feeling of walking back into the fold of a family that loves you after being away for so long.

"Everyone changes over time. You can't do anything about that. The question is …" He tapped her shoulder lightly with his finger. "Did you miss them?"

She took a deep breath. "I did."

"Then go with that. The rest will work itself out."

She gave him her sunshine smile, and he felt something a whole lot deeper than lust going on inside his chest.

"Thanks, Kareem. For coming and everything," she said.

"I'm getting something out of this as well."

"I know. We'll make it work." She took a deep breath then nodded. "Let's go in."

They got out of his car. She told him not to worry about the bags for now. They made their way up the stairs and rang the bell. A few minutes later a woman in her late fifties or early sixties, with brown skin, a face creased with laugh lines, and a simple, light blue dress answered the door. The woman's light brown eyes widened before a large grin came across her face.

"Miss Patrice, it's so good to see you again," the woman said with obvious affection.

Patrice returned the smile then reached out to wrap the woman in a huge hug. "Fran, you haven't changed a bit."

Fran gave Kareem a startled look before giving a stiff pat to Neecie's back. Neecie quickly stepped away. "I apologize."

A forgiving smile crossed Fran's face. "I understand, Ms. Patrice. Of course you're happy to be home."

Kareem flinched. The reprimand in the woman's voice clear. He guessed hugging the help wasn't allowed.

Neecie's smile lost some of its brightness as she took a step back. "I guess I am." She turned away from Fran to slide her arm through Kareem's. "Right, sweetie?"

Kareem had to suppress a smile. "Sweetie?"

She poked him with her elbow, and he gave her a half smile. "Where are my manners? Fran, this is my fiancé, Kareem. Kareem, this is our housekeeper, Fran."

If the tightening of Fran's mouth was any indication, he'd been correct to assume he wouldn't be easily welcomed into the family fold.

"Good afternoon," she said in a clipped voice. She quickly eyed him from head to toe. He could practically hear the tsking in her head before she looked at Neecie. "The family is in the study, Miss Patrice. If you'll excuse me, I'll get someone to take your bags to your rooms."

"Rooms?"

Fran again gave him a quick glance. "Ms. Janice put you two in separate rooms."

Kareem chuckled at the obvious attempt to put him in his place. Fran's eyes narrowed, and he tried to cover it with a cough. He stared at Neecie and raised a brow. Her answering smile started the crazy feeling in his chest.

"Please put Kareem's bags in my room. Kareem, you can give Fran your keys."

Fran opened her mouth, probably to argue, but Neecie straightened her shoulders and stared back. Fran's lips snapped together and she nodded.

"If you say so," Fran said, taking Kareem's keys. "We'll see what your parents say later." Fran did an about face that would make an army general proud and marched down the hall.

"Separate rooms, huh?" he asked after she walked away.

Neecie rolled her eyes. "They don't believe we're really together."

He leaned down to whisper in her ear. "We aren't really together." Her body trembled against his, and he smiled again. He was really going to enjoy seducing her.

"That's why we're going to convince them otherwise," she said softly.

"I'm willing to do whatever it takes to do that." He let the suggestion come through in his voice. Her eyes widened before she averted her gaze.

"Come on, let's get this over with."

They crossed wood floors polished so well they reflected his and Neecie's silhouettes. He got the same feeling he'd had in sixth grade when he took a trip to the Smithsonian—afraid to touch anything without being reprimanded for marring the many antiques and collectibles. He imagined Fran had maids hidden in corners to come out and wipe up any speck of dust or fingerprints.

Neecie stopped walking just before they reached a threshold at the end of the hall. Her body trembled, and her brows were drawn together. The sounds of voices wafted out of the room. Kareem rubbed her cheek with his knuckle. She glanced up, and he did a quick lift and lower of his chin. Neecie blinked, her eyes cleared. The sunshine smile returned, and she threw back her shoulders, lifted her chin, and nodded. In that moment he recognized she was a lot stronger than he'd given her credit for.

The study was a mirror of the rest of the house. A sweeping glance of the family inside was enough to say they fit the décor. Neecie was right—they looked like the perfect family. Sitting around a roaring fire, the bright sunlight filtering in surrounding them all with a halo of gold.

"Hey, everyone." Neecie's normally breezy voice nearly trembled with her nervousness.

Kareem unhooked their arms and rubbed the small of her back.

"Patrice!" A young woman with the same bright smile and friendly eyes as Neecie jumped up from a chaise. She rushed across the room in what was too fluid to be called a run and threw her thin arms around Neecie.

Good. At least someone in the house wasn't against giving her a warm welcome.

Neecie returned the hug with equal fervor. "Beth, I missed you so much."

Beth leaned back and wiped a tear from the corner of her eye. "Then never go away for so long again."

The rest of the family came over. He immediately figured out who was who. The mother shared the same features as her two daughters. She was slender like Beth, and her thick, dark hair was pulled up into an elegant twist.

"Welcome home, Patrice," her mom said. Her hug wasn't as big as her youngest daughter's, but the happiness in her eyes was just as real. Happiness that quickly disappeared when she lifted her chin and looked at Kareem. "You must be Roger." She held out her hand.

Neecie frowned and turned his way. He gritted his teeth to keep from swearing. "Roger is my first name. I go by Kareem." Her fingers were slender, but her grip was firm. She also didn't hesitate to drop his once the shake was done.

Her dad, an older version of Chad except with a beard and hair slicked back in waves, came forward and hugged Neecie as well.

"We missed you, darling."

"I missed you too, Father," Neecie said in a smooth, cultured voice.

Kareem tried not to scowl. She'd been gone for five years, and her parents greeted her as if she'd just returned from a weekend vacation. At his homecoming, his mother had smothered him with kisses, cooked every one of his favorite meals, and then insisted he try on all of the new clothes she'd purchased to make him feel at home again. Watching Neecie's cool reception, minus her sister, made Kareem feel guilty for brushing off his mother's obvious joy at having him back.

Milton Baldwin held out his hand to Kareem. "Roger."

Kareem took his hand and had no qualms about returning the extra pressure Milton put in his grip. "It's Kareem."

Milton gave a stiff nod and a quick up down pump of their hands. "If you insist." He turned to the rest of the family. "Why don't we all have a seat?"

Janice looked between the two. "Would you care for anything to eat or drink?"

"No, Mother, I'm fine," Neecie replied. She looked to Kareem. "Would you like anything?"

He scowled. She'd practically rubbed a hole in her pants in the car she was so anxious to see her family again, and now she was socialite daughter of the year. He didn't like it.

"I'm good."

"Very well," Janice said. "But we do have some snacks Fran brought in earlier." She turned and gracefully walked back to her chair. Milton and Beth followed.

Neecie moved to follow. He wrapped an arm around her waist and pulled her close. "Warm welcome," he said with a half-smile.

"They can loosen up when it matters."

He raised a brow, and she chuckled. Her body relaxed, and the tension left her eyes. They followed the family to the sitting area. Chad stood rigid next to the chess table before the fire, looking every bit the southern frat boy in a blue button up and grey slacks. His icy stare went from Kareem's hand on Neecie's lower back to Kareem's uncaring face.

"Melinda, you look great," Neecie said to the blonde woman sitting on a rose-colored couch that matched the loveseat he and Neecie occupied.

Melinda smiled, but her blue eyes darted nervous glances toward Kareem. "Thank you. So do you."

"How was the drive up?" Janice asked.

Neecie shrugged. "Relatively uneventful."

"That's good to hear," Janice said. "I worried with the light rain last night. You know how people drive on the highways after a rain."

Melinda nodded. "You're right. I always tell Chad that I refuse to drive anywhere when it rains."

The conversation continued to flow around the weather and traffic. What the hell was wrong with these people? The entire situation was like something out of a bad drama. The more he watched, the more frustrated he became. Didn't they want to know what she'd done for the past five years? How she came to work for him? Why she left in the first place? Where was the concern that she would disappear again? Or even the happiness to have her back?

Beth slapped her magazine on the table next to her chaise, cutting off Melinda's comments on her wish for snow. "How long after the party will you be staying, Patrice?"

Finally, someone who seemed to want to establish if Neecie planned to hightail it out of their perfectly decorated lives again.

"For a few weeks."

Her parents exchanged pleased looks. Milton turned away from the chess table to give Neecie a satisfied nod. "That's good to hear."

"Kareem and I are exploring a few options."

One of Janice's manicured brows rose. "What type of options?"

Kareem sat forward. "I'm thinking of opening another place in Charlotte."

Chad sort of chuckled. "Another barber shop?"

The condescending ice in Chad's voice didn't go unnoticed by Kareem. His shoulders tightened, and he fought not to let his anger with the arrogant asshole come through.

"Something a bit more than that. I'm looking into opening more of an upscale gentlemen's salon. Maybe include a cigar bar."

"Humph," Chad grunted. "Interesting idea."

Neecie sat up and placed a hand Kareem's thigh. "It's a great idea. You're a perfect example that men like to be pampered."

Her quick defense jolted his confidence. She had his back. Maybe just for show, but he liked her response just the same.

"A haircut by my own barber at the county club is my idea of pampering. Not in some corner barber shop," Chad said with a barely concealed sneer. "I can't believe you're washing men's hair. Patrice, your life would be so much better if you had stayed here instead of running off."

Neecie's plan to argue was written all over her face. Now they were getting somewhere. Kareem didn't like Chad, but at least the guy broached the subject of her leaving. Though now that he'd met the "perfect" family, he kind of understood her need to get away. She was too free to be pinned up like these people.

Janice stood before Neecie could respond. "That's enough, Chad. Why Patrice left isn't the issue right now. The issue is that she's home and," she turned to Neecie with a pointed look, "I hope it's for good." She took a breath before turning her cool glance on Kareem. "No offense to you, but I'd be lying if I said I didn't want Patrice to move back to Charlotte and be around her family. I know she said that the two of you are ... engaged, but I also believe that was a rush decision. Maybe a few weeks here will help clear things up."

Meaning, her family was going to use this opportunity to convince Neecie to stay away from him. Their engagement wasn't real and he didn't give a damn about what her family thought of him, but he did give a damn about Neecie. The thought of her losing some of her brightness and becoming as frigid as the rest of her family made him more uneasy than the idea of going back into the Runners.

He slid closer to her on the couch and ran his hand up and down her back. She didn't stiffen or shrug away. She looked at him and rewarded him with her smile. Right then they felt more real than anything.

"Rushed or not," she said, still staring at Kareem, "the decision was ours to make." She looked at her parents. "I ask that you all respect our decision when we're in town."

Milton cleared his throat and stood next to his wife. "Of course we will, darling. Now," he rubbed his hands together, "I'm sure you both must be tired. We'll get Fran to show you to your rooms, and then, Kareem, maybe the two of us can get to know each other a little better before dinner."

A pre-dinner drilling by the father. He hadn't been through that since ... hell, he'd never been through that. They type of females hanging around the Runners when he hit dating age didn't have concerned fathers hovering.

"Fair enough," Kareem said.

Neecie smiled at her parents. "I let Fran know to put our bags in my old room. There's no need for us to be separated."

Beth placed a hand over her mouth. Janice's eyes widened, and Chad crossed his arms over his chest. The tension ramped up to levels Kareem hadn't felt since prison. Anticipation that he would finally see something break their perfect facade made him sit straighter. They didn't want his dirty hands on their perfect daughter. Too bad, he had plans to put his hands all over her body.

A teenage boy came into the room. "Sorry I'm late; there was an accident."

All eyes swung to the door. Melinda popped up from the couch and hurried across the room.

"Joshua, are you all right?" Melinda ran her hands over Joshua's arms and legs.

Joshua shrugged out of his mother's hands with a smirk, looking like a miniature southern frat boy. "Not me, Mother, someone else had an accident and caused traffic."

Melinda pressed a hand to her chest. "Thank heavens."

Chad crossed the room to do his own visual inspection of his son. "I'm glad you're okay, son. We were just welcoming Patrice and her ... fiancé."

Joshua's eyes lit up and zeroed in on Kareem. "The convict?" he said with a bit too much admiration.

Kareem tensed, and heat infused his face. That was enough Baldwin family bonding time. He dropped his hand from Neecie's back and stood.

"I'm tired. I'll go find Fran and ask her where the room is." He looked at Neecie. "Enjoy this time with your family."

He took a step forward, then figured a loving fiancé didn't just walk away. Spinning back, Kareem bent and felt awkward as he pressed a kiss to her cheek. Neecie jumped, and her wide, beautiful eyes met his. She'd had his back against Chad, making him wonder how good things would be if she were really his girl. The feeling in his chest revved up, a strong longing he hadn't felt since trying to prove he deserved to be in the Runners. Before the feeling could take hold, he left the room. He walked down the hall, out the front door, and headed for the garden. He needed to clear his head.

CHAPTER 8

Patrice sucked in several sharp breaths after Kareem marched out of the study and hoped he wasn't going straight to his car and back home. Barely twenty minutes in and he'd already been insulted.

"Joshua," Patrice said with a hand on her hip, "Kareem is not a convict."

Joshua shrugged. "I didn't mean any harm. It's actually pretty cool he did time."

Her brother grunted and scowled. "You shouldn't find anything *cool* about that man."

Anger shot through Patrice. "Why are you determined to hate him? He made a mistake when he was younger and paid for it. Kareem turned his life around."

Her brother crossed his arms and returned her glare. "You can do better. You deserve better."

"What makes you think Kareem isn't better?"

Janice crossed to Patrice and placed a hand on her elbow. "Is he really?"

"He likes me for who I am." Patrice stepped away from her mother's touch.

Janice waved a hand from Patrice's head to her foot. "This isn't you. Your hair's all wild, your clothes are torn, and ..." Janice bit her lip, struggling for words.

Patrice waited for the old discomfort—the urge to do and be better, to match the perfection of her mother and sister. Instead, irritation tightened her neck and shoulders.

"And what, Mother?" she said, cocking her head to the side. "I've gained too much weight?"

Janice shook her head and immediately looked contrite. "Not at all, dear. You're curvy now. There's nothing wrong with that."

"No, there isn't," Patrice said with an edge of steel in her voice. "Kareem likes me, and I can guarantee he wouldn't overlook me throwing up after every meal."

Janice cringed. Milton ran a hand over his face. She didn't care that her family normally didn't discuss difficult things. Not talking about her old insecurities was the reason she ran away instead of facing them head on.

Milton leaned both hands on the fireplace. "Your brother mentioned that to us. It's not something we would have supported either, Patrice." Pushing away, he turned to stare at her. "If you had stayed and told us what was going on, we could have gotten you some help."

"It wasn't just that, Father, it was me. I needed to get away." She tapped her chest. "I needed to discover who I am and what I wanted."

Joshua chuckled and sauntered over to plop down on the couch. "You wanted a thug."

She glared at her nephew. He'd had the makings of a smart mouth at the age of ten; apparently he'd grown into a full blown smartass. "No, I just want to be happy."

Janice grasped Patrice's hands and squeezed. "We want you to be happy. Patrice, I hate that I didn't see the signs, and I'm angry Roland overlooked what was going on. But that doesn't mean you need to be with … this guy instead of finding someone who'll appreciate everything that makes you special."

"Mother, he isn't the convict Chad would paint him to be."

Chad crossed the room and leaned against the couch. "A carjacking and gang ties. That sounds like the perfect person to join the family."

Janice glared at Chad. "Stop, Chadwick." She turned back to Patrice. "Let's not fight about this. You're home, and I'm glad you're home. We're celebrating your father's and my anniversary tomorrow, and then we're going to spend as much time with you as possible. I want you to be happy here."

Patrice wasn't sure if that were possible, but the hopeful look in her mother's eye made her want to try. "If that's the case, then help us start Kareem's business here."

Janice's grasp slackened. "Dear, that's his dream, not yours."

"Doing this for him is doing it for me." Patrice pulled her hand away.

Milton walked over. "Are you sure he's not just interested in your connections?"

"Yes, I'm sure. He didn't know anything about my past until Chad stormed back into my life."

Chad smirked. "You say that as if it were a bad thing. I am your brother."

"And we're your family," Janice said. "We love you."

Patrice met each one of their gazes. "Then help us."

Her mother sighed before giving her the same serene smile that said she wasn't really listening. "I'll do anything to help you."

Patrice rolled her eyes. "I'm going to my room."

"Of course, dear. You can change for dinner. Afterwards we'll talk about the party tomorrow." Janice's eyes drifted to the riot of kinks framing Patrice's head. "Maybe we could have a mother daughter day at the salon."

Patrice turned away from her mother, not sure if she would be able to talk without letting out her frustration.

Beth jumped up from the chaise. "Wait, I'll go with you."

Patrice smiled and nodded, even though she wasn't really in the mood for company. But it was hard to say no to Beth's enthusiasm.

• • •

Patrice opened the door to her old room and stopped.

"I know, it's completely different," Beth said from behind. Her sister shuffled forward to stand next to Patrice in the doorway. "They did everything a year after you left."

Completely different was an understatement. All hints that Patrice once lived there were removed. Pictures of her in high school, posters of her favorite singers, even the soft pink wall color, gone. Her parents had never changed a thing while she was in college. Now pale mint green walls, white lace curtains, and white furniture gave the appearance of any formal guest room in America.

Patrice finally got her feet to move and entered the room. "Where's all my stuff?"

"In the attic, I think. When you stopped calling them after the first year they decided to redecorate."

Patrice plucked at the fluffy pastel green and white duvet on the four poster queen bed. "If they were so eager to get rid of any reminder of me, why did they invite me back?"

"They weren't eager to get rid of reminders of you. I think it was Mother's way of getting over you not being here anymore. It was too hard to see all your stuff and know you didn't want to be here anymore."

There was no blame in Beth's voice, but Patrice's throat constricted for the pain her abrupt departure had caused her parents. "From what Chad told me, they always knew where I was and what I was doing."

"We did."

"There was no need for an investigator. I called you and let you know I was okay."

Beth leaned a shoulder one of the bedposts. "That wasn't enough for Mother and Father. They were worried about you. Even though they wouldn't talk about it." A hint of hurt crept into Beth's voice.

Crossing the room, Patrice examined the connecting bathroom also redecorated with new marble and tile.

"I couldn't ignore my problem anymore." Patrice meandered around the room, picking up the various vases and books in the staged room. "I won't ignore problems anymore."

"No one is asking you to, but your leaving hurt us, Patrice. I understand why you left and I can appreciate your need for time, but you also have to accept that your departure had consequences." Beth ran a hand across the foot of the bed. "I blamed myself."

"Why on Earth would you blame yourself?"

"I knew about the bulimia." Beth's gaze lowered to the floor.

Patrice sucked in a breath. "Why didn't you say anything?"

"I didn't know what to say. You hid it well; I didn't notice until right before you broke up with Roland and left."

Roland knew, Beth knew, and no one said anything. She'd been right to leave. Patrice moved to stand before the window.

Below, Kareem paced in the rose garden. Her shoulders relaxed. He hadn't left, even though she wouldn't blame him if he called the entire thing off.

Patrice opened the doors that led out to the second floor balcony for a better view. "So many times I thought about coming home, but each thought brought back those old feelings of panic."

"What's different now?"

"Chad butting in the way he always does. Even though he made me angry, the anger reminded me how much I missed everyone." Letting out a heavy sigh, Patrice leaned her hands on the balcony's iron rail. "I can't run away from my problems forever."

"And you're not alone." Beth gazed down at Kareem. "I like him."

Patrice's jaw slackened. "You do?"

"Yes, I do. I can tell that he cares about you."

If only that were true. This wasn't real.

"Why would you say that?" Patrice asked.

"Because of the way he protects you." Patrice frowned, and Beth's light laughter filled the air. "He is protective of you—the way he put his arm around your shoulders when you first came in and the way he touched your back after Chad tried to be a jerk. He was itching to jump to your defense."

Beth came closer, and grabbed Patrice's arm with both hands. "Then there's the way he looks at you. I can see why you fell for him. Not only is he sexy in that dangerous sort of way, but his eyes are trained on you."

Patrice shifted her stance, but her sister's grip didn't lessen. In less than ten minutes Beth saw exactly why Kareem intrigued Patrice.

"He's always like that. With everything he does."

"Even so, if helping him keeps you around longer, I will."

"How can you help?"

"I'll talk to Lad," Beth said with a grin.

Patrice jerked her arm away. "Roland's brother? I can't go to my ex-fiancé's brother for help."

A don't be silly chuckle from Beth. "It's not like that. You're not the only one getting married." Beth held up her left hand, where a huge diamond glittered on her finger.

Patrice grabbed her sister's hand and inspected the diamond. "Seriously?" she said with a grin.

"Seriously." Beth's voice was filled with love and excitement. "And I know what you're thinking. Lad and Roland don't hate you."

Not quite the thought in Patrice's head.

"Roland made sure everyone understood your breakup was mutual. He had nothing but good things to say about you after you left. There's nothing weird between our families."

At least Roland lied for her. He'd begged her to change her mind and go with him to Europe. Eventually he'd accepted her decision but told her he thought she was making a mistake and they could work through her problems together. The pain and sincerity in his eyes had haunted her for the first six months after she left. When she was so homesick and lonely she didn't know if she'd made the right decision.

"He really said that?"

"Yes. He's going to be thrilled you're back. He's moved on and is dating someone else, and now you have Kareem so working with them won't be weird. Roland is the president of the state chamber of commerce, and Lad is a CEO at Chapman Bank. With their support you're sure to make your business a success."

Patrice twisted her foot back and forth. Her gaze drifted back to the rose garden, but Kareem walked toward the front of the house. Hadn't she asked him here to keep Roland at bay, now she was going to ask him to work with the same guy?

"I don't know, Beth. Going to an ex for help is never a good idea."

"He's more than an ex. He's a friend, and pretty soon he'll be family." Beth took Patrice's hand in hers. "He told me himself he'll always treasure the time you had, but he's no longer in love with you. I'll talk to Lad. Between the two of us we'll get you set up."

If she were really engaged to Kareem, she doubted he would be cool with going to her ex-boyfriend for help starting a new business. But they weren't really engaged. And she doubted Kareem would appreciate her ignoring a very good connection.

"I'll give Roland a call," Patrice conceded.

Beth bounced on her toes. "No need. He'll be at the party tomorrow."

Of course he would. "Then I'll bring it up to him then." And hope that her fake fiancé would agree that asking Roland for help was the right move.

CHAPTER 9

Kareem lit his cigar and leaned against one of the pillars in the gazebo of the Baldwin family garden. With the first drag some of the tension in his shoulders evaporated. Until he thought about the dinner he'd just sat through following a *get to know you* conversation with her father. The talk with Milton had gone how he expected: "Hurt her and I'll hurt you." That Kareem respected. But the dinner. That had to be the worst family dinner he'd ever experienced. And thanks to his parents' love for family meetings, he'd sat through what seemed like hundreds. An hour of polite conversation about the party the next day. As if their oldest daughter hadn't just walked back into the house after a five year exile.

Neecie's mother and sister whisked her away the second dinner was over to show her the dresses they'd ordered for the party. The dresses included a few Janice purchased in the hopes Neecie would come home. Neecie—he refused to call her Patrice—seemed somewhat excited about that. Kareem viewed the whole deal as their way of transforming his vibrant Neecie into a cold carbon copy of themselves.

Footsteps came from Kareem's left. "Want a hit?" Joshua's eager voice interrupted Kareem's solitude.

Kareem let out a heavy sigh. The kid had watched him like he was some type of hero all night. If only the privileged boy realized the hard life wasn't as sexy as music and movies portrayed it.

"Hit what, boy?" Kareem asked, standing straight and taking a drag from his cigar.

Joshua held up his hand. Even in the muted light of the garden he could see the joint in the boy's fingers. Kareem shook his head and chuckled without amusement.

"So you smoke weed, huh?" He didn't bother to hide the mocking in his voice.

"A little. Come on, you can't tell me you don't want this instead of that weak ass cigar."

"Actually, boy, I can. I don't do drugs." He frowned as Joshua lit the joint and inhaled. The pungent scent of marijuana filled the air. "And you shouldn't either."

"I'm not a boy," Joshua said, not realizing the declaration made him sound more childlike than adult. "And what are you, a spokesperson for the anti-drug crowd? I know you went to prison for carjacking. Then you got into some trouble inside."

Kareem's stomach hardened. He forced himself to breathe normally. Only three people knew exactly what happened that night in that cell. He and Tim hadn't told anyone. The third man was dead.

"What do you know about my trouble on the inside?" Kareem's voice was cool, but hard.

"All my dad can dig up is a fight, but there has to be more. Your family got it covered up pretty good."

"Your family is good at digging." Dread crept across his skin. The exact happenings of that night were too humiliating. To have Neecie's family know, and possibly use that knowledge against him or her, was unacceptable.

"Good enough." Joshua took a drag off the blunt. "My dad is on a mission to keep you away from Aunt Patrice." His voice tightened and went up an octave.

"Out of everyone in this house I'm least likely to hurt her." Kareem put out the end of his cigar on the bottom of his shoe and started toward the house. "Just say no, kid."

"Hey wait," Joshua said after Kareem took several steps away. Kareem stopped, and Joshua walked over to him. "You still hang with the Runners? Can you tell me about that? I bet you all got into some cool shit."

This boy had a serious problem with his understanding of cool. Kareem could relate to Joshua's curiosity. Society parties, school, and playing the good kid didn't compare to the allure of the streets. Kareem's same wish to be big, bad, and bold as fuck had led him to screw up his entire life.

"That cool shit earned me five years in prison. I'm not a part of that anymore."

"But you're still tight with them, right? My dad said you aren't a member but you're still affiliated with the group. That former members work in your barber shop and stuff."

Kareem's hands tightened into fists. Chad was balls deep in Kareem's business. If Neecie's family needed to get this involved in his background, no telling how involved they would try to get in Neecie's life.

"Goodnight, kid." Kareem turned his back and marched back to the house. Joshua called him a few times but didn't follow. Probably so he could finish smoking his joint. Wonder if the perfect parents and grandparents knew the boy was a weed head? This family needed a serious case of intervention. No wonder she'd run away.

The voices of the men in the study drifted down the hall when Kareem came back inside. Bypassing them, he made his way to the curved staircase. Thick carpet, so perfectly white someone had to clean the damn thing weekly, cushioned his footsteps as he made his way to the room he shared with Neecie.

His body heated. The room she insisted they share.

Kareem opened the bedroom door and stopped. Neecie jerked clothes out of her suitcase and marched them to the closet where she haphazardly hung them. More clothes lay strewn over the bed, along with shoes, scarves, and bottles of what he assumed to be beauty items. Her hair was a halo of curls around her head. The wild mass in all its glory made him itch to touch it.

He itched to touch her. Licking his lips, he took in the round curve of her ass in a pair of tiny grey pajama shorts. Each stomp across the room made her perfect tits bounce beneath the matching long sleeved top. She dropped one of her shirts on the floor and bent over to pick it up, revealing a glimpse of her behind. His cock jumped to attention.

She picked up the shirt and reached for a hanger only to drop it again. "Dammit! Now I'm fat and clumsy."

That broke him from his thoughts. "What did you say?" Kareem stepped into the room and slammed the door.

She sucked in a breath and spun around. "How long have you been standing there?" she asked in a breathless voice.

"Long enough to hear you say something crazy." He crossed the room to stand on one side of the bed. "You can't possibly think you're fat?"

Her shoulders slumped and she came over to sit on the edge of the bed. "I was being sarcastic."

"To who?"

"Myself." She made no sense to him, and his confusion must have shown. "I'm not the same size I was when I left five years ago. The two dresses my mom got for me don't fit."

"Did she call you fat?" As if he needed another reason to dislike this family.

Neecie waved a hand and shook her head. "No. Not directly. She was very ... surprised to discover I've gone up a few dress sizes."

"What size do you wear?"

She blinked several times and leaned back. "Excuse me? You don't ask a woman her dress size."

"I do when the woman's complaining about it. What's your size? Because from where I'm standing ..." He let his gaze drift over the smooth expanse of brown skin along her thigh on the bed. "There's nothing wrong with your size. I think half the men in the shop would agree with that."

She averted her eyes, her sunshine smile peeking out. "Guys like booty, but that doesn't mean it's easy to fit into a dress."

She stood and walked back to the closet. He eyed her booty. He'd prefer to see her ass in those sexy shorts over a dress any day.

"Besides, I know I'm not fat, and I'm not freaking out over my dress size." She took a hanger and put the shirt on the handles. Her hand hesitated as she put the hanger back on the rack.

"You used to." It wasn't a question; he could hear the discomfort in her voice.

"All through high school and college I was a cheerleader and dancer. You know, those good activities for well brought up young ladies."

"I don't know." Kareem sat on the edge of the bed and slid aside a pile of her clothes. "I remember the cheerleaders in my high school and what happened on the back of the bus during away games. If I were ever crazy enough to have a daughter, she'd play chess."

Neecie's bright laughter filled the room, sending that need to belong through his chest. A comic he was not, but he'd love to make her laugh again.

She came back over and sat on the opposite side of bed. "Okay, not all cheerleaders were freaky on the back of the bus. Besides I was in private school."

"Private school girls were the worst. They were always looking for a bad boy."

"And were you willing to play the bad boy?"

"I was sixteen and drunk on my own hormones. Hell yes, I played the bad boy."

That got another laugh out of her and a smile out of him. When her laughter died down, she gave him a warm glance.

"You should smile more," she said.

"I never had a reason to smile before." Until her. He saw the look of pity on her face and moved on. "So, you were a dancer and cheerleader. Did that make you obsessed with your weight?"

"That was only part of my obsession to be perfect. I was head cheerleader, had the lead in the school ballet, a 4.3 grade point average, and was elected student body president. And that was just high school." He cringed, and she chuckled. "College was a repeat of the same, except dancing was replaced with sorority activities. Everyone told me I had this perfect life ... and don't get me wrong, my life was far from terrible. I let myself get caught up in the hype. My life was perfect, my family was perfect, I needed to be perfect." She slapped her hip and gave him a small smile. "Extra curves ... not perfect."

"Maybe in your circles, but in mine, a girl with curves like yours would have gotten all of the guys' attention." She definitely had his.

"I'm going to consider that a compliment," she said with a grin. "I know they don't come very often from you."

"I don't want to hear you downing yourself." He dropped any hint of humor from his voice. "There's nothing wrong with you."

She reached over a stack of clothes to place her hand over his. "I appreciate that. But believe me, I know. It took five years and a lot of soul searching, but I'm no longer struggling with those insecurities."

Her hand slowly slid away from his. The soft glide of her fingers reawakened the stirring in his pants. Kareem flipped his over and took hold of her small wrist. Patrice's pulse tapped against the palm of his hand, and she sucked in a breath.

"Why did you insist on sharing a room with me?"

"We're supposed to be engaged. If you were ... anyone else we'd share a room."

"You say that with a lot of certainty."

"Because I am certain."

He tugged on her wrist to make her lean forward—and also to get a better view down the front of her shirt. "You also said I'm not supposed to sleep with anyone else while we're pretending to be engaged."

"Like I told you, it makes our relationship convincing."

Her lips parted in an unsteady breath. He'd never paid much attention to Neecie's lips before; she had too many other parts worth studying. They were thick, full, and right now more inviting than a cold beer at the end of a rough week.

"I know of a better way to make this more convincing." He pulled her forward again.

The pile of clothes fell over, and something heavy landed on the bed. Neecie's gaze lowered. Her eyes widened, and she tried to break his grip. He looked down to an egg-shaped cylinder attached to a small black box with the words *Magic Bullet* written in gold. Blood rushed in his ears, and his body tightened.

Patrice reached for the sex toy, but he moved faster, snatching up the toy and standing on the side of the bed.

"Give that back." She crawled across the bed.

He stepped out of her reach and held the beige cylinder up to study. "What's this?"

"None of your business, now give it back."

"I think I can make it my business." Kareem looked away from the bullet to her. "I know of a few things I can do with this."

Her tattooed foot twisted in the carpet, flexing the muscles in her sexy thighs. "Kareem, quit playing."

He took a step toward her and switched the toy on, filling the room with a quiet buzz. Patrice's nipples pressed through the material of her shirt. The need to possess her flooded his system, breaking the levees of decency that just tried to make her feel better. "I've got a feeling you're thinking of a few things I can do with this, too."

● ● ●

The look in Kareem's eye sent a shiver down Patrice's spine. She had to be the dumbest woman on the planet. Hiding her sex toy someplace more secure than between a pile of clothes on the bed should've been the first thing she'd done. Now the one thing she'd brought to curb the craving of pretending to be Kareem's fiancée was in the long, thick fingers of the very man she shouldn't crave.

"Tell me, Neecie," he said in a deep, sexy voice. "What all do you think we can do with your bullet?"

He stepped into her space, surrounding her with the sweet smell of his cigars and the underlying scent that belonged to him.

"I thought you didn't know what it was." She aimed for a confident tone; instead her voice trembled like a hot and horny porn star.

"Why don't you show me how you use it?" He placed the vibrating end against the base of her throat.

"I didn't bring it to do personal demonstrations for you." Desire throbbed through her veins with each pulse, heightening her awareness and arousal to a fever pitch.

"Too bad, because right now I want that personal demonstration." He placed a hand at her waist and lowered his head to whisper in her ear. "Do you trail it across your body?" He dragged the sphere down her chest to the swell of her breast.

This is where she should stop Kareem and say they were going too far, before they got out of hand. Aching nipples begging for his attention and slick heat spreading between her thighs kept her mouth shut.

"Do you?" his rough voice demanded.

She swallowed hard, forced sound out of her mouth. "Sometimes."

He groaned and brought the bullet to hover over her beaded nipple. "Do you touch yourself here?" He made slow circles around the protruding tip.

The pleasurable vibrations shot through her breast. Patrice's hands clutched Kareem's waist, and her knees nearly buckled. Stopping him no longer seemed an acceptable option. "Mmm, yes."

His tongue quickly darted out to tease the shell of her ear. "Where do you go next?" His warm breath tickled.

She tried to pull back, to break the spell, but he moved forward with her. "Kareem."

"Tell me." He pulled the bullet away from her nipple.

Patrice's body ached from the loss. Yearned for more of his game. "Down my stomach."

Her breasts were heavy, her nipples hard and longing for more. The faint pulses hummed thorough her body as Kareem leisurely trailed the toy down her stomach.

"Like this?" He made lazy loops with the vibrator across her stomach. "I want to know what you like."

Patrice sucked in a breath. "Yes ... like that."

The hand on her waist pushed past the waistband of her shorts and gently cupped her rear. When his firm palm contacted her skin he groaned.

"Then where?"

She squirmed against him. "Further down."

He shook his head. "Say it."

"Between my legs."

He let out a soft chuckle. "You won't talk dirty for me."

Patrice's face prickled with heat. Dirty talk made her sound stupid, not sexy. And right now she doubted she could get out anything other than low moans.

Kareem dipped the bullet into her belly button. Patrice's stomach caved in. The vibration tickled and teased.

"Do you play first or go straight for your clit?" Kareem's thick voice rumbled in her ear. "Tell me, Neecie."

Patrice spread her legs. "Both ... I do both."

She felt Kareem's nod against the side of her head. He slid his hands past the elastic waistband of her shorts and underwear. Patrice buried her face in the soft cotton of his black shirt, and breathed in his scent. Anticipation tightened her body. Desire buzzed wet and wanton between her thighs.

Soft lips kissed her ear. "What would you do now?" Kareem gently ran the vibrator back and forth against the swollen wet folds of her sex. "Go for your clit or play with your lips?"

Patrice squeezed her eyes shut. This was not how the night was supposed to go. Her legs spread, allowing the back and forth motion of the vibrator to tremble across the protruding tip of her sex. Why fight? She wanted to sleep with this man.

"Straight for it?" she said.

His hand tightened on her waist. "For what?" His own need trembled in his voice.

Patrice swallowed. "My clit."

"Eager, aren't you?" Pleasure filled his voice. She barely registered his words because, thank the stars, he finally pressed the toy against her clit. Steady pulses vibrated her body. Kareem worked in fast, light circles—just enough pressure to make her push her hips forward for more. Her shaky legs spread further, opening her entirely to his pleasure. Kareem pressed his entire hand over her sex, sandwiching the bullet between his strong hand and her wet heat.

Tremors of pleasure cracked and sparked deep in her midsection and across her skin. Her body jerked. The orgasm hitting every nerve she possessed. "Ah, yes, yes!" She trembled all over, her hands clutched his shirt, and her head fell backwards.

Kareem's mouth clamped down on her throat. He lightly bit her and sucked the soft skin. The movement was raw and shocking. More trembles wracked her body.

The sound of their ragged breathing and the buzz of the vibrator echoed in the room. When her grip on his shirt loosened, Kareem removed his hands from her shorts and turned off the toy. The silence pressed in around them, bringing awareness of what they'd done. Kareem lifted his head to stare at her. She smiled, wonderment and pleasure seeping into her bones and making her feel as if she were floating in air.

A line formed between his brows and he glanced away. Uncertainty blew away her rosy afterglow. She'd seen the casual way Kareem had tossed aside his ex. Heat rushed up her cheeks; here she was thinking what happened meant something. For him what they'd done was just another sexual encounter.

She tried to step out of his embrace, but he held tight to her waist. "I'm going outside on the balcony for a few minutes," he said.

"You didn't want to ...?" She glanced at the bed. *Man, I'm such a weenie. Just ask the man to screw your brains out.*

Kareem shook his head. "No. I need to clear my head."

She wasn't sure what that was supposed to mean. His arousal pressed into her stomach. Kareem wasn't totally unaffected by what happened, but that knowledge didn't stop her growing unease.

"Sure, I guess," she said.

He continued to watch her. She lowered her gaze. The entire episode was so surreal. She was still in his embrace, her body still hummed with the aftermath of her climax. This was supposed to be the precursor to ... something, but he needed to clear his head?

Kareem slowly let her go and took a step back. She glanced up at him. The heat in his gaze sent another tremble across her skin.

He closed his eyes and turned away, then spun back and brushed a thumb across her cheek. Kareem lifted her chin with his knuckle. "Not tonight, Neecie, but soon." His voice was low, urgent.

He tossed the bullet on the bed, then stalked out on the balcony. Slowly, Patrice crossed the room to pick up the toy. Her hand rose to the spot on her cheek he'd touched. They'd gone too far, too fast. They wouldn't be together forever, but from the way her body hummed for more, she wanted right now more than forever. Wanted the hot sex and to see the glimpses of humor Kareem let through. Lord help her, but she was going to make Kareem her lover.

CHAPTER 10

Kareem's strong fingers gripped her hips and bent Patrice over the bathroom counter. Her legs spread wide, and he steadily drove in and out from behind. Her hands clutched the cool granite. The edges pressed painfully into her palms to keep her from falling over with the force of his thrusts. The mixture of pleasure and pain sent another rush of desire to her core. Too soon her body convulsed around his rigid cock. Her toes curled on the cold tile floor and her vision blurred.

Patrice's eyes popped open. The green and white pillowcase on the bed greeted her instead of the reflection of her and Kareem in the bathroom mirror. Her heart thumped; the sticky aftermath of her orgasm throbbed with the beat. Morning sunlight brightened the room, meaning the third sex dream she'd had about Kareem had at least woken her up during the daytime. The other two woke her in the middle of the night and she lay staring at the dark ceiling of the bedroom waiting for sleep to return. Or for Kareem to join her. Not once in her fitful sleep had she woken to find him beside her.

She ran her hand across her eyes and groaned, rolling over to the side of the bed Kareem should have occupied, and froze. Kareem sat in one of the wingback chairs on the other side of the room. He'd turned the chair to face the bed, and was watching her. Powerful shoulder muscles were revealed by a dark sleeveless t-shirt. Thick dreads hung loose around his shoulders, begging for her to grab them and pull him down on her. All of the desire from her dream turned into a shiver across her body.

Holding the sheet to her chest, Patrice slowly sat up. "What are you doing?"

"Watching you."

"For how long?" Edginess crept into her voice. There'd been a lot of moaning and groaning going on in her dream. If he'd sat there long enough he must have heard every one.

"Long enough to wonder what you're dreaming about."

She wished the sheets would catch on fire. "I don't remember."

"You remember," he said in that no nonsense voice. He leaned forward in the chair and rested his elbows on his knees. "Tell me one thing. Were those good moans, or bad moans?"

His voice hadn't changed, nor did his eyes give anything away, but she sensed that he was concerned about her answer.

"They were good moans."

"Were you dreaming about me, or someone else?"

As if she could think of anyone else right now. "You."

His nostrils flared and he gripped his hands together between his knees. "I'm not good at the sleeping together, making love, cuddling type of thing you deserve."

The exact words that should tell her to pretend last night hadn't happened. Forget all of her wild dreams about Kareem bending her over things, or how enticing the hard, demanding edge in his voice was. She wanted roses, and love songs, and cuddling one day.

Today, she wanted him.

Patrice bent her knees to hug them to her chest. "Right now I'm interested in the no strings attached you're offering."

His left knee bounced up and down and his eyes narrowed slightly. "There will be strings. We're pretending to be a couple.

No strings for me usually means I don't see you the next day. Or ever again."

Again, words that should scare her off. They didn't. "Why can't we have some fun while we're helping each other out?"

He shook his head. "Neecie, you deserve all of the stuff those guys sing about in those love songs. Not what I can give you."

Patrice's back snapped straight. "Don't tell me what I deserve, or need, or should want. I've had that my entire life, and I walked away from it. Now that I'm home, I'll probably begin hearing what I deserve from my family all over again. I didn't ask you here to give me the same treatment."

Kareem's leg stopped bouncing, but otherwise he didn't react. Just watched her with those expressionless black eyes. Patrice fought not to fidget and met his stare head on. After several seconds, Kareem's gaze dipped to her cleavage. He licked his lips, and the memory of the way he'd licked her ear then bit her shoulder added moisture to her already wet shorts.

Slowly Kareem rose from the chair and crossed the room to the side of the bed. "Fine."

Patrice blinked. What exactly had they agreed to? That he wouldn't tell her what she deserved, or that they would be doing more of what happened the night before?

"I don't think your family is going to willingly help open the salon," he said with a shrug.

She released her knees and sat up on her heels. She wasn't sure if they'd settled the first conversation, but even she wouldn't go so far as to beg a guy for clarification that he'd sleep with her.

"Beth wants to help."

He strolled back to the chair where a black long sleeved t-shirt rested on the chair. "Your sister?" His voice had an *I'm not impressed* quality.

"Her fiancé is CEO of Chapman Bank, and his brother is president of the state chamber of commerce."

Kareem stretched his arms to put on the shirt. The black undershirt lifted to expose a flat stomach and a trail of dark hair. Patrice's tongue ran across her bottom lip.

"We join the chamber," Kareem said, slipping on the shirt. "Make the connections we need, then go to your brother-in-law for help with the loan."

"Umm ... yeah, pretty much." Better to get him on board with the plan before revealing one of the people they were relying on was her ex.

Kareem nodded and tugged on the edges of the shirt to straighten it out. "Your nephew knows everything there is to know about my past. I've got the feeling he's going to make it known to anyone who'll listen." He crossed back over to the bed. A thick line formed between his brows. "Will that be a problem?"

Patrice shook her head and crawled to the side of the bed. Standing on her knees on the mattress, she reached out and smoothed the line between his eyebrows. Kareem jerked back. Patrice let out a frustrated sigh. "It will be if you keep scowling at everyone who looks your way. Part of business is being charming and agreeable."

"That's not me."

She grinned and held out her arms. "That's why I'm your business partner. I'm the charming one, you're the one with the big ideas. But I will need you to at least try to be somewhat approachable."

His mouth quirked and a dash of humor brightened his eyes. "I get it. Smile, nod, listen to conversations about nothing."

"And tell people about your idea. Now's the time to sell the dream. Why your salon will be different from the barber shop down the street. Let them know the benefits of having a modern, masculine place that offers traditional grooming services but with style."

The line came back between his brows, but not as deep. "You really did read my business plan."

"I did, and I love your idea. But I can't sell it by myself. You're going to have to crack a few more friendly smiles."

He gave her that stare she was starting to realize meant he processed her words but was unlikely to agree or disagree.

"I've got to go out for a while," he said. "Will you be okay this morning?"

Patrice plopped back on her heels. "I agreed to the mother daughter spa day."

"Good." Kareem came closer and trailed his fingers down the side of her neck to the top of her cleavage. A line of sparks followed his fingers. He tugged on the hem of her shirt. "I'll be back as soon as I can." He dropped his hand and gently patted her hip, then turned to walk out.

Patrice frowned at the door, confused about what exactly was going on between her and Kareem.

CHAPTER 11

After spending the past few years styling other people's hair, Patrice thoroughly enjoyed letting someone else take care of her. The stylists at the spa were amazing. Though at first she'd had a moment of panic when the owner Tina gasped at the sight of Patrice's thick, natural hair. Tina had cut, relaxed, and grown Patrice's hair since she was a little girl.

"I still can't believe you cut off all your hair," Tina said as she sectioned Patrice's freshly washed hair into sections.

"That was five years ago. My hair's grown a lot since then."

"What made you do it?" Tina pulled out her blow dryer.

Patrice's palms became slick. "I just wanted something different." She eyed the blow dryer. "I haven't straightened my hair in years."

Tina gently squeezed Patrice's shoulder. "Then this will be fun!"

Tina turned on the blow dryer. Seconds later the pull of her brush followed by the heat of the dryer tugged at the back of Patrice's head. Patrice's fingers gripped and loosened on the chair's leather armrests. Cutting off her hair had been part of the process to "find" herself when she'd left, stripping away everything that defined the old Patrice. Including the long, straight hair everyone complimented her on.

Her mother sat in the salon chair next to Patrice getting highlights from Tina's assistant. Beth sat beneath the overhead dryer but looked back and forth at them as if she could hear every word in the noisy salon.

"You can do something different without cutting off all of your hair," Tina said over the roar of the dryer. "No one can see how beautiful your hair is if you keep it tied up in those scarves or twisted against your head."

Heat not related to the blast of hot air forcing out every kink in her hair shot up her spine. "I've gotten a lot of compliments about my natural hair. There are a lot of women who are clients of Fresh Cutz because they saw me cutting hair and wanted their hair to look like mine."

The dryer turned off and Tina spun Patrice's chair around. She placed a hand on her slender hip and raised a perfectly arched brow. Even in a black t-shirt, dark jeans, and wearing an apron, Tina managed to look sophisticated and beautiful the way any stylist who charged over $100 for a wash and set could.

"Wait a second, *you* cut hair?"

"I do."

"Why?" Tina asked.

"Because I like it. Cosmetology and barbering were my interests before I left."

"There are other ways to get involved in the beauty industry without working in some corner barber shop," Janice said in a perfectly smooth voice.

"I'm sure there are, Mother," Patrice said.

Janice held up a hand, and the assistant stopped slathering color. Janice leaned toward Patrice. "In fact, I met Lorelei Meadows at a ladies luncheon the other day. She's opening an office for her modeling agency in Charlotte and mentioned hiring in-house beauticians. I know how much you used to devour her beauty tips."

Devour wasn't a strong enough word. Lorelei was one of the biggest names in modeling, fashion, and beauty, and was one of the first agency owners who advocated and promoted plus size models back when a size negative zero was the only thing considered beautiful. Patrice had loved, and still followed, her advice on ways to work all assets to their best.

"You met Lorelei?" Patrice couldn't keep the awe out of her voice.

A satisfied gleam came to Janice's eyes, and she leaned back and signaled for the woman to start on her hair again. "I did, and invited her to the anniversary party tonight. She RSVP'd, so I'll be sure to introduce you to her. Maybe you can work at her agency and be around the beauty industry you love."

In a more fitting atmosphere. Janice didn't say that, but Patrice heard the implication. "I can't turn my back on Kareem. We're here to start our own venture."

"Oh do tell," Tina said, going back to blow drying Patrice's hair. If she hadn't gone to Tina for years, she'd assume her beautician's tendency to turn on the blow dryer after asking a question meant she never wanted to hear the answer. But Tina's ears could pick up conversations from across the room when every blow dryer in the building was going.

"My f ... fiancé." She nearly tripped over calling him that. "He's a master barber. He wants to open up a high-end salon for men."

"I thought it was your goal as well." Janice was quick to catch that. Add supersonic dryer blasting hearing to her mother's ears as well.

"It is, but the idea originated with Kareem." Patrice made eye contact with Tina in the mirror. "We're looking at possible locations to open *our* salon here in Charlotte."

Tina grinned and nodded while her hands efficiently straightened Patrice's hair. "Good for you. You'd be surprised how many guys ask me to cut their hair but hate the thought of coming into my spa. I think it'll be a niche that needs an outlet."

Janice's lip pressed together and her freshly manicured nails dug into her arms. Patrice appreciated Tina's support, even if her mother didn't.

"How's your son, Tina?" Patrice asked to get the topic off of her.

"He's a big brother now." Tina's face lit up, and she went into several stories about her seven-year-old son and five-year-old daughter.

Two hours later, Patrice stood in front of the mirror and stared at the woman she hadn't seen in nearly five years. Her flat ironed hair hung to her shoulders, not as long as before she left, but long enough to satisfy both her mother and Tina that cutting her hair wasn't an apocalyptic event. Makeup, something else she'd only worn sparingly since leaving, enhanced her skin, eyes, and lips. Her face couldn't breathe. The makeup sealed her now invisible pores like a clear plastic film.

Beth came over and gave her a hug from behind. "You look fantastic. You can't tell me you didn't miss this?"

"There are some perks I can't deny." Patrice rubbed the arm Beth had draped around her neck.

Beth raised her eyebrows. "Is it enough to make you stay?"

"I have a life back in Columbia, Beth. Even when Kareem opens his place here, it doesn't mean I'll be in Charlotte full time. We'll have the other shop to run as well." And when this farce ended, she could return to Columbia and try to forget the imprint Kareem was sure to leave on her heart.

Beth let her go and moved to block Patrice's view of the mirror. "Why not? Your family is here, your fiancé will be here. There's no reason to leave."

"This is different."

"How?"

"Kareem never said he wanted to live here. I couldn't leave him."

"You left Roland," Beth countered.

Patrice sighed. "Roland isn't Kareem."

"I believe I heard that last night," Beth said with a sly grin.

A shocked laugh burst from Patrice's lips. "Excuse me?"

"I came by your room last night to talk and heard some of your, shall I say interaction, with Kareem." Beth fanned herself. "I guess I can understand why you're hesitant to leave him behind."

Heat crept up Patrice's face, and she playfully pinched Beth's arm. "Can we talk about this somewhere else?"

Beth cocked her head to the side. "Remember when we watched *Dirty Dancing* as kids? Then later agreed Johnny was good for a summer affair but he'd make a terrible husband?"

"Yes, but ..."

"Kareem is your Johnny. He's the summer fling, the bad boy who's a good lay after you went away and got your head together."

Patrice shifted her stance and propped a hand on her hip. "What happened to wanting to help us start the business? I thought you were on my side."

"I am. Believe me, I am. And I'm not changing my promise to ask Lad to put in a good word to help Kareem start his business. He obviously means a lot to you, and you mean something to him."

Patrice had to fight not to lower her gaze. She wasn't sure what she meant to Kareem. He'd given her an orgasm then walked away as if he'd just passed the salt at dinner.

"Helping him doesn't mean I won't try and convince you that staying home and being with your family is what you need to do. We miss you, and it just makes more sense for you to be here with us."

"More sense for whom? I was happy away."

"You can be happy here." Beth grasped Patrice's hands. "Work on his place, but talk to Lorelei tonight at the party. Tell her about what you'd like to do, I'm sure she'd be thrilled to have you work for her. You'd be able to work in beauty and fashion, be close to us, and figure out your next moves." Beth gave her another hug, when she leaned back, she wore their mother's perfect smile. "Think about it."

Beth let Patrice go and glided away. Patrice gazed back at the familiar stranger in the mirror. One who would look perfect working at a Lorelei Meadows modeling agency.

CHAPTER 12

When Patrice returned to her parents' house with her mother and sister after leaving the spa, the first thing she noticed was Kareem walking toward the rose garden.

"Your fiancé really likes that side of the house," Janice said after she pulled her Mercedes into one of the slots of the garage.

"He likes being outside." Patrice had no clue if that were true or not, but her excuse sounded better than a vague *I noticed the same thing.*

She jumped out of the back of the car. "I'll see you in the house," she called over her shoulder, and she made her way to the garden.

She rounded the corner to the rose garden. Kareem sat in one of the wrought iron chairs with his back to her, his black leather jacket blocking the cool breeze of the afternoon. His head was bent over, and his shoulders moved as if he were either writing or drawing. The grass, still green in the middle of fall thanks to fertilizer and irrigation, cushioned her steps. Tip-toeing toward him, she held her breath, hoping to get a peek at what he was doing.

She bit her lower lip and stretched her neck to see when he snapped the notebook shut.

"What's up, Neecie?"

Her breath came out in a huff and she fell back on her heels. "How did you know it was me?"

"I smelled you."

The smile that was starting froze, and she lifted her sweater to her nose and sniffed. "Smelled me?"

"Yes, you smell like hair products and fruit. You always smell like fruit." He lifted a leg onto the chair and turned to face her.

For a split second his dark stare struck her speechless. Kareem had a way of looking through her. His sharp gaze penetrated the layers to see the yearning she didn't want anyone to know about.

"I smell like fruit?" she finally asked after snapping herself out of the Kareem trance.

"Yeah," he said, but his voice sounded like he'd already moved on. He stood and faced her with a scowl. "What happened to your hair?"

She ran her hand through the silky straight strands. "They straightened it."

"They who?"

"Okay, she straightened it. My mom's stylist. You don't like it?"

"No."

For a split second she felt like she should have asked his permission—not surprising with the censure practically oozing from his voice, which in turn sent anger surging through her system.

"Good thing it's my hair," she snapped.

"It's not your hair; it's your mother's hair."

"What it that supposed to mean?"

"It means exactly what you implied. They straightened your hair. Your mother and her stylist. Now you look like them."

"I'm her daughter; of course I'm going to look like them."

The glower on his face grew darker. "You know what I mean."

"No, I don't. What did you expect to happen when I left for the spa this morning?"

"I like it better curly."

That robbed her breath. First she smelled like fruit and now he liked her hair curly. Kareem gave a pretty good impression of a guy who paid a lot of attention to her.

The anger drained from her body. "I didn't know you had a preference," she said, crossing her arms and twisting her foot on the ground. "Or that you cared."

His frown relaxed then tightened again. "The curly hair, the scarves. It suits you."

"Do I look terrible with straight hair?"

He studied her, his gaze tracing over her face and followed the fall of her hair to her shoulders. "Not terrible. Just not like Neecie."

She smiled at the compliment. He crossed his arms, and his features froze. "Did you straighten it for him? Your ex-fiancé?"

She clenched her teeth to keep from swearing. She didn't want to get into a discussion with Kareem about Roland.

"No, I wasn't thinking about him when I did it. Why would you think that anyway?"

"According to your father, this guy was perfect for you. Why did you break up with him?" Kareem completely ignored her question, a habit of his that annoyed Patrice.

"That's none of your business."

"It is my business." He took a step forward, crowding her space and filling her senses with his inviting cologne. "I can't walk around making the same mistakes this *perfect* guy made. Your family will wonder why you're with someone so *imperfect* if that happens."

"Believe me, you wouldn't make the same mistakes he did."

"What was his mistake, Neecie?" he demanded.

She couldn't tell him about her bulimia, wouldn't let him know about how truly screwed up she used to be and refused to let him see her as weak.

"We just didn't work out, okay? I needed space, so I broke things off and left. We parted as friends." She met his stare, knowing he searched for any indication of a lie.

"Anything else I should know about?"

She shook her head. Now was the time to mention Roland possibly helping them. "What did you do today?"

He watched her for what seemed like an eternity. Her heart's tempo increased with every passing second.

"Went into town, came back, and played tennis with your father." Kareem shrugged.

Patrice held up a hand. "Hold up, hold up, hold up. Tennis?"

"Yeah, tennis," he said, way too no nonsense for Patrice's understanding. "I used to play in high school. Before not playing and pissing off my dad became more interesting. I surprised your father and your brother."

"Chad played?"

Kareem's lip lifted. "And we didn't kill each other. Surprisingly." His start of a smile melted away. "They think I'll hurt you."

"Will you hurt me?" she blurted out. She already knew the answer. Yes, he'd hurt her—if she didn't keep her mind right and realize they were only pretending.

"Are we really together?" he asked with a half shrug.

The anger revved back up. Pain joined in. "No, we aren't."

She spun on her heels to stomp toward the house. The sound of his determined footsteps registered a second before his hand grasped her elbow and spun her around to face him. The notebook she was dying to look at a few minutes earlier hit the ground, and he pressed her body against his.

"Wrong answer, Neecie." He didn't raise his voice, but the power behind his words hit her with the force of a punch to the gut. Instead of frightening her, her body heated as desire crept across her skin. "After last night you are mine. No exes, no new guys, no one else, understand."

His sudden bout of possessiveness combined with his hard muscled body made her angry and aroused. But his demand was no different than hers.

"I understand," she said. "But answer my question. Will you hurt me?"

The angry scowl on his face flickered to something else. She'd call the look insecurity, but couldn't fathom Kareem insecure about anything. The tension in his body seeped away, and longing filled his dark eyes. Kareem lowered his eyes and pulled back. After several breaths, his gaze returned to hers. The emotion gone.

"Only if you ask me to."

"That makes no sense." She opened her mouth to argue, and he placed a finger over her lips, robbing her ability to speak.

A deep line formed between his brows, and he slowly traced his finger around the edges of her mouth. Patrice tried to breathe as the pads of his finger gently caressed the fullness of her lips. Gradually his hand slid across her chin and neck. The light, tickling touch sent sparks of excitement through her chest.

His nostrils flared, yet she didn't think he breathed. She lifted her chin and slightly opened her mouth, hoping he'd eradicate the inches between them and kiss her. Taking a step forward, the sensitive tips of her breasts brushed his chest. The touch resonated deep in her midsection and lower. Kareem sucked in a breath. His hand stretched to cover her neck then slowly lowered to settle over the irregular pounding of her heart.

Patrice gripped his upper arm, fingers flexing across the rock hard bicep. She tugged forward, and though he outweighed and could easily overpower her, his body shifted forward until they pressed together. His hand eased up to the back of her head, long fingers slipped through the straight strands of her hair. Her pulse fluttered, and time seemed to stop as Kareem ever so slowly lowered his head. Patrice's lids fluttered closed. She rose onto her toes, and she lifted her chin.

Kareem's soft lips brushed her cheek then lightly pulled her ear. "Tonight, Neecie." His desire thickened voice sent trembles through her body that gathered at the pulse point between her legs. "I'll give you everything you want, tonight."

Her eyes popped open. Disappointment that he hadn't kissed her warred with her excitement in his sensual promise.

"We'll make love tonight," she said.

Kareem ran thick fingers across her lower lip. "No, we'll have sex tonight. I need you to understand the difference. I like it hard, and fast, and more than once. I want you chanting my name. I want you to sweat so hard your curls come back while I drive so deep you come hard and fall asleep afterwards. I'm going to leave no doubt in your mind that in the bedroom, we're together. Do you understand?"

Patrice didn't know if she should be excited or put off. The hard tips of her breasts and slippery wetness between her thighs craved what he offered. Her brain registered the truth. He wanted to have sex with her, but that was all.

She nodded. Kareem shook his head.

"Say it," he said. "Tell me you understand."

"I understand." *That I am a crazy, sexually frustrated fool.*

• • •

Patrice leaned over to look in the mirror while she slipped on a pair of diamond stud earrings. Kareem strolled over and lightly grasped her waist. The heat from his palm radiated through her entire hip. She jerked and dropped the earring. They made eye contact in the mirror. The corner of Kareem's mouth inched up into a knowing half-smile, and Patrice's breath stuck in her throat.

Kareem gently squeezed her hip. "Are you ready?"

Patrice's hand slightly trembled as she picked up the earring. The guy had her so wired she didn't know what to do with herself.

"I am." She turned to face him. Kareem's hand slipped away from her waist, but he stayed in her space, overwhelming her senses and warming her body. He smelled divine, his broad, strong shoulders filled out a crisp black dress shirt, and his dreads were twisted back.

"Are *you* ready?" she asked.

Kareem ran a hand across his lower lip and smirked. "I've attended my fair share of society parties. I know the drill. Smooth jazz, cocktails, and fake laughter."

"Ahh, but you've never been to a Baldwin family party. You might have more fun than you expect."

"Doubtful." His gaze slowly wandered down her body.

Shifting her weight to one foot she placed a hand on her hip for his inspection. The long sleeved black maxi dress she'd brought for the party had a scooped neckline and white asymmetrical stripes along the skirt. A thin white belt accented her waist. The material clung just enough to show off her curves, and she'd let her hair hang in a thick curtain to her shoulders.

"Are you finished with your inventory?" she said with a grin.

Kareem's gaze returned to hers. "Let's go." He turned toward the door.

Patrice dropped her arm and considered hitting him in the back of his head. She flipped her hair and followed.

Kareem stopped at the door and faced her. "You look good, Neecie."

Her stomach went gushy, and her heart skipped in her chest. "Thank you. You aren't half-bad yourself."

One side of Kareem's mouth lifted and a spark flashed in his dark eyes. "Come on, girl." Putting a hand on her waist he ushered her out of the door.

They drove his car the short distance to the large clubhouse in her parents' neighborhood. Janice loved parties, but wasn't fond of the cleanup afterwards.

A large crowd mingled inside of the clubhouse where a brass band played music before a large dance floor. Tables decorated with crystal and blue hydrangea, the flower that made up her mother's wedding bouquet, surrounded the floor. Though it was chilly outside, the patio was closed in with a clear tent draped in white lights.

Beth spotted them first and did her skip glide across the room to hug Patrice. "You look beautiful, and sexy." She winked. Beth glanced at Kareem, and her smile dipped at the edges. "Kareem, you're dressed in all black again."

He shrugged. "I like the color."

Beth gave Patrice a questioning look, but Patrice didn't have the answer. If he wouldn't let her see his notebook, she doubted he'd answer why he only dressed in black.

Patrice wrapped her arm around his waist. Already his body was stiff as granite. "The color looks good on him."

Beth's bright smile returned. "Of course it does. Come on, let's mingle."

Speakers amplified the band's jazz music for the outdoor guests. Kareem bumped her with his elbow and pointed to the speaker. "Jazz."

She held up a hand. "Just wait. It gets better."

"Oh my God, Patrice Baldwin, I haven't seen you in years!" A thick female drawl came from Patrice's left.

Patrice spun around to a tall, slim beauty with caramel skin. "Rhonda!" She grinned and embraced her old high school friend. "You look fantastic."

Rhonda ran a hand over her blue grey suit. "Pilates twice a day and a strict diet." Rhonda's gaze traveled to Patrice's hips. "And you look healthy. Who knew you could pull off curvy so well."

Patrice gritted her teeth. She fought not to run sweaty palms across her dress. "Thanks, Rhonda," she said in a flat voice.

Kareem wrapped an arm around her shoulders and pulled her back against his hard chest. "Neecie does more than pull off curvy; she owns it."

Rhonda brought a hand to her heart. "Oh … and you are?"

"Kareem Henderson, her fiancé." Kareem held out his free hand.

A light came into Rhonda's eyes as they swept appreciatively across Kareem. "Well, isn't that fantastic. Congratulations, girl, you've got yourself a hottie."

Patrice blinked several times. "Thanks."

Beth chuckled. "I said the same thing, Rhonda."

Within seconds other old friends surrounded her and Kareem, giving air kisses and congratulating her on her new engagement. Kareem's lips hovered between a tight smile and pressed-together lips, both of which she preferred over his scowl.

With every introduction her old connections eventually brought up how nice she looked. Usually after a quick inventory. Patrice could practically hear the questions. *What happened to her figure? She used to be so thin!* Surprisingly the silent judgment didn't bother her, and as the night went on she found herself annoyed yes but also happy. Leaving and becoming comfortable with herself had been the best things she'd ever done.

Kareem pulled Patrice away from the group to just inside the clubhouse. "These people were your friends?"

She frowned and nodded. "They were."

"No wonder you ran away."

They made eye contact, and she grinned. After a second a devastating grin crossed his face and made her insides quiver, Kareem took a step closer, and Patrice leaned against the door.

"You know I'd take your curves over their stick figures any day?" He leaned in and spoke low.

Heat swept through Patrice's midsection, and she pressed her thighs together. "Oh really?"

Kareem's dark eyes dropped to her cleavage. "Really."

"Patrice, dear, come over and let me introduce you to Lorelei Meadows," Janice's voice broke through the moment.

Patrice looked heavenward and sighed. When she met Kareem's gaze again he winked and her stomach fluttered. "I'll be right back."

Kareem stepped out of her space. "Have fun. I'll mingle and check out all the excitement you promised me."

"Is that sarcasm? Don't tell me Kareem Henderson has a sense of humor."

"Apparently you bring it out in me." He cocked his head toward Janice, who stood watching with narrowed eyes. "Go talk to your mother."

Kareem nodded at Janice. "Lovely party," he said then strolled away.

Patrice studied the sexy way his slacks draped over his ass. He walked toward the back of the room, and people moved out of his way—maybe because he walked with purpose, not slouched or hesitant, but with a stride that said don't get in my way unless you have a reason.

A sharp pinch slashed through her upper arm. "Ouch!" Patrice rubbed her arm and faced her mother. "What was that for?"

"Because it's not ladylike to drool," Janice said, but then she smiled.

"I wasn't drooling." Patrice ran a finger across her wet lower lip.

"Of course you weren't dear," Janice said with humor. "Come along."

Janice led Patrice across the room to a group of women. Patrice recognized Lorelei immediately. The modeling queen wore a stylish garnet pantsuit, and her long reddish brown hair was pulled up into a complicated knot on the side of her head. Lorelei towered over the women in the group.

"I've heard so much about you, Patrice," Lorelei said after the introductions. "Your mother said you're interested in modeling."

"Not so much modeling," Patrice replied. "I've always been interested in the fashion and beauty industry but from behind the camera doing hair and makeup. I used to read your tips in *Radiant* magazine religiously."

"Have you studied or worked in the beauty industry?"

"Not on your scale. I've gotten my cosmetology license and studied to become a master barber in South Carolina, I just haven't completed that. I worked in a beauty salon in Jacksonville until I moved to Columbia and started cutting men's hair."

Interest lit up Lorelei's green eyes. "Really, why the switch?"

"Men care about looking good just as much as women, but they're usually easier to please. And it's just easy to chat with guys."

Lorelei placed the tips of her fingers on Patrice's arm. "You wouldn't believe how many male models love having their hair washed and cut by women. Why don't you come by my office one day next week? We can talk about you possibly apprenticing at my agency. If I like your style, then we'll see."

Patrice could barely keep the grin off her face. "I'll call and make an appointment."

Patrice met Janice's eye, who grinned as if Lorelei had offered her the job. "I'm so glad that worked out," Janice said.

The conversation switched to another topic, and Patrice searched the room for Kareem. She hadn't spotted him when a hand tapped her shoulder.

She spun around then froze. "Roland." She said his name, exhaling.

"Hello, Patrice." Nostalgia hit hard hearing the smooth cultured voice she used to listen to for hours on the phone at night throughout her teens. She used to tremble and sigh with wonder when he'd wait for her at her locker or waited by her dorm on the weekends he visited her at college. Roland's dark eyes and chocolate skin had matured in a way women paid hundreds for through cosmetics.

"It's good to see you," she said.

Roland spread his arms, stretching open the jacket of his charcoal grey suit. Patrice automatically accepted his hug. Hugging Roland was as natural as hugging her sister or parents. His arms were both foreign and familiar. After breaking the embrace, Roland pulled her hands into his. His hands were warm, but sweaty, and his eyes wary.

"You look wonderful." Unlike the barely veiled sarcasm that came from others when they said the same, Roland's voice rang with sincerity.

"Thank you, Roland. You look good, too."

"I came with my girlfriend." He pointed to a woman with beautiful mocha skin watching them while she danced with an older gentleman. "I decided to wait before introducing you. I was concerned you wouldn't want to see me." The wariness in his eyes increased.

Patrice shook her head, glad to know Roland had brought a date to the party. Dousing her fear he had hopes to rekindle their relationship. "I know I left in a rush ... and broke things off, but that was never about you. Not really."

Roland's face relaxed. "I understand that now. I always worried you were out in the world hating me."

"I never hated you. We share too much history for me to hate you."

He squeezed her hands. "You have no idea how much it pleases me to hear that." Roland glanced over her shoulder and slowly let her hands go.

A hand slid across her lower back to grasp her waist a second before Kareem's imposing figure towered at her side. He didn't have the polish, or sophistication, but the smell of the oil he used on his hair and the hardness of his muscles swept away her nostalgia and instantly electrified her body.

She bent her head back and smiled at him. Kareem wore a smile, but the dark glint in his eye and the coiled tension in his body made her want to run and hide. He turned hard, flat eyes on Roland. Yeah, getting him to accept her ex's help was a dumb idea.

CHAPTER 13

"Kareem, this is Roland Simmons." Neecie held out her hand to the country club cutout who'd held her hand too long, in Kareem's opinion.

Kareem accepted the guy's firm, and sweaty, handshake. "Kareem Henderson."

Roland gave him a glossy politician's smile. "Ah, the lucky guy. Congratulations on your engagement. You've got a wonderful woman." Roland studied Neecie with adoring eyes.

Kareem gritted his teeth. This was the former fiancé. Neecie didn't need to say anything; their friendly greeting, the warm smiles, the way the guy couldn't keep his eyes from roaming over her body with the knowing look of a former lover said it all.

Kareem moved his arm from Neecie's waist to gently rub her lower back. "She is special."

Neecie gave him a tight smile. "Roland and I have known each other since we were kids."

"Old friends, huh?" Kareem said.

Roland chuckled and tilted his head. "You can say that."

Neecie took a deep breath. "We were once engaged."

Kareem squeezed her hip. "So you're the guy. I'd say I'm sorry things didn't work out, but you know."

Neecie's body stiffened, and Roland's easy smile turned brittle. They exchanged wary looks that made Kareem narrow his eyes.

"Yes, well," Roland said and cleared his throat. "I guess I can't fault you for that."

Beth strolled over arm in arm with a guy who resembled Roland. She introduced him as her fiancé, and Roland's brother, Lad. "Father is about to give his speech."

Kareem squinted down at Neecie. "Speech?"

"Yes, my father always gives a speech at parties." He raised a brow, and she patted his chest. "I promise the fun starts after the speech."

So far he'd gotten what he expected at this party. Rich people trying to impress each other and tossing thinly veiled insults. Old money too far removed from the times when their families may not have had everything they wanted. The pretentious people made him appreciate his father for trying to force appreciation and humility down the throats of his children—and made him appreciate Patrice's ability to walk away from everything and start her life on her own.

The tap of Milton's fingers on the microphone filled the room. The crowd focused their attention on the head of the Baldwin family on stage. "Those of you who know me are aware that I'm not big on giving speeches." The crowd laughed. "All right, you've got me. We know not to give a judge a microphone. But I won't take a long time with this. Janice, dear, thank you for a wonderful thirty years of marriage. I only hope we have thirty more. We also get to celebrate having all of our kids here tonight. In case you didn't see her." Milton pointed to Patrice, and out of nowhere the spotlight shined their way. "My lovely oldest daughter Patrice is here. With her fiancé, who is quite the tennis player."

Neecie smiled and waved, and Kareem forced what he hoped resembled a real smile on his face.

Milton cleared his throat and got the crowd's attention again. "Now for the fun of the evening. Most of you know how I met my beautiful wife." A few catcalls and cheers came from the room.

Neecie grinned at him and tugged on his shirt. Kareem's interest piqued.

"For those who don't, here you go. It was 1977 at the old dance studio in Midtown. There I was, this dapper young man." Milton tugged on the front of his tux, and the crowd chuckled. "Hanging out with friends when this song came on." The lively stream of the first bars of "Get Down Tonight" played. The formerly stuffy crowd cheered. "And then I saw the love of my life out on the dance floor." Milton did a fancy two-step that made the crowd whistle and cheer.

Kareem laughed with the rest of the crowd. If he hadn't seen Milton dancing on stage with his own eyes he never would have believe the man capable of letting loose.

"I think I like your father," he said.

Milton pointed to Janice. "Sweetheart, let's show these people we still have the moves."

Janice clapped her hands and waved Milton down. He joined her and spun her around before the two danced together.

Kareem watched the couple with new admiration. "Your parents could've been on *Soul Train*."

Beth leaned over and bumped his shoulder. "They were! Don't worry, you'll hear the story about how they tore up the Soul Train Line." Beth turned to her boyfriend. "Come on, Lad, let's dance."

Lad grinned and pulled Beth onto the quickly filling dance floor. In a matter of seconds the conservative anniversary party turned into a high-class disco.

"Want to dance?" Neecie's hopefulness almost made him agree.

"You know I don't dance," he said.

Neecie's lips tightened. "Or maybe it depends on who asks."

He kept his face impassive, but inside he felt like she'd kicked him in the balls. The accusation flashed in her eyes. He would have danced with Sandra.

"Lucky for you, it appears Felicia is still dancing with her father," Roland said. "Which leaves me without a partner." He held out his hand to Neecie. "If you can keep up with my moves."

Neecie's giggle at the lame joke made Kareem's stomach tighten.

"I remember your moves. They're not hard to keep up with."

Roland eyed Kareem. "Do you mind? I don't want to step on your toes."

The guy's existence stepped on Kareem's toes, but he wouldn't give him the satisfaction of knowing.

"Go ahead."

He watched, once again, as another guy danced with Neecie. She smiled and laughed as Roland twirled and spun her to the disco music. Tension slowly took over Kareem's body. Neecie was pretty damn comfortable with the guy she supposedly brought Kareem here to keep at bay. Her excuse for him coming could have been a lie. She could have asked him here to make her ex jealous. Pitting men against each other had never seemed to be her style, but honestly he didn't know much about her outside of the shop.

He wanted to know more. What made her so romantic? Where did she go after she left her family? Why in the hell did her smile make him so happy?

Roland dipped Neecie in his arms and then pulled her in close. Kareem snapped. No way in hell would he let another guy twirl his woman on the dance floor. But he refused to dance to this music.

Kareem stalked over to the DJ booth and flagged the guy over. "You got any reggae?"

The DJ grinned and nodded. "Sure do, man. Any requests?"

Kareem mentally flipped through the various songs he liked that Neecie might appreciate. "'Is this Love.' Bob Marley?"

"I got you," the DJ said, pointing a finger.

He stepped away from the DJ booth and went back to watching Neecie and her ex on the dance floor. He slid his hands into the pockets of his pants, tapped his toe in his shoe, and waited for his song to play.

Joshua lumbered over with two other boys at his side. The teenagers reeked of marijuana, their boldness shocking Kareem. One of the boy's blue eyes was red-rimmed, going against his Richie Rich blond hair and good looks. The other boy had darker hair, and red also sported his green eyes.

"Hey, guys, this is my soon to be new uncle," Josh said. "The one I told you about."

The blond kid grinned. "We've heard good things about you. Maybe you can help us with our plan."

Kareem raised a brow. "What plan?"

The darker-haired kid elbowed the blond guy. "Shut up. You guys can't keep your mouths closed about anything."

Instead of elbowing back the blond kid chuckled, and Joshua joined in. Kareem scrutinized the three teens and shook his head. "Sounds like trouble."

Joshua tugged on the front of his pants and gave a shrug. "Only if you get caught."

The blond one chuckled. "And if we do, once we say our names we're good." The boy and Joshua gave each other a high five.

Watching the three idiots was like watching bad replay of Kareem's teenage years. "Don't do anything stupid, Joshua."

Joshua smirked. "Yeah, whatever."

Kareem balled his hands into fists. He wanted to smack some sense into the boys, but what use would it serve other than feeling really damn good. Joshua was Chad's problem, not his. Pivoting away from the chuckling knuckleheads, Kareem headed back to the dance floor.

He tapped his hand on the outside of his leg and checked his watch. His stomach hurt more than it had the night he'd been arrested. Going to jail and dancing with Neecie both made his nerves stretch like taut wires. On the dance floor, Roland ran a hand down Neecie's back to rest on her waist. She stepped back, putting more space between them, but the smile never left her face.

Neecie looked right at home in Roland's arms. Kareem's eyes narrowed, and a vision of Roland kissing Neecie filled his head. Roland would have kissed Neecie that afternoon in the garden, not panic because he didn't want her to realize kissing made him uncomfortable.

The sounds in the room faded, and the corners of his vision blurred. The air seemed to thin and Kareem sucked in several breaths, but his throat wanted to close up. He shifted from foot to foot and pulled on his collar.

"This next song is a request," the DJ's voice boomed.

Kareem blinked and took a deep breath. The room came back into focus, and he registered the sounds of Bob Marley playing. A few enthusiastic mummers rose from the crowd. Kareem locked eyes with Neecie. With purposeful strides, he broke through the crowded dance floor. Kareem eyed Roland, who dropped his hand from Neecie's waist and stepped back. Good, the guy knew what was best for him.

The smile on her face slowly drifted away. Kareem's brows drew together. He wanted her smiles, needed her sunshine.

When he reached her, questions swam in her eyes. Was he angry? Had she done something wrong? If only she knew he'd done wrong by letting her go on the floor with Roland instead of him. Kareem slid his arm around her waist and pulled her soft body against his. Neecie sucked in a breath; the questions gave way to something else, and her lids lowered.

Small hands clasped his arms right above the elbow then slowly traveled up the rigid muscles of his biceps to finally rest on his shoulders. Kareem caught the rhythm of the music and swayed her gently from side to side. Stretching fingers across the span of her hips, he brought her forward and guided her movements with his.

The corners of her full lips tilted up in a sensual smile. His heart bumped heavily. Tightening her arms around his neck, Neecie brought her warm body closer. Her hands gently tugged one of his dreads from the band. With a slight tug she pulled him closer into the safe circle of her body. Locking eyes, Kareem lowered his forehead to rest on hers. The sweet fragrance of her perfume, mingled with the smell of her sweat, heated his blood.

As they swayed to the music, her hips pressing forward, his cock stirred and swelled. Kareem wished he knew the right words to tell her what he longed for. How if he were the type of man she wanted he'd kiss her softly, hold her hand, and make love through the night. But as the music played, and her breasts pressed against the hardness of his chest the darker side of him stirred. The side that wanted her pinned beneath him. The side that wanted to hear her cry out his name and submit to his desires. The side that wanted to seduce away her sweetness and hear dirty words come out of her pretty mouth while he drove in and out of her without holding back.

Kareem gripped a handful of her dress at the small of her back. Neecie's lips parted with a silent sigh, and she trembled. Her soft brown eyes turned urgent. She lifted her head, and the tip of her tongue edged along the pink seam of her lower lip. The move was an unmistakable invitation. Kareem went with what felt natural and brushed his lips across hers, a quick taste that jolted his system. Neecie pressed closer, almost as if she'd dissolve into him.

Tilting his head to the side, Kareem raised a brow. He'd promised her tonight, and he wanted her now. Patrice jerked her head up and down once. As the last bars of the song filtered in the air, Kareem kept a hand on her waist and ushered his woman off the dance floor.

CHAPTER 14

Kareem didn't bother to be polite or apologetic as he pulled Neecie through the crowd and down one of the halls off the main floor of the clubhouse. He could take her back to her parents', but that required waiting for the valet to bring the car. Right now his hardening cock wasn't big on being patient.

He strode down a hallway marked "Employees Only," his hand firmly around Neecie's waist. She didn't play silly and ask where they were going or what was he doing. That was one of the things he liked about Neecie. She didn't play coy, and she understood what was up. The hall ended with a pair of double doors labeled "Conference Room." Kareem tested the knob, which easily twisted.

Gently Kareem placed his hand on her lower back and pushed Neecie inside. With a final click, he closed and locked the door. Neecie approached the wood table visible in the silver slits of light filtering through the blinds. Wide, unquestioning eyes met his. Kareem's skin tightened, suddenly unsure. She trusted him, wanted him, and he didn't want to hurt her. The need to fuck her battled with his desire to make love. Tremors raced through his taut muscles. He clenched his fists to keep from groping her.

Neecie stepped forward and reached for him. Kareem's heart jumped, and he stepped back. "Take off your dress."

Her brows drew together. "I thought—"

"We are, but first I want to see you naked." He tried to keep his voice calm, to hide how much he wanted to pounce on her.

Kareem held his breath. Slowly her hands removed the belt then lifted the skirt of the dress. Seconds felt like hours while she pulled the dress up and over her head. His breathing echoed like screams in the quiet room as she revealed softly rounded curves. The dress fell quietly to her feet, leaving only air and lacy, black underwear between him and Neecie's curvaceous body.

Kareem's control snapped. In one long stride he closed the distance between them. Her arms opened. She lifted her head and eyes fluttered closed. Spinning her around, Kareem wrapped his arm around her waist and pressed his hard dick into her soft behind. Hungry lips latched onto the sweet skin of her neck.

An excited gasp escaped her mouth. One of her arms reached up to grasp his head; the other clutched his pants above his thigh. Kareem's hands roamed over every one of her silken curves, palming her tits until her hard little nipples teased the palms of his hands. His mouth watered, and he sucked on the side of her neck, an image of pulling her nipples between his lips flashing in his head. Soon, he'd do that soon enough. One hand slashed across the gentle curve of her stomach. Her legs widened, and he grinned into her neck. Eager little thing.

Kareem gripped one of her hips instead. The perfect anchors to an ass he'd watched sashay across his barber shop too many times. The hand on her hip jerked her backwards, and the other pinched her nipple.

"Ahhh yes," Neecie cried out.

Her head fell to the side, and Kareem ran his tongue down then up her throat. The salty sweet tang of her skin tightened his balls almost to the point of pain. Neecie jerked at the twist of his dreads. His scalp pulled, and they tumbled around them. Her fingers plunged through the thick locks.

Hell fucking yeah, she wanted this hard. Kareem jerked down the front of her lacy bra. Material ripped, and his cock jumped. Looking over her shoulder, he wished for more light to see the tempting bounce as her tits fell free. He filled his hands with the pliant mounds, pinching her nipples until she moaned and twisted against him. She jerked, and his hand slipped. Kareem nipped her shoulder.

A long moan escaped her. "Again, do that again."

Kareem's heart jackhammered his ribcage. "You like that."

"I dream about that." Her voice was a low, erotic moan.

Kareem placed one hand around her neck and pressed her into his body. The other plunged down the front of her skimpy panties. God in heaven she was so fucking wet! Spreading her soaking lower lips Kareem sank two thick fingers knuckle deep into her pussy. "What about that?"

Her hand on his thigh clenched. "Ahhh, yes!"

Kareem eased his fingers out then pushed back in. "Too deep?"

Patrice bucked and moaned. Her hard swallow pressed against his hand at her throat, and the thin slivers of light revealed the bounce of her breasts with every heaving breath. "Not deep enough."

A shudder rocked him. He turned her head and grazed the tip of her ear with his teeth. "I can go a lot deeper."

"Please do," she said in a trembling, sexy plea.

The erratic beat of her pulse played against the tips of his fingers around her neck. She was his. Wet, hot, and ready for the taking. "Tell me to fuck you."

Patrice's mouth fell open and her tongue played in the corner. Her eyes opened to slits and met his over her shoulder. A warm palm left his thigh to caress his aching hard on. "Make love to me, Kareem."

If only he knew how. He closed his eyes and removed his fingers from the sweet slickness between her thighs. In a quick movement he ripped the lace of her panties and spread her legs further.

"That's not what I said." Using the flats of his fingers he lightly slapped her swollen clit.

The hand at his cock tightened. "Kareem!"

"Don't make me punish you." He slapped her sex again. Each wet smack sent an answering twitch to his groin.

She twisted and pushed her hips forward. Kareem visualized what he couldn't see. How each light hit would cause the nub to grow and swell. He sucked in a breath, intoxicated by the smell of her desire.

Smack. "Say it." Smack.

The twisting of her hips grew frantic. "Kareem, shit, yes!" She clutched his dick so tight shots of pleasure and pain jolted up his spine.

"Ohh, I love it when your pretty mouth says dirty things." He slapped her slippery center harder. "Say it, Neecie," he damn near growled against her ear.

"Fuck me, Kareem!"

Kareem pushed her forward and bent her over the conference room table. One hand spread her legs wide; the other ripped open the button on his pants. His hand trembled with the burning anticipation to bury himself in her sweet heat. Kareem sucked in a breath and bit his lip. Control, he needed to keep some control.

Patrice popped her ass backwards and stared at him with narrow, desire-fogged eyes. Kareem froze. This was Neecie. She was sunshine, happiness, and sweetness. And he'd turned her into his horny sex toy.

Guilt scratched at the edge of his reason. Neecie pushed back and brushed her butt on the dripping tip of his dick. He'd worry about the consequences tomorrow. Pulling a condom from his back pocket he ripped the foil packet open, rammed the thin latex on, grabbed her curvy hips, and slammed into her.

Patrice slapped the table. "Oh my God, yes!"

Kareem bit his lower lip to keep from crying out. Slick wet walls sucked him deep and cradled him in scorching heat. Grabbing her hips Kareem gave her what she wanted. No holding back, no sense of control, he just drove in and out of the place he could spend eternity. At first she took the thrusts, but soon she moved with him. Pushing back whenever he pushed forward. Taking him further and further until the heavy sac of his balls slapped the underside of her sex.

This was what he promised. Rough and hard. No softness or sweet words. Bending her over sent a rush through him. She called out *his* name; he controlled her pleasure.

Her climax came quick. "Oh, God, yes, oh, God, yes!" she chanted over and over.

Her tight walls seized, pulling him in and clenching tight. His skin tightened then exploded. An orgasm more powerful than he'd ever experienced drained him dry. Patrice collapsed forward, arms spread eagle and hair covering her face. The table's glossy surface fogged with each heavy breath. Kareem quickly pulled out and stepped away, watching her try and regain her senses. He grinned.

The doorknob rattled. Kareem tensed and swiveled around. A muffled curse came from the other side and the footsteps drifted away.

"We're going to get caught," Neecie said, pushing up on her forearms.

"They left," he said. "But we better get out of here."

The near interruption broke his moment of triumph. What was wrong with him? Bringing her in here and bending her over the table like some hoe from the club. He could have waited for the car and slept with her in a bed. Instead he'd used her. Pulling her away from the dance floor and dragging her in here without bothering to be discreet or hide what was on his mind.

Neecie finally stood and glanced at him over her shoulder. He turned away. He removed the condom, wrapped it in one of the tissues from a box next to the door, and threw the wad in the trash. As he zipped up his pants a wave of shame prickled his skin. He hadn't bothered to even take off his clothes.

Neecie's soft body pressed against his back. Kareem jerked out of her embrace. When he faced her, pain replaced the trust from earlier. *Shit, I'm screwing with the wrong girl.*

"So ... what, I can't hug you?" She tried for lighthearted, but there was discomfort in her tone.

"I don't like to be hugged. Or surprised."

She crossed her arms over her chest. Her bra barely covered her breasts thanks to his eagerness to get the thing off. Her panties were nonexistent. Seeing her half-naked only made him want to bend her over again.

She scoffed. "Or kissed."

Kareem clenched his jaw. She noticed. "Did I hurt you?"

"No."

He jerked his head toward the door. "Do you want to go back to the party?"

"No."

Good, because he didn't either. "Put on your dress. We're going back to the house."

"Why, so you can ignore what we just did like last night?" Neecie spun around and snatched her dress off the floor.

His stomach clenched. That had been the plan. Forget what he'd done and try to make things better tomorrow.

Scowling, Kareem stalked over and hauled the dress out of her hands. Her eyes darted to him before they jerked away. Her body trembled, and damn if he didn't get excited. *I'm such an asshole.*

Bunching up the material of the dress, Kareem slid the garment over her head. "We're going back to the house so I can have sex with you again." Her bright eyes jerked to his. He took a step forward, and she stepped back. "And again." He stepped forward. She stepped back. "And again." He stepped forward. Her foot slid backwards. Kareem grabbed her waist and jerked her body against his. "Do you have a problem with that?"

She shook her head, and her eyes flared with interest. "No."

He lightly slapped her behind. "Good. Now hurry up and finish getting dressed before whoever that was comes back."

Her sunshine smile brightened the room. His chest filled with warmth. He was an asshole, but if she wanted more he was powerless to stop.

CHAPTER 15

Patrice grinned and stretched out in the bed. Morning sunlight filled the room with a cheery glow that matched her mood. Patrice reached out for Kareem on the other side of the bed. Cool, empty sheets met her hand. Her contented smile withered away. She pushed back the thick covers and sat up, scanning the room for Kareem and seeing only empty space.

Disappointment dimmed her mood. She tried to push the feeling aside. Just because they'd gone at it like porn stars the night before didn't mean he would be waiting for her with breakfast and roses the next morning. Like the leading role in a porno, he'd disappeared. Patrice pushed back the covers and trudged across the room to the bathroom.

Stiff, long untouched muscles protested and she stretched her arms and lower back to release the tightness. Despite being upset Kareem wasn't there, the memories from the night before brought back her smile. Having sex like a porn star had definite perks.

Patrice used the bathroom then went to the sink to wash her face. She splashed cold water on her eyes and shivered at the instant invigoration. Catching a glimpse of herself in the mirror, Patrice gasped. She grabbed a handful of her frizzy hair, pulled it behind her head, and leaned into the mirror. Dark marks lined her neck, shoulders, and chest. Each discoloration brought a memory of the exact nip, bite, and suck of Kareem's eager lips against her skin. Her free hand ran across a large mark above her breast and stabs of heat raced up her neck and spread to the cheeks.

I love your tits. Kareem's rough declaration before he'd done that then lapped at her nipples rang through her head, a phrase that would have turned her off if any other man had spoken the words. Her fingers trailed down to her nipple hardening beneath the thin material of the tank top Kareem insisted she put on after shivering in her sleep. Wetness slipped between her legs, and her eyes fluttered closed. The images of Kareem played in her head. The way he held her, dominated her, made her talk dirty and beg for more. The hand in her hair pulled the thick strands, reminding her of the way he'd tugged while plunging in and out from behind.

"Thinking of me?" Kareem's low voice jolted her from her fantasy.

Patrice's eyes flew open. She dropped her hands and ran them across the smooth marble of the sink. Kareem leaned against the bathroom door, eyes assessing and making her self-conscious as hell.

She spun and crossed her hands over her breasts. "Just inventorying the marks."

Kareem pushed away from the door and crossed the room in a few determined strides. "Marks?" He grabbed her chin and lifted. After surveying her for several seconds his hand dropped. Kareem's face pinched, and his eyes shifted away.

Immediately Patrice regretted saying anything. "There's only a few."

"I'm sorry." Regret laced his voice.

"Don't be. It's just a few hickeys."

Kareem scowled and spun her around to face the mirror. "It looks like I chewed you like a piece of rawhide."

The self-loathing in his voice made her heart drop to her knees. Kareem stepped back, and she spun to grasp his shoulders.

"Stop it. Don't pull away from me, and don't feel bad about the marks." He thankfully stopped struggling to get away. "Did you hear any complaints from me last night?"

Kareem brushed the back of his hand down her neck. "I should have treated you better. You deserve better."

She pushed his chest, but his hard body didn't budge. "I deserve what I ask for. I asked for and want you, Kareem. Why is it so hard for you to see that?"

"Neecie—"

She stood on her toes and kissed him. Kareem's body froze. She brushed her lips across his. He didn't pull away and sparks flew through her veins. Not once during the course of the night had he kissed her. And she'd been either too out of breath from before or after the sex to care. Patrice pressed forward, slipping out her tongue to trace his lower lip.

Kareem lifted his head and pulled back.

Patrice looked at the floor to hide the disappointment.

"Get dressed." He lifted her chin with a finger. "We're going out." He spun to walk out of the bathroom.

Patrice stood frozen then rushed to follow. "What? Go where? Why?"

"Because I don't want to sit in this house with your parents and sister after I spent the night making their daughter scream and moan. Fran has already turned up her nose twice when I walked in a room."

Patrice covered her face with her palms. "Don't tell me they heard."

"Do you want to stick around and find out?"

Her head popped up. A small but sensual smile graced his face. Patrice's heart cut cartwheels.

"Not a chance."

He nodded. "Exactly. So take a shower and get dressed. I'm taking you to a football game."

• • •

"Yes! That's how you do it, baby! Whoo!" Kareem yelled.

Patrice dropped the popcorn in her hand, and her mouth gaped open. She stared at Kareem standing next to her in the Bank of America stadium cheering on the Carolina Panthers. When Kareem slapped high five with the people behind him and chest bumped the man with black and blue face paint next to him Patrice laughed out loud. Who was this man, and what had he done to Kareem Henderson?

The kicker made the field goal, winning the game. Another round of cheers and hand slaps went through their section. People grabbed their items and prepared to file out of the crowded stadium.

Kareem faced her. "That was a good game."

She chuckled and nodded. "It was."

"I didn't think we'd be able to pull it off." The grin and excitement in his voice brought back the image of the carefree guy.

"It was a nail biter," she said.

He placed his hand on her lower back and guided her into the throng of people. The thick crowd made maneuvering nearly impossible. Kareem wrapped an arm around her shoulder and pulled her close to his side. His body heat slowly overcame the chill that seeped into her bones from the fall winds.

"Did you have fun?" he asked. His eyes sparked with happiness, no longer dark and flat.

She continued to grin like a contestant on *The Price is Right*. "I did, but not as much fun as you. I didn't know you were such a Panthers fan."

"I like football, especially live. I haven't been to a game in years."

"You really got into the game. I don't think I've ever heard you cheer." She raised a brow. "Or give high fives, or chest bumps."

Kareem rubbed his lower lip. "It wasn't that big of a deal. We're at a game; it's what you do."

"It's not what you normally do. I like seeing you so happy. I like your smile. It's sexy and should definitely come out to play more."

He pulled her a little closer. "Sexy, huh. Maybe I'll let it out to play with you." His grin knocked away any remaining cold in her body.

Patrice raised one of her fists and yelled, "All right, Panthers, keep pounding! Roar!" The rest of the crowd, already hyped from the win, cheered.

Another round of high fives and chants kept the smile on Kareem's face. Instead of going back to her parents', they walked to the Epicenter for a drink at one of the many bars located there. Kareem kept his arm around her shoulder. The action chased away her some of her concerns about the night before, but she still needed to guard her heart. Kareem happy and laughing, cheering a football team and slapping high fives just like any other ordinary guy started her to believing he could be in a relationship like any regular guy. Obviously the afterglow from a great night clouded her judgment, but somewhere between dancing to Bob Marley and watching him cheer, her *this is just a fling* wall started to crack.

They snatched the last two seats at the bar in Wild Wings, cramming themselves into a corner at the end. "I'm going to need to stay here for a while before I'm ready to walk back to the car," Patrice said.

Kareem slid his barstool close to hers. "Your feet hurt?"

"My everything hurts." She shifted in the chair and rubbed her lower back.

His gaze dropped to her neck. All marks were hidden beneath a blue turtleneck, but regret from earlier slipped into his eyes, drawing away the life. Patrice slapped a hand on his muscled thigh. "What do you want to drink?"

"How about two beers?"

"Sounds great to me."

He ordered then stared at the television over the bar. The bartender brought their beers, and Patrice studied Kareem as he brought the bottle to his lips, focusing on the scar above his lip that started beneath his right nostril and cut across the left side of his mouth.

"How did you get that scar?"

His hand jerked so faintly she wouldn't have noticed if she weren't already so intently focused on him. "You want something to eat?"

She shook her head. "I want you to answer the question."

He took another swig of his beer then cleared his throat. "Prison."

She took a deep breath. Dozens of questions popped to the surface, but bombarding him would only mean he'd clam up. "Was it an accident?"

"No."

"Someone cut you on purpose?"

He sipped, then glared at her. "Yes." The hard clipped answer said that was the end of the discussion.

She nodded, and Kareem turned back to the television. Patrice brought the beer to her lips but pulled back before sipping. "Why did you go to prison?"

Kareem's nostrils flared with his deep inhale. "Carjacking."

"I know that, but why? Why did you try to steal a car?"

He didn't answer, just swigged the beer. His tongue did a quick sweep of thinning lips, and he forcefully brought down the bottle. Patrice's brows drew together. Apparently, she'd crossed a line. She swiveled her chair toward the bar and studied the label on her beer.

Several minutes passed before he let out a heavy sigh. "Are you going to sit there and pout until I give you an answer?"

Her eyes snapped to his. "I'm not pouting."

"Yes you are, and it's not cute."

Patrice straightened her shoulders. "Well, clamming up and not talking to me about your past isn't very cute either. I thought we were ..." He raised a brow, and she shut up. She pulled the paper on her bottle.

Another few minutes passed before he leaned in. "I was young, bored, and looking for excitement."

She turned her seat to face him. "Were you really in the gang, or just hanging around them?"

"There was no hanging around." Kareem paused. His hands moved back and forth as if he were grasping for the right words. "I met my boy Omar freshman year of high school. He introduced me to the Runners, and the rest is history."

"Again with the Cliff's Notes version. Your family is successful. Why would you even consider hanging out with a gang?"

Kareem rubbed his lower lip then ran a hand over his dreads. He spun in the chair and leaned an elbow on the bar, facing her. "Hanging out with Omar and the rest of the Runners was exciting. I even started my dreads then, just because my dad would hate it and the head of the Runners wore the style." His voice lifted with some of that long ago enchantment. "They introduced me to stuff I never saw at any of the parties my parents made me go to and did stuff the kids that hung in my circle wouldn't dream of. They taught me how to use a gun. Had so much money from running guns they could buy anything they wanted. And the women ..." The corner of his mouth lifted, but there was no joy in his smile. "They introduced me to sex."

Patrice studied the frayed edge of the label on the beer bottle. "Was there a girl that you liked who was part of their group?"

He scoffed and sipped his beer. "If you're asking if there was a girl I loved, no. Sex was everywhere, but love played no part in it. The girls at school, they all wanted to hold hands, be romantic, and put a claim on me. The freaks who hung with the runners, that's what we called them, weren't about that. They would do anything to be with one of the guys. Doing whatever felt good with whoever."

Patrice swallowed hard and stared at the button at the top of his black polo shirt. "Was there one freak in particular who did whatever with you?"

"Neecie, you don't understand. I lost my virginity with two other guys and one of the older freaks."

Patrice's head shot up, and her stomach twisted. "You what?"

The flatness returned to his eyes, but he didn't look away. "That's the way it was. All the time. There was no place for love, and unless you were one of the main guys or earned enough cred, you didn't get to stake a claim on one of the freaks." He shrugged. "We shared."

She tried to swallow but her mouth went dry. "Sooo, what you ..." She didn't really know what she wanted to ask.

"I never had a girlfriend. Never lusted for the head cheerleader or took some girl out to dinner or the prom. If I wanted to have sex, I either joined in or waited until I could get with one of the fr—"

"Women in the gang." She held up a hand. "I get it."

Kareem shifted in his seat and spun the beer bottle on the bar. His eyes shifted to then away from her. "Are you disgusted now?"

Patrice shook her head and guzzled from the bottle. "No ... just ... taking it all in."

He grunted and watched the television. Patrice peeked at him from beneath her lids. Maybe she should be disgusted. He'd spent his teenage years learning about sex with no connection to love or affection. But disgust wasn't what she felt. She felt sorry, and any hint of pity would have Kareem sprinting out the door. Would he even know how to have something else? Was she crazy enough to want to be *that woman*? The woman who took on the project of dating a hard to love, flawed man?

Yeah ... kinda.

Patrice closed her eyes and quickly shook her head. That type of thought would have her crying for months after this thing ended. Nope, better to just keep her heart out of things. Time to throw some plaster on the cracks in the walls guarding her heart.

"What did your family say? About the gang?" she asked.

The tension in his body diminished a little. "They didn't know how deep I got involved. While I was in high school I wasn't allowed get into the deep stuff. I basically counted money and relayed messages. Looked the other way when things went down I wasn't supposed to know about. As I got older, I handled more deals. Jacking the car was something we'd done before."

"What happened?"

"Me and this guy, Red, ran up on a man at a red light. It should've been easy. Just break the window, pull the man out, and take off with the car. But the guy had a gun. Red was shot in the chest, me in the leg when I ran." He sighed and shrugged. "Instead of going back to tell the runners I went to my parents. Stupid really, but after seeing my boy bleeding in the street, I just wanted to be home. I tried to hide the injury, but my mom caught me washing off the blood in my bathroom. They took me to the hospital, the police put two and two together, and I ended up in prison." He stared unfocused at the television. "I should've been graduating from college." He gave her a humorless laugh. "That's what my dad said that night in the hospital."

"And you were hurt in prison?"

A shutter came across his face. "I thought I was hard. I didn't realize how soft I actually was until I had to fight off murderers and rapists."

She reached over to lay her hand on his thigh. "Did anything bad happen to you?"

He moved his leg out of her reach. "Nothing good."

"Is it why you don't like for me to touch you?"

The smile returned to his lips, but avoided his eyes. "I like it when you touch me."

"You like having sex with me, but you didn't let me touch you or kiss you. Just now, I placed my hand on your leg and you pulled away. Unless you initiate it, you don't like to be touched."

Kareem's shoulders went rigid. "I spent five years where the only reason someone touched you was for ulterior motives. Sick, twisted, ulterior motives. Sometimes people coming up on me ..." He scowled and waved at the bartender then held up his empty bottle.

"Touching triggers you."

Kareem drummed his fingers on the bar. His gaze darted around the room, seemed to go out of focus. He pinched the bridge of his nose.

Patrice put her hand on his arm, which vibrated with tension. "What happened to you?"

He jerked away. "Let's get out of here."

"You just ordered another beer."

He stood, pulled a twenty out of his wallet, and waved the wrinkled bill at the bartender. "This'll cover it." He slapped the twenty on the bar. "Let's go."

They left the warmth of the bar to go back into the busy square of the Epicenter. Patrice wanted to know more, but she'd pushed too hard today. At least now she had some answers. All she knew about prison she'd learned from cable television. No matter how disturbing, the real experience could only be worse. Heaviness settled over her heart and thoughts of what could have happened to him in there played in her mind. She glanced at his clenched jaw.

The sound of reggae music came from one of the clubs next to the bar they'd just left. She shook away the dark revelations and suddenly needed to get back the happiness from before.

"They're playing your music."

Kareem blinked and focused on her. She wondered what he'd been thinking about, but honestly wasn't ready to hear more.

"I hear it. Did you want to go in there?"

"Only if you'll dance with me again." Kareem narrowed his eyes and opened his mouth, but she held up her hand to stop his argument. "And you can't say you don't dance because you already danced with me."

He chuckled and the sound made her belly flop. "That wasn't dancing, Neecie." He took a step forward and overpowered her with his dark eyes and presence. "That was foreplay."

She took a step until they almost touched. She wanted to reach up and touch him, or wrap her arms around his shoulders, but after his confessions she restrained herself. They were just having fun and helping each other out. She needed to remember this wasn't a real relationship. That he didn't know how to have a real relationship.

"I'd like more foreplay, please."

The flatness left his eyes, and humor, maybe warmth, livened up the dark centers. Kareem wrapped an arm around her shoulder. "Then hell yeah, we'll dance again."

CHAPTER 16

"Where are you going?"

Kareem continued tucking his shirt into his pants and glanced at Neecie over his shoulder. She leaned against the door of the bathroom wearing nothing but his black tank top from the night before and a smile. Her hair was messy, and his marks were all over her body.

Something stirred deep in his chest. She was his. "Downtown," he said. "I want to find out the process for a business license and verify what I read online about getting my master barber certification in North Carolina. I may swing by a realtor's office and start scoping out places."

Interest brightened her eyes. "Do you mind if I come with you?"

He finished with his shirt and checked his reflection in the mirror. "I doubt it'll be much fun. Don't you want to hang out with your parents?"

Neecie sauntered into the room and jumped up to sit on the counter. "I'm here to help you, and that's what I want to do. Besides, I'm going to meet mother's friend Lorelei while we're downtown."

"The model? I didn't know you were interested in that."

"It never hurts to hear what she has to say," Patrice said. "Plus, Beth gave me a lead on a friend who's willing to help. We can go by his office."

Kareem spread her legs and stood between them. "Who's he?"

"The head of the chamber whose brother is a bank president," she said with a cocky grin and slid her arms around his neck. "I told you I have connections."

Running his hands up the smooth skin of her outer thigh, Kareem gripped her hips. No underwear. The corner of his lip tilted up. He'd expected her to turn away after he confessed his sins the day before. His sexual past disgusted him at times. Last night she hadn't pushed him for more, which made him question what decent task he must have done once to result in landing a good woman like her.

"So you do." Kareem slid his hands toward her inner thigh, brushing damp curls. He raised a brow. "What were you thinking about before coming in here?"

A naughty grin spread on her sweet face. "You."

"I can tell." He pressed a finger into her wet opening. Neecie's eyes rolled backwards, and her mouth opened. Her tongue played with the corner of her mouth. His dick became as hard as the marble countertops. Sweet Neecie, now all wet and wicked for him.

His free hand untucked his shirt and unzipped his pants. "We're making another stop."

Neecie trembled; her breasts rose and fell from short, shallow breaths. "Where?"

Taking a condom from the counter, Kareem opened the packet and covered himself. "To a clinic so I can prove to you I'm clean. I'm tired of condoms."

"Oh." The breath rushed out of her and Kareem pushed into her, hard and deep. "Ooohh."

Using one hand to press her chest backwards and the other to pull her hips forward, Kareem closed his eyes and succumbed to Neecie's sunshine.

• • •

The young administrative assistant in the swanky chamber of commerce office smiled at Kareem and Patrice. "Mr. Simmons will be with you in a few minutes. But he said you can wait in his office instead of out here."

Kareem's muscles seized, and he gripped the black leather satchel strap on his shoulder. Mr. Simmons? Roland Simmons? He glared at Neecie, who smartly avoided his glare. This was the damn friend she wanted help from? Her perfect ex-fiancé? He should've asked more questions that morning, not gone for one more round between her deceptive thighs.

"If you'll follow me." The assistant came around the cherry wood desk.

Neecie's gaze darted toward him, then she scampered to follow the assistant. Kareem followed, but saw and heard nothing but the pounding in his ears. If she planned to use him for sex while she tried to reconcile with her ex, he would walk out today. He didn't need her help to make his business grow.

The assistant escorted them to a large corner office. "Make yourself comfortable."

Tight edges encompassed Neecie's smile. "Thank you."

The assistant left the door open after her exit. Kareem grabbed Neecie's upper arm and glared.

"Your friend is your ex?"

She placed a hand on his chest. "Let me explain."

Her body shook and Kareem immediately released her. "Why didn't you tell me?"

"I wasn't sure if you'd accept his help if you knew who he was." She rubbed her arm and Kareem felt like an asshole.

"You thought it would be better for me find out this way?"

She cringed. "I just don't know how to take you, Kareem. Judging your reactions is nearly impossible."

"Here's a tip: the truth goes a long way to getting the reaction you want out of me."

"I'm sorry. I deserve that. I promised I'd use my connections to help you." She waved her arm to encompass the room. "Roland is one of my connections."

"You should have said something." He pointed and took a step toward her. "Trust doesn't come easy for me, Neecie. I have to know you have my back and that you're not here to rekindle an old flame."

"I do have your back. This isn't about Roland. We're through. Kareem, I swear I thought you'd say no if you knew, but you have to admit, he's a good connection."

He ran a hand over his face and wanted to rip out his dreads. "Good connection or not, I deserved to know. This isn't some shit you spring up at the last minute, Neecie."

"I know, I'm sorry. Please don't be angry. I won't lie again, but I just wanted to help."

"I don't want his help." He spun to the door.

Neecie's small hands tugged on his arm. "Don't be stupid, Kareem." He swerved back to her. She dropped her hands and backed up a step. "Well, walking out of here would be stupid. Roland has the business connections you need. His brother is the president of a bank and can secure your loan. Beth already said they agreed to help. This is how things work. It's just business, I promise, nothing else."

Her eyes, her voice, all rang with sincerity. But he'd been lied to and deceived too many times to trust.

"Just hear what he has to say," she whispered.

Kareem gritted his teeth. He wanted to leave and say to hell with Roland and her. But honestly, he had planned to join the chamber. He would have discovered later her ex ran the damn place and still would have had to work with him.

"Lie to me again and we're through."

She twisted her foot on the ground, a movement he found sexy, and right now he hated that he still wanted her so damn bad.

"I won't. I mean it; I have your back."

He nodded. Her smile tried to melt away the rest of his anger, so he turned away and sized up the office. Everything about the space oozed perfection, from the organized shiny cherry wood desk to the wall of degrees and accolades hung in absolute symmetry. Kareem clenched his jaw. A far cry from the black history calendar he got from the funeral parlor across the street thumb tacked to the wall of his office.

Kareem plucked at the leaves of one of several potted palms and crossed to study the items on a bookshelf. Carpet muffled her steps, but Kareem felt Neecie's energy come up behind him, and he smelled her fruity perfume. His anger drifted away. Damn her for making him so weak.

She pushed her hair, mostly back to the kinky curls he liked, behind her ear and leaned in to look at a row of pictures. He recognized one of the women in a frame as the woman Roland had been with after dancing with Neecie. Neecie gasped then lightly laughed and picked up a picture. "Oh my, God, I can't believe he still has this."

"What is it?"

She turned the picture his way. "College graduation. We took so many pictures that day, but my sister said we had to do our jail pose. This was it. We look ridiculous."

In the picture, a younger Neecie stood to one side in a graduation gown with her arms crossed over her chest and a twist to her lips. Roland stood behind her, also in a graduation gown opened to reveal a loosened tie and untucked white shirt. Roland held up both hands and flashed the peace sign.

"You do look ridiculous," he said.

Neecie's lips turned up in a nostalgic smile that made him uncomfortable. "That was a fun day."

"Was it the day he asked you to marry him?"

She gently placed the picture back on the shelf. "Why would you say that?"

"Those are usually the kinds of occasions that warrant big declarations."

Neecie closed the space between them though not quite touching. He wanted to push her away, refuse to succumb to the strong draw this woman had on him.

"Big declarations aren't always good declarations. I broke things off with Roland for a reason. He's not the man I want." She lowered her voice, and the hungry gleam he'd put in her eye over the weekend returned.

Kareem drew his hand up her arm to her elbow and pulled her against him, allowing him to gaze down the V-neck of her black and beige striped dress.

Roland strolled into the room and stopped at the door. "Normally I'd apologize for interrupting, but since it's my office," he said with a friendly smile.

Neecie stepped back and Kareem considered keeping her from pulling away. But he wasn't down with playing tug-o-war with a woman. The man Neecie chose was completely up to her.

Neecie pointed to the shelf. "We were just admiring your pictures."

Kareem slid his hands in his pocket. "Neecie pointed out the one from your college graduation."

Roland nodded and crossed the room to them, a wistful smile on his face. "That was a very special day." He gave a smile that belonged on a toothpaste billboard. "Our parents were very proud."

Neecie shifted closer to Kareem. "Yes, they were."

An awkward pause. Kareem cleared his throat and raised a brow at Roland. "Why don't we get started?"

"Of course." Roland held out his hand to the two leather chairs across from his desk.

Roland sat and stretched his arms out on the desk, revealing gold cufflinks with the chamber of commerce's seal. "So, tell me more about your idea."

Neecie nodded and slid forward. "It's kind of a different idea."

Kareem placed a hand on her arm and called on the pleasant businessman's smile and attitude his father once tried to instill in him. The movement pulled the tight skin around his scar, a reminder he wasn't smooth and polished like his father.

"Not that different." Kareem leaned back in his chair and put the right foot over his left knee, feigning comfort. "My plan is to open a gentlemen's lounge."

"A lounge." Roland lifted a brow.

Neecie sat forward again. "They're not unusual."

"What I'm proposing isn't very different from many of the places you probably frequent already," Kareem said with ease.

Roland leaned back in his chair. "How so?"

"We've all been to a barber shop and had to wait on uncomfortable chairs in a cramped space," Kareem said. When Roland made a face, he held up his hands and chuckled. "Okay, maybe not for you, but I've frequented corner shops all my life. And if the haircut is good enough, you have politicians, businessmen, and others who started in the neighborhood still getting haircuts at the corner shop they're familiar with. There's no reason why a trip to the barber shop can't be something more. To wait in a place with leather seats, a bar stocked with high-end liquors, and flat screen televisions playing the best game."

Roland leaned forward and picked up a gold pen. "That's a lot in one place."

"It only sounds like a lot. Think about it, women go to spas and spend all day there. Why? Because there are services that cater to their needs. There's no reason men can't have the same. A place where you can have a conversation with your boys or a business partner in the lounge, try one of the cigars in the smoking room, or just sit back and relax, watching the game, before letting one of our master barbers cut your hair."

Roland tapped the pen on the desk, but interest lit his eyes. "Any other services?"

"If things go well, there's no reason not to include other spa services. Massages, maybe."

"What makes you think it'll work?"

Kareem pulled his business plan out of the satchel and passed the copy to Roland. "The research I've done suggested Charlotte is the perfect market. Your city is the banking capital of North Carolina, you have a professional football and basketball team, and a rising growth in young professionals. All the types of men who are not only in need of grooming but aren't afraid to have it done with style."

Roland flipped through the plan, and Neecie gazed at him with open admiration. He was tempted to wink at her. He knew how to be charming when needed. Most of the time being charming wasn't needed.

Roland looked up from the plan. "This is well thought out."

Kareem's practiced grin became easier as he thought about the hard work Sandra had put in to help him make his plan shine. "The person who worked with me on it knows her stuff."

Neecie sat back in her chair. Kareem glanced her way, but she studied her nails.

"Have you already thought of locations?" Roland asked.

Neecie looked up. "We haven't started looking yet."

Kareem held up a hand. "There is a location in midtown that might work." In the corner of his eye he saw her brows raise.

"Financing?" Roland asked.

"I've got some money saved and hope to get a business loan for the rest."

Roland closed the plan and nodded. "My brother can help with that. I know of several places available in midtown. I'll put you in contact with my real estate broker to show you around."

Roland pulled out a business card and handed it to Kareem. His brother's contact information was embossed in shiny black letters. They spent a few minutes going over the details of meeting with Lad and possibly Roland's realtor, though Kareem preferred working with someone else. He didn't need any more help from Neecie's ex.

"Patrice," Roland said when he and Kareem finished talking. "What will be your interest in this?"

Neecie glanced from Roland to Kareem, her brows drawn slightly together.

Kareem reached over and squeezed her hand. "She's one of my master barbers, plus she's always wanted to work in this field. I couldn't imagine doing this without her."

"That's sweet," Roland said.

There was no malice in his voice; still, Kareem didn't sense any warmth. "We've taken enough of your time. Thank you for your help today, Roland."

Kareem stood. Roland remained seated until Neecie got up from her chair. Kareem felt like he'd been kicked in the gut from the subtle reminder he wasn't a gentleman.

"It's been a pleasure, Kareem. Any friend of Patrice is a friend of mine."

"I'm a lot more than her friend," Kareem said, his voice going hard.

Roland appeared unsure, then his politician's smile reappeared. "Of course. I meant no harm." He held out a hand.

Kareem accepted. Roland twisted his wrist to turn Kareem's hand in to a subordinate position. Kareem held firm, keeping their hands even. "Of course you didn't."

Roland quickly released his grip. He turned warm eyes on Neecie. "It's good to see you again. Hopefully we'll catch up soon."

Neecie nodded, but her smile was cool. "Thanks again, Roland."

Kareem and Neecie left Roland's office. Outside the sun shined but didn't do much to cut the crisp feel of the fall afternoon.

Neecie pulled her burgundy leather jacket tight. "That went well."

"Better than I expected."

"I told you he would help."

Kareem pulled out his telephone and checked the time. "You did." He shuffled from foot to foot and slid the phone back in his pocket. "But I wish you'd told me *before* we arrived at his office. And ..." He drew out the word and stopped shifting. "You didn't think I could handle myself."

Neecie stopped scrolling through her phone and her hand fell to her side. "That's not true."

"It's very true. Look, I know I'm not the most ... verbal guy, but my family is full of salesmen. I know how to sell an idea."

"You're right, I did have some reservations."

Kareem hiked the satchel strap on his shoulder and crossed his arms. Her admission didn't really ease his annoyance. "Can you trust me to handle myself now?"

"Yes."

"Good. Now let's get out of here." He glanced at the concrete chamber building. Roland probably watched from behind the mirrored glass, searching for cracks he could wiggle his way through in the Kareem Henderson, Patrice Baldwin façade.

Kareem walked to the corner and waited impatiently for the light to change.

Neecie grabbed his hand and pulled him around. "Hey, listen. I do trust you, and I'm sorry about springing Roland on you this afternoon. I just ..." She lowered her eyes and twisted her foot. "I just want you to succeed at this, and I didn't want you to refuse to see him just because of our past."

"I get that, Neecie. Just be honest next time. Eventually I would have had to work with him. And you were right, his connections are good. We're cool."

He tried to turn away but she held his hand tight. "Did you mean that about me being one of your master barbers?"

"Yeah, I did. You know, if you want to."

She grinned her bright smile. "I do. But won't it be weird when we don't get married?"

The thought of marrying Neecie made him feel like he stood on the edge of the Grand Canyon with a gun at his temple. The thought of giving her up made him feel like he'd fallen. In the end, he'd have to give her up—or else watch her brightness dim because of him.

"You're right," he said. "We can end the engagement shortly after the lounge opens up."

"Oh ... we could."

"I mean, we can't keep up this scheme forever." He watched for any signs that she didn't see him only as the bad boy she'd brought home to piss off her parents and live out the fantasy of sex with a thug.

She met his gaze and cocked a shoulder. "Yeah ... you're right. We'll end things right after the lounge opens."

Kareem nodded and ignored the sudden tightness in his chest. "You want to go back to your parents'?"

She glanced at her watch. "I actually need to get over to meet Lorelei."

He shook his head. "Be careful there, Neecie. I don't like the way they try to hint around that there's something wrong with your weight."

"Don't worry. I won't drink the Kool-Aid. Those days are gone," she said with a frown.

"Those days?"

Her frown cleared and her sunshine reappeared. "Nothing. Just trust me when I say they aren't going to be sucking me back into my old ways."

His gut said there was more, but he didn't push. It wouldn't do him any good to get any more wrapped up in Neecie and her past than he already was—no matter how much he wanted to figure her out.

"I'll see you when you get back." He took a step back, then glanced at the mirrored windows hiding the man everyone said was perfect for Neecie. Kareem leaned in and brushed his lips across hers. Her body leaned forward. Kareem pulled back before the jolt could draw him in. Make him try and kiss her when he didn't know how.

She crossed her arms. "Sure. See you in a few."

Kareem turned around and crossed the street without checking the light. The crosswalk indicated he could pass, but a part of him wondered if getting struck by a car would hurt as much as realizing he was getting in over his head with a woman far out of his league.

CHAPTER 17

A crash from the family room distracted Kareem on his way out the door to the car. He stopped and frowned in the direction of the noise. No one came down the hall. He hadn't seen Fran since she'd kicked him out of the kitchen when he'd come in to make a sandwich. Crazy, since she scowled the entire time she delivered a sandwich to him in the bedroom. Milton and Janice were still out, and Neecie hadn't returned from her meeting with the model.

This left him to investigate the crash in the family room. Someone breaking into the house was doubtful, still, he kept his footsteps silent in case whoever was breaking shit didn't want to be discovered.

Kareem slowly rounded the corner into the family room. The chairs before the fireplace were empty. Frowning, he spun toward the area with the piano. Neecie stood on the tips of her toes reaching for a leather-bound chest on top of the bookshelf. Another box and an array of books littered the floor around her feet. The probable source of the previous crash.

Her fingers brushed the edge of the box directly above her, edging it forward. Kareem pictured a waterfall of books raining down on her head and his heart nearly stopped.

Rushing forward, he placed a hand around her waist and jerked her backward.

"Hey!" She spun around and frowned. "What's wrong with you?"

"What's wrong with you? That box could fall on your head."

"The other one didn't."

Kareem gritted his teeth. The noise he made sounded very much like a growl. "Did that mean you had to try again to crush your skull?" He walked over to the bookshelf and reached up. The case wasn't as heavy as he thought but had enough weight to have hurt her.

"I'm not trying to crush my skull. I'm trying to see what board games are up there."

He pulled down the chest and set it safely on the floor between them. He scowled at her, his heart still hammering from the idea of her sprawled on the floor knocked unconscious. Neecie crossed her arms beneath her breasts and looked every bit the petulant child.

"Then ask someone to help next time," he said. "You're tiny; this would have hurt you."

"I am not tiny! I'm average height."

"For a hobbit." He flipped open the top of the chest as Neecie sputtered behind him. He glanced back at her and the corner of his mouth turned up. "Don't get mad; you know you're short."

"Maybe you're abnormally tall." She pushed him aside and fell to her knees in front of the chest. "I grabbed the wrong box the first time, but nothing bad happened."

"Not this time." Kareem lowered himself next to her. Several board games filled the chest. "Don't do that again. I couldn't stand it if you hurt yourself."

Her sunshine smile brightened her face, and her eyes became something warm and soft he wanted to wrap himself in forever. Kareem cleared his throat and pointed to the boxes. Just a few hours ago they'd both agreed to a deadline for this deal.

"Why are you looking for games? You need to clear your head?"

"What makes you think that?" Her voice went defensive, and she pulled the games out of the chest.

"You played Jenga when you needed to clear your head the other week. Doesn't take a rocket scientist to figure out you're doing the same thing here."

"Aren't we observant?"

"Quit pouting and tell me what's up. Did things go badly with that model? Did she insult you?" His neck tightened and the need to defend Neecie sprang like lion in his chest.

"Want to play backgammon?" Neecie pulled out a smaller wooden case and unfolded it to reveal the dark and light brown long triangles and a row of white and black round pieces.

"Here's the thing. I'll play if you tell me what's bothering you."

Neecie set up the pieces on the board. "It's no big deal really. I've always wanted to work in the beauty industry. And working with Lorelei will be a great experience."

"But?"

"I don't know, she just has a weird way with her employees." Neecie picked up the dice and shook it. "Black or white?"

"Black."

She raised a brow, and her gaze dropped to his black shirt. "When did you start wearing all black?"

"Are my clothes a problem?"

"When?"

If he were that type of guy, her constant questions would have him sighing and rolling his eyes. "After prison. You got a problem with that?"

"No."

But he could see in her eyes she wanted to know why. He didn't have a good answer; black just felt right after five years in hell. "What's weird about her ways with her employees?"

"More Cliff's Notes, huh?" Her cute smile returned and she rolled the dice. "Fine. Some of the things Lorelei says to her employees kinda got to me."

"Is she cursing them out or something?"

"No, not that." She rolled a six and moved her piece. "She snaps at them." Neecie snapped her fingers. "Literally. And then she told another girl that she looked *fluffy*, and this woman was much skinnier than me."

Kareem grabbed the dice and tossed them onto the board. "Did she say anything to you?"

"As cute as it is that you've got that *I'm going to fix things* tone in your voice, don't worry. I made it clear I'm not down for being called fluffy, and she didn't snap at me once." Neecie bent a knee and rested her cheek on it. She wrapped an arm around the bent leg and frowned. "It makes me wonder if she will one day."

"If she does, to hell with her. Don't let Lorelei or anyone else make you doubt yourself. You're beautiful, sexy, and perfect just as you are. There are other modeling agencies and other ways to stay in the business. And if we have to knock on the door of every one of them to help you find the right place, we will."

"We will?"

Damn, he'd said *we*, letting it slip that he'd thought of her long term. "I mean you." He moved his piece and slid the dice back to her. "You're tenacious. You got me here, didn't you?" He softened his words with a half-smile. Her eyes always went warm when he smiled.

"I did, didn't I?" Her eyes gave him what he expected, bringing back the longing he tried to ignore. "See, this is what I mean. You look out for people. You're not as scary as you want everyone to believe."

"Oh, I'm not?"

"No. Besides, how scary can you be if you open a high-end barber shop?"

Kareem shrugged and looked at the board. "Being scary isn't why I'm opening the place. Mr. Keisler owned the corner barber shop where some of the guys from the Runners got haircuts. He knew what we were in, but he didn't preach." Kareem lifted his eyes back to hers. "He listened, gave advice on females, talked me out of dropping out of high school, and covered my ass when he shouldn't have. I learned a lot in that shop, and after I got out, I realized everything he said was true. Fresh Cutz was my way to do something similar."

"And Henderson's Gentlemen's Lounge?"

Kareem rubbed his scar and pointed to the board. "Roll."

"Oh, no, I'm not rolling until you answer." She curled the dice in her hands and pressed them to her breasts.

"You know I have no problem reaching over there for those."

Her chest rose and fell, and heat flared in her eyes. "Answer."

"You're going to laugh."

"I promise I won't."

He looked around the room, then dropped his head. He couldn't believe he was actually going to tell her. "Okay, fine." He met her gaze. "I wanted to create something classy. Some place where men can get pampered without feeling ... you know, crazy for doing it. Guys like beautiful women, they like to look good, and they like hanging with their boys. I figured my place can be all that."

"That's nothing to laugh at, Kareem. I think you're making a great move."

He pinched the bridge of his nose and ran a hand over his dreads. "Sometimes I wonder if it'll work."

"It will, for all the reasons you named." She placed her hand on his thigh. The warmth comforted him in a way that had nothing to do with desire. "I believe in you."

Unsure of what to say or do. Kareem shifted until her hand fell away. He cleared his suddenly thick throat and motioned to the board. "Let's play. Or are you afraid I'm going to beat you?"

Neecie's chuckle sent light through his body. "Say that at the end of the game, mister."

CHAPTER 18

After a week with Neecie's family, Kareem enjoyed being in his shop the next weekend—back with his normal clients and in his small office with the yellow walls and black history calendar. No matter how things went with the lounge in Charlotte, he'd keep Fresh Cutz. This was his first business, the place that provided sanity when he needed it most.

"When you heading back up to Charlotte?" Lee's voice came from the office door.

Kareem rose from his chair. He came around the desk and leaned a hip against the side. Crossing his arms, he regarded Lee. They'd met in the Runners, and Kareem gave Lee the way out after he witnessed a murder. Lee worked hard and never looked back. Instead, he'd married his son's mother and spent his time looking out for his family.

"Going up at the end of the week to check out a few places," Kareem said.

Lee frowned and raised his chin. "Look, Kareem, I never wanted to believe you'd toss us to the side. Al thinks this stuff you're doing in Charlotte means you're closing the shop. I didn't want to believe you'd leave us out in the cold like that."

"I'm not closing the shop." Lee relaxed, but Kareem held up a hand. "But I won't be working here. Once I open the new place in Charlotte. I'd like for you to run Fresh Cutz for me."

Lee's eyes narrowed. "What exactly is this new place?"

"Something a little more upscale. Still a barber shop, but with other services, manicures, meeting space, and a cigar lounge."

"That don't sound like a place our folks would go to."

"I'm reaching out for new clientele."

"You too good for us now?" Lee asked, anger in his voice.

Lee's reaction was exactly the reason why he kept his idea to himself for so long. "You know me better than that. I'll always love this place, and there's no way I'd forget it. But I want bigger things. This place in Charlotte, with the connections I'm making, will bring in businessmen, athletes, and celebrities if it all works out. It's just the next step in the game. And it's a step I want to make." Kareem stood and shrugged. "We both left the Runners because we wanted something better. This is my better."

And he was making the connections he needed. Being *charming* wasn't as hard as he'd expected, once he let his guard down and realized networking was just another form of hustling. One that thankfully came with a lot less collateral damage.

Lee studied him, and several seconds later the tension left his face and he nodded. "I can't hate on you for taking your game to the next level. Doesn't mean I won't miss you around here. You keep us all straight."

"Now you can. Again, I'm putting you in charge, if you want it. Which means a percentage of the booth rentals along with what you make cutting hair."

Lee's brows rose. "For real?"

"I wouldn't ask without looking out for you."

Lee grinned and held out a hand. "Deal, man."

Kareem shook his hand and grinned. He spent another few minutes asking Lee about his family, then talked with Al, Joe, and Rico out front and let them know what was going on. After telling Lee he'd get with him before he left about renting out his and Neecie's booths, Kareem drove to his parents' house.

He had a key but chose to ring the doorbell. His parents weren't expecting him, and after his dad's heart surgery, he felt weird to just barge in unexpected.

Loretta opened the door, and her beautiful, heart-shaped face broke into a radiant smile when she laid eyes on him.

"Kareem, boy, what are you doing ringing the bell?" She grabbed his hand and pulled him into the house.

"I didn't want to scare you and Dad," Kareem said.

"You not coming around scares me." She wrapped him up in a tight hug, surrounding him with the softness of her lavender cashmere sweater and the smell of her Red Door perfume. Normally he pulled away quickly, but days with the Baldwin family made him appreciate her. No matter what he did, Loretta always welcomed him home. His arms wrapped around her shoulders, and he pulled her in tight.

"Oh, well, that's a first," she said when let her go. When he pulled back, moisture brightened her eyes. "When did you become a hugger?"

"Nothing wrong with letting the people you love know it," he said and shrugged. She leaned in for another one, but he diverted her by wrapping an arm around her shoulder and urging her down the hall. "Where's Dad?"

The look she shot him said she knew he'd avoided the second hug, but her smile didn't waver.

"He's out with David taking a look at the new store in Lexington," Loretta said, wrapping an arm around his waist. "Ever since he decided not to sell the business, he's taken more of an interest in how David's running things."

"Is it driving David crazy?" Kareem asked. Their dad's idea of taking an interest usually meant telling his kids how to do things his way.

"Actually, no. He's only observing." She looked his way with a raised brow. "Surprising to everyone in the family." Her arm around his waist squeezed him. "But Sandra's here with me until they get back."

They arrived at the kitchen, and Kareem let Loretta go ahead while he lingered at the door. Sandra sat at the granite island, her hands wrapped around a coffee mug. A smile crossed her face when she saw him.

Sandra's smile still hit him in the chest, but not with the same force as before she and David finally worked out their differences.

Kareem crossed the room to stand next to her. "What's up, Sandra."

"Hey, Kareem." She put down the mug, which looked to be filled with hot chocolate. "It's good to see you again."

"It hasn't been that long."

Loretta pulled another coffee mug from the cabinet. "Do you want some hot chocolate, Kareem?" She used the mug to point toward the fridge. "I made spaghetti earlier, and I can fix you a plate. When was the last time you ate?" She put the mug on the counter and scooted over to open the fridge. "We've also got some leftover chicken and dumplings from yesterday. Your dad will be upset if you eat it, but I'll deal with him."

Loretta's fussing comforted him after the lukewarm acceptance of Neecie's family.

"I'm not hungry, Mom," he said with a smile. "I picked up something before I went to the shop, but hot chocolate will be good."

She stopped dead in her tracks and gaped at him.

He shrugged. "You used to put marshmallows in it when I was a kid, remember?"

Loretta nodded and gave a smile. "I remember. You would eat them first then chug down the chocolate."

The love that radiated from her gaze made Kareem shift on his feet. He'd drawn away from his family for too long. "I'll still eat them first." Loretta chuckled, and Kareem looked to Sandra. "What brings you here?"

She blinked a few times. "Hanging out with Ms. Loretta while David and Mr. Henderson are out." She turned in her seat to face him. "How long are you in town for?"

"The rest of the week. Then I'm going back up to Charlotte."

Loretta tuned away from the stove where she'd put milk in a pot. "What are you doing in Charlotte? Some type of gentlemen's lounge or something?" Loretta asked. She stirred the milk.

He looked at Sandra. "Did you tell them?"

Sandra bit her lip and stared down into her hot chocolate. "They were worried."

Or David pried it out of her during loving couple pillow talk. "No big deal." He looked to his mom. "Yeah. I am."

Loretta poured the warm milk into a mug and added chocolate syrup. "I'd rather hear it from you."

She dropped several small marshmallows into the mug from the bag on the counter and came over to sit across from him at the bar. She slid the mug his way.

"Then I'll tell you." He pulled out one gushy marshmallow and popped it into his mouth, then spent the next few minutes telling his mom about his plans. The pride and joy in Loretta's face made him wish he'd opened up sooner.

Loretta reached across the counter and placed a warm hand over his. "I'm so proud of you, Kareem. You deserve to be happy."

He nodded. "That sounds like something Neecie would say. She's helping me out."

Loretta's eyes widened, and she squeezed his hand. "I knew I liked that girl for a reason. Exactly how is she helping you out?"

A part of him considered telling his mom the truth about his arrangement, but the idea of watching the pride on her face morph into disappointment kept his mouth shut.

"She's from there. Knows people."

Loretta raised a brow and tilted her head to the side, a hint of excitement sparkling in her eye. "Is that all she's helping you with?"

"What does that mean?"

"Well, first the rehearsal dinner then the wedding, now the two of you are in Charlotte working together. It sounds to me like there's more going on."

Sandra perked up. "And David did mention something about you two being together."

He had told David to pass that along. "Something like that."

Loretta grasped his hand again and grinned. Sandra beamed at him. Guilt tickled his insides for not telling the entire truth.

"So you really like her?" Loretta asked.

"I do like her. She's cool," he said. Loretta got a glow, and he could practically hear the wedding march playing in her head. "I like her, but I'm not marrying her."

News of the daughter of a North Carolina Supreme Court judge was unlikely to reach his family's ears, but he didn't doubt Chad might eventually reach out to his family to confirm the story. "But we are ... kinda serious."

Loretta nodded in Sandra's direction. "Maybe she can be a bridesmaid and catch the bouquet at your reception."

This conversation now had his mom's hopes up to the moon and reawakened the longing he had trouble locking away lately. Kareem focused on Sandra. "You and David finally picked a date?"

"Yes, a very close date."

"Why the rush?"

Sandra glanced at Loretta, who only grinned back. Sandra placed a hand over her stomach. "Pretty soon I won't be able to fit into a dress."

"My first grandchild," Loretta said, clasping her hands in front of her.

Kareem looked from his mother to Sandra. His guts turned to razorblades, slicing through the happy contentment of the afternoon. Jealousy. That damn emotion. Once again, David, the good son, had it all. Good woman, successful business, and soon a family. He could see them all together: the perfect couple and family.

Shit, I want that.

The image in his mind shifted. The happy couple: him and Neecie, and a little girl with Neecie's sunshine smile.

"Aren't you going to say something?" Sandra asked, looking uneasy.

Oh, yeah, dumb silence wasn't usually the standard response to a pregnancy announcement. Kareem gulped the hot ass cocoa.

The liquid scalded his tongue, and Kareem cleared his throat, then stared into the eyes of the woman giving his brother something Kareem kind of wanted. "Congratulations."

CHAPTER 19

Kareem glanced around the rental space in Phillips Place in Charlotte's South Park area. Immediately, he visualized changing the space to suit his needs. He saw a stocked bar, upgraded barber stations, and polished wood and chrome as if the features were already there.

"Well, what do you think?" Roland strolled up next to him with an *I'm so pleased with myself* voice.

Kareem hated to add to Roland's overinflated ego, but on this he had to agree. The place was perfect. "Not bad."

Kareem glanced at Neecie as she wandered over to run her hand along the old salon's receptionist area. He locked in on her fingers trailing across the wood and remembered the way she'd run her hands over him the night before. One month in, and he only wanted her more. He wasn't quite sure why the feeling didn't bother him considering the deadline on their time together.

"What do you think, Neecie?"

She glanced around and placed a hand on her hips. The movement opened the short white jacket she wore and stretched the green blouse over her perfect tits. "It isn't bad."

"Not bad?" Roland crossed the room to stand beside Neecie. "The place has most of the set up you need, and the location is great."

Kareem nodded and pointed to the right side of the room. "I could add the bar over there. Maybe add a hall and close in some space toward the back for the cigar lounge."

Kareem moved to Neecie's other side and stood in her space to feel her warmth and smell her fruity perfume. "What do you think?" He lowered his voice so that only she could hear.

Neecie's sexy little smile came out, and she placed a hand on his chest. Her familiar touches were something else that came easy after a month.

"I think you could really make this place shine," she said. "There's plenty of room to add the meeting space."

Kareem pushed away one of the kinky curls bursting from her yellow beanie cap. "You think I can make this place work?"

"I know you can," she said with earnestness, adding fuel to the confidence that burned through him the moment they walked in.

A woman like Neecie could make a man feel capable of anything. She said she had his back and proved true to her words, giving control of her body in the bedroom and supporting his decisions concerning the business, leaving him to wonder how he would be able to let her go when everything was done.

"Then I think this is it." Kareem turned to Roland, who quickly wiped away the frown on his face. Kareem's own smile disappeared. Roland hadn't said anything outright, or made any moves on Neecie; they'd even had brunch with him and his girlfriend, but Kareem didn't trust him.

"You finally hit the jackpot, Roland." Kareem wrapped an arm around Neecie's waist and pulled her into his side. Roland's good natured smile tightened around the edges. "I'm going to put in an offer."

Roland rubbed his hands together. "Great. I'm glad I could help you two find a location."

"Anyone else looking at this place?" Neecie asked.

"It hasn't even been listed yet," Roland's *I'm pleased with myself* tone returned. "I called in a few favors when I heard the owner wanted to sell. If you're interested, you can have first dibs."

Kareem didn't like him, but Roland damn sure made himself useful. "I'm interested. Let's make some calls and seal the deal."

Neecie bounced on her feet. "I'm so excited for you, Kareem."

He squeezed her waist. "Don't get too excited. I'll wait until opening day for that." He glanced around again; the renovations shouldn't take too long. With the right contractor, his place could be up and going in six to eight weeks.

Roland clasped his hands behind his back and rocked back on his heels. "About that. You want to cater to a certain clientele, I'll tell you now it'll be hard to convince people with expendable money to give your business a try."

"I'll put in a good word for him," Neecie said. "And Father will as well."

"That'll do some good, but you and I both know it'll take more than that." Roland's regretful tone didn't sound sincere to Kareem. "Let's face it, no one in the Charlotte scene knows him, and you've been away for five years."

Kareem narrowed his eyes. "What are you saying?"

"You need an investor. A partner who will make it easier to convince the prestigious clientele you're seeking that you're offering a sophisticated experience they can't get anywhere else."

"Exactly who were you thinking?" Kareem said.

Roland shrugged as if the answer were obvious. "I'd love to help. Believe me, I wouldn't offer if I didn't believe in your business plan. This place can be big. I'd like to help you see it happen."

Or, he'd like to find a way to stay close to Neecie. "Sure, I'll think on it." Kareem let his negative vibes come through.

Neecie turned wide eyes his way. "Kareem, he makes a good point. I have been away for a while, and since my brother is unwilling to help, Roland as a partner—"

"I said, I'll think on it." His voice hard, Kareem tightened his grip on her waist.

She frowned and tried stepping away. Kareem held firm. "Thanks for showing us the place, Roland. If you give me the broker's name, I'll have my real estate agent contact them."

Roland's brows raised. "I'll be happy to work out the details."

Kareem bared his teeth in the semblance of a grin. "I'd rather let my guy handle it."

Roland nodded. "No problem. I'll hook you two up."

Kareem raised his hand from Neecie's waist to her stiff shoulders. He gave a gentle squeeze. But she didn't lean into him.

"Ready to go?" he asked.

She stiffly pulled out of his reach. "Yes."

• • •

"How long are we going to keep up this silent treatment?" Kareem asked once he pulled the car into her parents' driveway.

Neecie glared at him from the corner of her eye. Her arms were crossed tight, and her leg bounced frantically in sexy black leggings that had him ready to get her upstairs.

"How long before you apologize for cutting me off in front of Roland?"

Kareem scoffed and snapped off his seatbelt. "I didn't cut you off."

The tightly crossed arms popped loose, and she pointed a green polished nail at him. "Yes, you did. You basically shut me up when all I tried to do was make a point."

"Yeah, a bad point." He pushed open the door and got out of the car.

She quickly followed, slamming her door. "It was not a bad point. What Roland said made a lot of sense."

"I don't want him to be a partner." He marched around the car toward the house. Neecie blocked his steps.

"Why? If we bring him on it'll bring more of the connections we need."

"He can bring those connections without being a partner. If he likes the idea, and wants to help, then he'll put in a good word with the people he works with. I don't see how giving him a share of my dream is the only way to make that happen."

Her shoulders relaxed, and she took a step back. "I know this is your dream. I'm just trying to help you make it happen."

"I'd rather make it happen without him."

"He only wants to help you."

Kareem shook his head. "No, Neecie, he only wants to help you."

Her head jerked back. "Don't be crazy. Roland hasn't said or done anything to warrant that. He has a girlfriend."

"That doesn't mean a damn thing." He sidestepped her and headed toward the house.

"I'm not finished," she said, her footsteps hurrying up from behind.

"I am. This conversation is over."

Neecie's hand jerked his arm. She couldn't turn him, but he faced her anyway. "There you go shutting me down again. This isn't how things go."

"What things? You want your ex to be a partner in my business. I'm not going to do that."

"I'm asking you to listen to my reasoning. Not shut me down without hearing me out. Accepting help isn't losing control."

"Not wanting Roland as a partner doesn't mean I'm afraid of losing control."

"I think it does." Neecie stepped to him with hands on her wide hips. "You're afraid to let people in."

Kareem scoffed and pushed past her. "I'm done."

"What are you afraid of, Kareem?"

He spun back to her. "I'm not afraid of anything."

"Yes you are, but you won't admit it. You're afraid of accepting help. You're afraid to feel." Her eyes darted to the side then met his. "You're afraid to kiss me."

"What the hell does me kissing you have to do with this conversation?"

"Nothing." She pressed a hand to her eyes. "Everything." Her hands fell. "You don't trust me with what you're thinking or feeling." She took a step forward. "I hear you at night, when you're mumbling and angry in your sleep. I see when you try to hide the way you sometimes blank out around people."

Buzzing louder than a hundred hair clippers vibrated in his ears. Neecie saw too much, wanted too much. His face hardened, and he gave her the stare that usually resulted in people backing down. "I don't know what you're talking about."

A month ago she would have looked away. Today, she boldly met his eye. "You know exactly what I'm talking about. Let me in. Let me—"

"Shut up, Neecie." He sliced his hand through the air. Her mouth snapped shut. Blood pounded in his ears. His hands became slick with sweat. "My secrets, my *fears* as you call them, are my business. Know your role."

Neecie sucked in a breath. Pain flashed in her eyes.

"I didn't mean it like that," he said.

"No, you made it very clear what you mean." She rushed forward and grabbed the keys out of his hands.

"Where are you going?"

"Anywhere but here." She stomped around to the driver's side of his car and yanked open the door. Kareem had every right to tell her she couldn't take his car, but his lips froze together. She needed to hear him, needed to know that some things were off limits. He needed to realize that things couldn't work. One month in and he was getting crazy ideas—ideas that made him think a guy like him could make it work with a woman like her.

CHAPTER 20

Patrice returned to her parents' house two hours later. Fran greeted her at the door with pinched lips and eyes glowing with concern.

"Are you okay, Ms. Patrice?"

Patrice tried to smile and nodded. "Yes, Fran, I'm fine."

It wasn't a lie. Two hours of riding revealed how unfair she'd been to Kareem. They were together only in the bedroom. Other than that, he'd made no promises or given any indication of wanting a real relationship. Just because her emotions were tangled around him didn't mean he owed her any of his secrets.

"Are my parents at home?"

Fran shook her head. "No, ma'am. Your father had court today, and your mother is busy with plans for the women's luncheon."

Good, she didn't want to face them. "Is Kareem still here?"

Fran sniffed and wrinkled her nose. "He is."

She left Fran with her scrunched-up face and slowly made her way upstairs. Asking Kareem to consider Roland's offer to be a partner was a mistake. She'd brought Kareem here to keep Roland off her back, not accept every offer he made help. No wonder Kareem didn't trust her with his secrets.

Patrice entered an empty bedroom. The doors to the outdoor balcony were cracked, and the sound of reggae music drifted inside. Patrice crossed the room and went out onto the balcony. Kareem sat in one of the chairs, sketching in his notebook. A cigar and his smartphone, the source of the music, lay on the table next to him.

"How did your drive go?" he asked.

Patrice leaned against the rail in front of him. "Pretty good. I had some time to think."

Kareem flipped the notebook closed, picked up his cigar, and took a drag. "Me too." With his black hoodie and jeans, dreads tied loosely at the base of his neck, a dark, sexy air hovered around him.

He put the cigar on the table and watched her through the haze of exhaled smoke. "What did you think about?"

"You. And me," she said. Afternoon shadows covered the balcony and worked with the chill seeping into Patrice's hands and feet. She crossed her arms, pinching her hands between her body and forearms.

"I shouldn't have gotten mad at you earlier," she said. "For the record, I don't want you to take on Roland as a partner."

"Are you sure? You got pretty pissed when I didn't consider it."

"The truth is, I got pissed because you cut me off and didn't consider what I had to say. This was never about Roland. I apologize, and I'll stay out of your business."

Kareem's hand rubbed the scar above his lip. "See, that's the thing, I don't want you to stay out of things."

Patrice's eyes narrowed and Kareem shifted from one side to the other in the chair. "I like your support," he said. "Your ... confidence in me. Liking your input pushes against my dislike of having people try to control my decisions. You've never held back your opinions before. No need to stop now."

"So, we're good?"

"Yeah, we're good." He picked up the cigar but only rolled it back and forth between his fingers. For several seconds they didn't speak, which usually meant he considered the conversation over. She pushed away from the rail to go back inside.

"And, Neecie, I'm sorry if I hurt your feelings." His eyes were no longer flat and emotionless, but alive with seriousness. "I never want to hurt you. I'm just not ready to give up my secrets yet."

She nodded, but inside she yearned to know all his secrets. Pull back more of the elusive layers of Kareem Henderson. Heal his pain and give him nothing but reasons to relax and smile.

Patrice twisted her foot back and forth on the balcony. "Can you at least give up what you thought about while I was gone?"

His gaze zeroed in on her foot and the corner of his mouth lifted. "You. And me. How you drive me crazy and have since the day you walked in my shop."

"I drive you crazy? How?"

He pointed at her with the hand holding the cigar. "Look at you. You're sexy as hell. Of course you drive me crazy."

Hot prickles of desire scattered across her skin. "I didn't know."

"You weren't supposed to know." He inhaled from the cigar then stubbed it out. "You're sexy even when you're not trying to be. When you're irritated, you get this little line between your brows and purse your lips like you want to be kissed." He leaned forward, placing his forearms on his knees. A sad smile crossed his lips. "It makes me think about kissing you, really kissing you, but I've never really ..." He frowned. After a second he pointed to her leg. "Then there's that thing you do with your feet."

She stopped twisting her foot. "My feet?"

"Yeah, you twist them. It makes the muscles in your legs and ass tighten. I like it."

The thought of Kareem checking her out over the past year every time she did the unconscious movement sent flames to her belly. "You're not good at poetic words." The quiver in her voice hindered her attempt to be lighthearted.

"I'm good at saying what I'm thinking."

"What else are you thinking?"

For several seconds Kareem's dark, hungry gaze brushed across her breasts, hips, and thighs. Her skin tightened. Her nipples hardened and slick wetness dampened her panties.

"That I'd like to see you naked."

Patrice's sharp inhale echoed on the balcony. "We can go inside."

Kareem leaned back in the chair, legs spread wide. "Not inside, out here. I'd like to see you naked in the afternoon sunlight."

"Why?"

Eyes filled with unchecked longing rose to hers. "Because you'll be beautiful in sunlight."

Patrice's tongue did a quick dart across her lips. Take that back, the man was poetic in his own way. "You'll see me naked in the sunlight, but what do I get?"

A spark of eagerness replaced the longing. "Some of the control you say I deny. You can do whatever you want to me."

CHAPTER 21

Patrice's heart did an unsteady rap behind her ribs. Anything she wanted. She wanted to hear her name on his lips. Watch his eyes roll to the back of his head. See his hands clench the arms of the chair. Kiss without him pulling away.

"Anything?"

"Within reason." He shrugged and a wicked grin relaxed his handsome face. "Take your clothes off and find out."

Not quite a promise, but enough to make her clench the muscles of her sex. "Aren't you going to take off your clothes?"

"After you're done."

Patrice considered the pros and cons. The only con was the cold, which the heat in his eyes quickly zapped away. She shrugged off her short, white leather jacket and let it fall to the floor. He raised a brow and nodded. Slowly she handled the buttons of her blouse. Cool air caressed her and goose pimples sprang over her skin. Her nipples puckered against the green silk of her bra. Patrice slipped the blouse off her arms, and the material landed on top of her jacket. Kareem's dark eyes followed every movement. Despite the cold, heat sizzled in her veins.

Her hands touched her bra's front clasp. Kareem shook his head. "The pants first."

Her gaze dropped to the growing swell behind his zipper and mini tremors vibrated low in her stomach. "I thought I was in control."

"You can do what you want to me, after I watch you get naked."

Patrice removed one boot then the other. She went for the waistband and again he shook his head.

"Turn around as you pull them down," Kareem ordered, in a low deep voice.

Turning her back to him, Patrice hooked her fingers in the waistband of her leggings. She glanced over her shoulder, then bent over to ease the black material down her legs. A breeze swept across the wet hairs between her legs, and she sucked in a breath. She eased one hip to the side then the other, letting the air caress her overheated slick folds. From between her legs she watched Kareem. His lips parted and nostrils flared watching her with eager bright eyes. She ran her hands up her legs and gradually stood. When she spun around the bulge in his pants had grown.

The heat in his gaze singed her skin. Patrice unclasped the front of her bra, spilling her breasts. The hard chocolate tips jutted out, eager for attention.

Kareem's breathing came in shallow bursts. "Perfect," he said, almost with awe. "Are you wet?"

Her face heated and she nodded. "Yes."

"Good." He sat up in the seat. "What do you want?"

She cleared her throat and licked her lips, suddenly unsure of what her next move should be. "Take off your hoodie and your shirt."

He did, not as slowly as she'd removed her clothes. His flat nipples pebbled in the cold air. The muscles in his chest and abs jumped with each of his deep breaths. Strong arms strained with power and he clutched the chair.

Patrice's hands tingled. "I want to touch you."

He nodded. "Come touch me."

The tile balcony floor was cool beneath her hot feet as she shortened the distance between them. Patrice stood between his strong, wide legs and softly swayed her hips to the steady beat of the music playing from his phone. Shaky fingertips ran across his muscled shoulders. His skin was softer than cashmere over solid power and cool in the afternoon air. More scars from tiny cuts littered his chest. Each one made her ache for his pain. She ran her hands over his shoulders and down his arms, enjoying the twitch of his muscle wherever her touch landed.

"What else do you want?" he asked.

"Are you hard?"

A small chuckle rumbled through his chest. "I think that's obvious."

"Let me see." She licked her lips. "Pull it out."

She prepared to step back to give him room, but Kareem wrapped one of his feet behind hers. He eased down the zipper, and her throat tightened. The tendons in his hand flexed as he pulled the length of his arousal from the opening in his boxers.

Her sex clenched, and her throat dried out, remembering how deep he would go and how much he made her shout out in pleasure.

"Now what?" His voice held a hint of a challenge.

"Jack it."

Hooded eyes widened before a sly grin spread his full lips. Kareem started with hesitant strokes, then he caught the slow rhythm of the music. Up and down, nice and easy until the head of his penis swelled and wept.

"What do you want now, Neecie?" he asked in a tight voice. His nostrils flared. "Tell me."

His urgent tone pushed her forward. "I want to taste you."

Kareem's eyes rolled back. "God, please do it."

It was the first time she'd ever heard Kareem beg. Her knees became putty, and she lowered until they pressed against the cold floor. She jerked his pants down. He helped her get them past his waist, and his hand went back to stroking. Pushing his hand to the side, she wrapped her fingers around his thick, hot flesh. Dark eyes bore into hers, and she kept eye contact as she eased him into her mouth. His skin was salty, and the potent smell of arousal infused her senses.

"Like you want it, Neecie," he ground out.

Tightening her grip, Patrice took him deep and sucked hard on the way up. Kareem's hands clutched the sides of the chair. His breaths ragged, and his leg shook. "God, yes, Neecie," he said in a sex drugged voice.

Patrice's tongue played with the seam of the blunt head. Her other hand lightly stroked the heavy sack beneath. Her mouth and hand glided effortlessly over his rigid length, and she licked and sucked with eagerness. She watched Kareem's mouth fall open. The desperate sweep of his tongue across his lips. The rise and heavy fall of his head as she pleasured him. Her nipples ached, and her core dripped in anticipation.

He grew harder in her mouth. A hand shot out to jerk the beanie from her hair before his fingers dove into the thick curls, pulling her away from her work. "Ride me, Patrice."

She ran her tongue across the underside of his dick once more. Kareem trembled. "With pleasure."

Patrice straddled him and slowly eased all of his thick glorious cock into her wet center. Their gazes locked. Unyielding hands gripped her hips and slammed her down with a hard upward motion of his hips. Patrice gripped his wrists and shook her head. "Let me feel you." She rotated her hips to the beat, felt Kareem deep.

Her hands slid up his arms, shoulders, and finally cupped his face. Kareem met her slow hip rotations with small deep strokes. She clutched him tight. Long fingers dug into the soft flesh of her behind. He licked his upper lip, swiping across the scar.

"Let me kiss you."

A slight hitch in his deep strokes hinted at his unease, but he nodded. Pulling him forward, her hands still cupping his face, she pressed her lips to his. The hair on his chest scratched her sensitive nipples. The erect bud of her clit brushed against the rough patch that surrounded his cock. Slow trembles started in her lower belly. Sliding her tongue across his lower lip, she tried to deepen the kiss, rotating her hips faster as her orgasm built. Kareem's tongue darted out and met hers in a tentative dance. Her heart fluttered. Then his head fell back.

"God, yes, Neecie!" His cock jerked and heat shot high inside of her.

Her body shattered. Patrice bit her lip, swallowing her own shout and collapsed against Kareem's chest, sated but still yearning for more.

CHAPTER 22

Lively conversation and big band music filled the Ritz-Carlton ballroom for the Charlotte Chamber's annual silent auction. Kareem, in an all-black tuxedo that pronounced his sexiness, held Patrice's hand where they stood next to one of the cocktail tables. She'd worn a sleeveless gold dress that swayed around her feet to match his tuxedo. Lad and Beth entertained them with the story about Lad's surprise proposal. Seeing her sister so happy pleased Patrice, and Lad's storytelling abilities were humorous, but Patrice's cheek-aching grin came from Kareem's hand clasping hers.

Kareem squeezed her hand and stared at Lad. "You really got on the news and proposed during the evening weather report?" His deep chuckle unleashed an army of butterflies in Patrice's stomach.

Lad wrapped an arm around Beth's shoulders and hugged her tight. "She watches every night and loves the weatherman. I decided if she's going to drool over a weatherman then he might as well be me."

"Oh, Lad, you know I don't drool over John Allen." Beth playfully hit Lad's shoulders.

"Really, then you don't care that he's here tonight?" Lad asked.

Beth's eyes went wide and she leaned up on her tiptoes. "Where?"

Lad laughed and kissed her cheek. "See what I mean?"

Patrice and Kareem joined in the laughter. Patrice glanced up at the relaxed smile on Kareem's face. He still held his secrets, but in the weeks since the balcony he'd seemed more open with their relationship. She just wasn't sure if they were still pretending or not.

Kareem turned his smile her way and love slammed her gut.

Buzzing started in her ears. The air in her lungs burst out. Forcing more in seemed impossible. She loved him!

Kareem's brows drew together. "You okay?"

Patrice blinked several times and nodded. "Yeah, I'm fine." She picked the last piece of double chocolate cake off the plate on the cocktail table. "I probably shouldn't have had that third piece of cake." She shoved the last bit in her mouth, but this time didn't savor the rich flavor.

Grabbing her half-finished glass of champagne she downed the contents to force the cake past her dry throat.

Worry filled Beth's eyes. "They were small pieces. Nothing to get upset about."

Patrice waved a hand. "You're right." Kareem eyed her and heat filled Patrice's face. *Oh, God, I love him.*

Patrice fanned her face. "Is it a little warm in here? I'm going to the bar for some water."

Kareem shifted at her side. "I can get it for you if you're not feeling okay."

"No, no, I'm good. Walking around will help." She smiled at him, and he rubbed her chin with this thumb, his eyes searching and concerned. Even in a tux and clean-shaven, Kareem's dark sexiness pulsed off him like sunbeams. Her love smacked her in the face.

When did I fall in love with him? The when didn't matter; the pain of when things ended scared her.

"I'll be right back." She spun away and dashed through the throngs of people into the cooler lobby air.

Patrice speed walked to the bar and clutched the polished wooden surface. "Ice water, please," she nearly screamed at the bartender.

A few people next to her stared with surprised glances. Patrice gave them tight smiles.

A hand clasped her shoulder. Patrice jumped and spun around. Beth snatched her hand back and Patrice relaxed.

"Oh, sorry," Patrice said.

Beth studied Patrice's face, her lips pressed tight. "Are you okay? When you talked about the three pieces of cake and ran out ..." Beth swallowed and leaned in. "I thought you'd relapsed."

Patrice frowned then Beth's meaning hit. "Oh, Beth, you don't have to worry. I've gotten over that particular weakness."

Beth slid into the space next to Patrice and rubbed her sister's back. "You never want to do that again? Ever?"

Patrice shrugged. "The first year was hard. I relapsed, but it got easier as time went on. I haven't wanted to in nearly a year."

"Then why did you rush out? Your face, you had that same *oh shit* look you used to have before you ... you know."

The bartender brought Patrice's water. Patrice gripped the cool glass and took a long sip. "I had an *oh shit* moment, but it had nothing to do with the food."

"What's wrong?"

Patrice opened her mouth to tell Beth, then snapped it closed. She was supposed to be in love with Kareem already. "Nothing, just worrying about things. And hearing you talk about your wedding plans. I don't know, maybe I got nervous."

Kareem's big, warm arm wrapped around her upper torso from behind. "Nervous about what?" His dark voice brushed against her ear.

Patrice shivered and brought a hand up to his arm. She squeezed the hard muscles. "Wedding plans. Listening to Beth reminded me of all we have to do."

Kareem stiffened. He tried to pull his arm away but she held tight. "We'll worry about that later."

"Right, later."

Beth watched the two of them with her head tilted to the side. "When are you going to set the date?"

"Soon," Patrice said. "I don't want to steal any of your thunder."

"I don't know, you two are doing that already," Beth said, a sly twist to her lips.

"How's that?" Kareem asked.

Beth leaned close. "Lad and I are crazy about each other, but we tend to keep things off the balcony." Beth winked.

Patrice's jaw dropped. "Who saw?"

"Fran, but I think she only complained because she was jealous." Beth pushed away from the bar. "You and Johnny have fun." She waved her fingers and glided away.

"Johnny?" Kareem asked.

She'd thought Beth was over that *Dirty Dancing* reference. "Inside joke." Patrice covered her hot face with her hands. "Oh my God, my parents know about the balcony."

Kareem chuckled and nipped at her ear. "I think they already know we have sex."

"But not on a balcony," she whispered, peeking between her fingers at the people next to them at the bar. Thankfully, no one paid attention to them, or at least they pretended they weren't. Dropping her hands Patrice turned to face Kareem. He braced his hands on the bar on either side of her. "I can't look my father in the eye ever again."

"Act like you don't know they know, and I promise they'll do the same." Kareem leaned in, and the strength of his body tugged at her midsection. "And if we find a corner in this hotel I'd wouldn't mind getting a chance to flip up your sexy skirt."

Patrice twisted her foot, and tingles traveled from her core up her spine. "We're here to network."

The slow upward pull of his lips twisted her loving heart. "Networking isn't on my mind right now." He pushed away from the bar. "I'm going to the men's room, wait for me here."

She nodded, and tried not to show her relief that he was walking away. She needed a moment to recover. Her heart beat so hard she feared her ribcage would fracture.

"I'll be here."

He ran a finger across her lower lip, and his brows drew together. He wanted to kiss her. She'd figured that out whenever he did the movement. She licked her lips and lifted her head. Kareem dropped his hand. "I'll be right back." His lip and scar quirked, and he walked away.

Patrice turned back to the bar and considered ordering a shot of tequila.

"Patrice, there you are." Roland's voice came from behind.

Exhaling heavily, Patrice faced Roland. He'd spent the night catering to his girlfriend, Felicia, but now approached with a guy who was vaguely familiar. She left the bar and took the few steps to Roland.

"Patrice," Roland said, "let me introduce you to Wade Livingston. He just won the election for the open city council seat."

"That's where I recognize you from," she said, holding out a hand to shake Wade's. "The television ads."

The tall, dark-haired guy gave her a winning smile and returned her handshake with a firm grip. "I hope that's not the only reason you remember me," Wade said with a good-humored laugh.

She dropped his shake. "If I were registered in the area I would have considered voting for you, but I went home to South Carolina to vote."

Roland placed a hand on Patrice's shoulder. "I told Wade about our plans to partner, and he wanted to meet you."

Patrice's smile froze. Partner? She'd never agreed to that and knew Kareem would rather eat angry fire ants.

"Our partnership?" she said in a questioning voice.

Roland kept on smiling when she knew good and damn well he'd heard her hesitant tone. "Yes, in fact, many of my colleagues are intrigued by the idea."

She narrowed her eyes. She didn't need the *I told you so* to emphasis on the words. "Wade, you're welcome to come by and check out the space anytime. We'd love to have you as a customer."

"Excellent," Wade said and waved at someone to their left. "Excuse me a second."

She stepped out of Roland's reach and placed a hand on her hip. "*Partnership?*"

He shrugged and raised he brows. "I thought we'd agreed on that."

"No, you brought it up, and Kareem and I decided against it."

"That's news to me. After you both willingly accepted my help I figured we'd come to an agreement." His brows furled over confused eyes. "My connection with Wade proves I can bring in the clientele you are searching for. The hints I've dropped with many of the businessmen I meet with on a regular basis have only resulted in more interest in your place."

"Kareem and I can do this on our own."

"Oh, really? Tell me how, Patrice." Roland crossed his arms over his chest and stared down his nose.

"He joined the chamber, and my father introduced him to many of his friends. Plus, we're hiring a public relations firm to assist with the opening and marketing of this place."

"That's not enough, and you know it. Your guy needs my help."

Patrice's hands fisted against her hips. "My guy appreciates your help but doesn't need it."

"What's with you, Patrice? All I'm trying to do is help your dream succeed, and you're giving me a hard time." Roland took a step forward and placed a hand on her elbow. "I only want to make you happy."

An uneasy feeling went down her spine. "Roland, it's not your job to make me happy."

"We were once engaged and loved each other. I know we're not those same kids, but there's enough affection left to want to see the other do well. I stood aside and ignored your needs before. I want to make things up to you."

Her anger faded. "There's nothing to make up. Please understand, I can't let my ex hang around offering to make my dreams come true."

Roland raised a brow and a spark went off in his eye. "If Kareem were secure in your relationship, he wouldn't feel threatened by my offer to help." His smug tone irritated her.

"I didn't say he's threatened."

Roland nodded. "I know you didn't." The smug tone remained, and Patrice felt ill.

Wade walked back over. "Sorry about that, but I had to speak with him. Patrice, be sure to let me know when your salon opens."

Pushing aside her unease, she gave Wade a small smile. "It's my fiancé's place, and I'll be sure to include you on the invitations for our soft opening in a few weeks."

Kareem walked up and slid his arm around her waist. He wore a pleasant expression, but the muscles in his body were tight.

"Kareem, meet Wade Livingston. He's new on the city council."

Kareem shook Wade's hand. "I noticed your ads. Nice to meet you."

"Same here. Roland was telling me about the salon you're opening. Good luck."

"Thank you."

Wade then pointed to Patrice and Roland. "With partners like these, this place is bound to be successful."

Kareem's hand on her hip tightened. "That's what I hear," Kareem said.

Wade looked at his watch. "I'm going to do another round before the auction starts. Again, nice meeting you two."

"I should get back to Felicia," Roland said. "Patrice, Kareem, we'll talk soon." Roland threw a knowing glance Patrice's way before leaving with Wade.

Kareem ushered her to the side of the room and faced her with angry eyes. "Since when did we become partners with Roland?"

"We're not. He came over talking partnership with the new councilman on his arm. I tried to say something when Wade walked away, but I don't think he took it very well."

"Why not? What's hard to understand about we're not partners?"

"He just says he wants to help."

"Then help, but don't tell everyone we're partners. I don't like the guy."

After Roland jumped to insinuate Kareem was insecure, she questioned his friendliness. "I understand, and we'll both make it very clear that he's not a partner. He just wants—"

"If you say he wants to help one more time I might punch a hole in the wall." His voice was sharp and angry. "Quit making excuses for him."

Patrice placed her hands on her hips. "I am not making excuses, and we're not having this argument again." She tugged on the lapels of his jacket. "Seriously, let's not go there. Let's go back to where we were before—when you talked about dragging me off into some secluded corner."

The corner of his mouth quirked, but his eyes went flat. "Maybe later. Come on, let's go back into the ballroom." He turned and walked away, leaving her behind.

CHAPTER 23

Kareem sat at the newly-constructed bar in his lounge and stared at the brushed nickel fixtures Neecie picked out for the hair wash areas. The sound of music from his phone echoed in the empty space. The construction workers were long gone, as he should have been. He wasn't ready to go back to Neecie's parents.

He stared at the new walls and remodeled floors. Just a couple more weeks and the place would open. This was his dream. His lounge. Opening this place and revamping his life was what he should be focused on. Not untying the knots Neecie created in his stomach.

Instead, his chest ached and his stomach clenched when he thought about letting her go once the place opened. He wanted to keep her in his life. But could he really make her happy? Could he really trust her? Roland had backed off after the auction, but the entire partner thing still stunk to him. And as if they already didn't have a butt load of crap to overcome, she'd started looking at him with that *let's fall in love* expression of hers.

Damn if he didn't like it every time she did.

A loud knock on the door interrupted his thoughts. Frowning, Kareem checked the time on his phone. Nearly ten, and too late for someone to knock on the door of this place.

He slid his hand into his book bag and pulled out a Glock .45. Rising from the bar, he held the gun behind his back and cracked open the door. The tension in his shoulders dissipated when he met Chad's disdainful gaze.

"What do you want?" Kareem's attempts at being charming didn't apply to Neecie's pompous brother.

"I was in the area and saw the light on. I figured I'd check out this place you and my sister have worked so hard on," Chad said in his stuck up tone of voice.

Kareem stepped back and opened the door. "Coming by to add your two cents about what we should do?"

Chad stepped through the door and inspected the place. "No, I'm just coming to satisfy my curiosity."

Kareem closed the door; when he turned around Chad's eyes were on the gun.

"Planning on shooting me?" Chad asked in a cool voice.

The corner of Kareem's lip lifted. "I don't like you, but I don't want to shoot you." He made his way back to the bar and slipped the gun in the backpack. "Unexpected knocks on a door at this time of night usually mean bad news."

"Thieves don't typically announce themselves by knocking." Chad followed him over.

Kareem leaned a hand on the bar and faced Chad. "Best way to surprise someone is by catching them off guard. Knocking gives the impression it's someone you know."

Chad raised a brow. "I forgot you were a thug."

Kareem's shoulders tightened. "Came to check out the place *and* insult me?"

"No, insulting you is just an added perk," Chad said with a half-smile.

Kareem let out a dry laugh and shook his head. If the guy weren't such an asshole, he might actually like him.

"Why are you really here, Chad? We both know you don't give a damn about this place." Kareem held out his hand to indicate the rest of the room.

"I may not give a damn about it, but I do care about Patrice. She's spent all of her free time working with you on this." Chad crossed the room and inspected the contractor's work. "I'm even hearing some positive interest in a few of my circles. I need to know what they're talking about when they ask me what my sister and her *fiancé* are up to."

"Last time I checked, you had a kid. Maybe you should concentrate on watching him instead of playing overprotective parent to Neecie." Kareem leaned his back on the bar and watched Chad. "And while you're at it, stop calling me her *fiancé* as if it weren't real."

"It isn't. I've known that from the start," Chad said with a flippant wave of the hand.

The dismissal irked Kareem. "You're using that as an excuse. We're together. There should be no doubts by anyone about that."

Chad slowly spun on his heels to face Kareem. His polished loafers left a trail in the construction dust. "And you made damn sure to stake your claim on her. You treat my sister like a tramp, not like your fiancée."

Kareem pushed away from the bar. "I don't treat your sister like a tramp."

"Yes, you do. You handle her. And make sure everyone knows you've put your filthy stamp on her." Chad sneered, his body rigid. "Do you think we don't know about where you took her at my parents' anniversary? Or that the staff isn't buzzing about the little peep show you two had on the balcony?"

"That wasn't about making a show for anyone." It was just to see if his sweet Neecie would really get naked for him on a balcony. Disgust warped his stomach.

"Save that crap for the next guy. You paw at her, lead her around like she's your personal Playboy bunny. Never once have I seen you show my sister the least bit of affection."

Mentally he ran through all of his interactions with Neecie. "I've shown your sister more affection than any woman I've ever known."

"You're using my sister for your own sick, twisted games. It sickens me to see her falling in love with you. And you treat her like a whore."

Kareem's expression didn't change, but his stomach flinched. Hadn't his sick fantasy been to watch her sweetness give way to his desires?

Kareem took a step toward Chad. "Neecie isn't a whore."

Chad didn't back down. "Then stop treating her like one. For some reason Patrice loves you. But it's very clear you don't feel the same. You're in lust, and when this is all said and done you'll move on and she'll be heartbroken."

That was the plan they'd agreed to. The plan that had his stomach in knots. "The last thing I want to do is break your sister's heart."

Chad appeared dazed for a second and then his gaze sharpened. "If that's true, then go ahead and call off this farce of a relationship. She deserves better. She deserves a man who'll love and cherish her. You're not the man to do that. I ignored her problems the last time, but not this time around."

"I care about your sister." Kareem couldn't control the need that came through his voice.

Something flickered in Chad's gaze, but he blinked and hardened his stance. "But she deserves to be loved."

Chad strolled to the door. When he turned around his gaze did one last sweep of the place. "I can see the potential. This place may actually turn out successful. I don't hate on any man for having dreams." He met Kareem's eye with a serious expression. "Unless he uses my sister to get there. You don't deserve her, Kareem." He jerked open the door. "Let her go."

CHAPTER 24

Kareem burst through the door of the bedroom he shared with Neecie. She lay on the bed, asleep, her e-reader resting on the pillow next to her head. The sense of purpose that had driven him from his lounge back to their bedroom seeped out of him. He slowly crossed the room and stared down at her. Sleep enhanced her sweetness. Loose, curly hair framed her face, the strap of the white camisole hung off her shoulder, and she clutched a pillow to her chest. Every night he watched her sleep, afraid to lie beside her and possibly awaken her with a nightmare if she snuggled too close, forcing him to reveal his issues.

Easing down on the side of the bed, Kareem ran his hand along her cinnamon brown thigh.

He gave her a little shake. "Neecie, wake up."

She turned over onto her back and opened her eyes. Once the remnants of sleep cleared, she glanced at the clock then back at him. "Kareem, what's up?"

"I need to ask you something."

Her sunshine smile brightened his heart. "You couldn't wait until morning?"

He shook his head and tugged on one of the curls in her hair. His gaze traced across her features, down her neck, to one of the marks he'd left the night before. Disgust twisted his stomach. "Do I treat you like a whore?"

Her brows drew together, and she pushed the hair from her face. "What are you talking about?"

"Answer me. Do you think I treat you like a whore?"

Neecie pushed herself up on the bed and leaned against the headboard. She scratched the side of her head and frowned. "Of course not. You're not that bad."

Kareem fought not to flinch. "How bad am I?"

"I know what to expect from you. You told me how you were, and I understand."

"But do you want more?"

Hope flashed in her eyes before her lashes lowered. She plucked at the green and white comforter on the bed. "I'm not expecting you to give more."

Kareem licked dry lips. His heart thrummed like a hundred hair clippers. "What if I want to give you more?"

Her eyes jumped to his. He saw her excitement, her hope, but he also saw wariness. "Kareem, I'm not asking you to change. I understand."

"No, you don't." He jumped up from the bed. The band around his dreads pulled his scalp tight. Kareem jerked at the elastic until it snapped, and his hair fell loose around his shoulders. Pressure built in his chest, pushing against his ribcage with so much force he felt ready to pop. He'd have to tell her.

Patrice drew her knee up to her chest. Wide, understanding eyes pleaded for him to talk. "Help me understand."

The pulse in his temple pounded. His dry mouth suddenly flooded with saliva, and bile rolled in his throat. Closing his eyes, Kareem sucked in a deep breath. Then another. And another. He withdrew from the feelings, the disgust, the loathing.

Warm hands closed around his forearm. He jerked away and opened his eyes to the wary expression on Neecie's face.

"I'm sorry," he said in a strained voice.

She crossed her arms and shook her head. "You were blanking out again. What happened? Trust me."

"Sit down," he said, pointing to the bed. "This will be easier if you sit and I ... pace."

Neecie sat and Kareem paced from one end of the bed to the other.

"I went to jail because I lost control." He swallowed hard then continued. "It wasn't until the judge made his decision that I realized all of the so-called freedom I thought I had was actually me giving the Runners control over my life. I told you what happened, and I don't want to talk about that again. Not right now anyway."

He looked around the room, thought about grabbing a cigar to ease his nerves, then changed his mind. Fran would light him on fire if she came in to clean and the smell of smoke clung to her precious fabrics.

"For five years I had absolutely no control over anything. I was told when to eat. When to sleep. When to shower. I hated it. I was scared, but I covered it with resentment and anger, letting them both consume me." He paused; the fear that once clenched him hovered at the edge of his mind. Kareem shook his head. "I couldn't let anyone know how scared I was, so I talked a lot of shit. Bragged about what I did with the Runners. All to hide how terrified and hopeless I felt every damn day I sat in that prison."

"Then one day, in the middle of my daily shit talking, this guy laughed. They called him Cide. Short for homicide because he'd killed close to a dozen people ... some young kids." The sound of Cide's mocking laughter played in Kareem's head, making his skin itch. "He called me a bitch. So what did I do? Told him 'I got your bitch.' Got ready to fight the meanest asshole in there when I should've kept my mouth shut. The corrections officers came and broke things up before they could get bad."

Neecie shifted on the bed. He spared a glance her way, saw the frown on her face, the question in her eye. Kareem breathed deep, noting the fresh smell of the plug in air freshener, Neecie's fruity perfume, anything to block out the rank memory of the smell of that jail cell.

"Later, Cide caught me in the showers." He let out a dry laugh. "Typical. That don't drop the soap bullshit is real. One second I'm showering, the next Cide has me pinned to the shower. Said he was ready for me to be his little..." He lost sight of the room. He smelled the cloying scent of the jail soap, felt the clammy mildew on the wall. His heart pounded with the fear he'd had that night.

"I fought, hard. But all I could hear was him calling me a bitch ... telling me he'd show me what a real man could do."

Neeice gasped. He couldn't bear to look at her. "He slammed my face into the sink then pulled out the knife he'd made. That's how I got this." He ran a finger over the scar above his lip. "Things went fuzzy after that. I knew for sure it was over."

"Stop," she said.

But he couldn't. "Cide had me, but Tim, my cellmate, came in. He jerked Cide away and nearly knocked him out. All I could think was how much I wanted to kill him. Wanted to make him suffer. I grabbed the knife off the floor."

"You killed him?" her horrified voice asked.

He shook his head. "Tim held him up. Told me to do it. Real quick, two stabs right in the chest." Kareem slapped his chest. "Puncture the lungs. Hate, embarrassment, anger, they all filled me. But I froze. Cide called me a punk. Tim snapped his neck. Just like that; it was over, and a man was dead. The corrections officer decided to show his face. Tim took the blame for everything. Said he caught Cide attacking me and did what needed to be done. My parents hired a lawyer who prevented my part in the fight from adding to my sentence. Tim is still serving life."

"Do your parents know?"

Kareem shook his head. "No. Just that there was a fight and a prisoner died. I didn't need their pity." He met her eye. "I don't need anyone's pity."

• • •

Patrice stared at the stiff wall of Kareem's shoulders. The pounding of her heart was the only reaction adequate enough for what he'd revealed. Pain filled her chest for the young man he'd been—the adult he'd become.

He watched her, uncertainty and anger in his eyes. The hard line of his jaw dared her to cry. To feel sorry. Though her heart hurt, she refused to let the emotion overwhelm her or overshadow him taking this step.

Standing, she crossed the room and placed her hands on the hard lines of his chest. "I'm proud of you."

Kareem's lips parted and his head tilted slightly to the side. "Because I went to prison? Wanted to kill a man, but instead froze and let another man do what I was too scared to do?"

She ran her hands across his shoulders stiff as granite. The light scratch of his dreads on her skin sent a shiver across her body.

"Because you overcame everything life threw at you. Gangs, prison, assault. You could have chosen to let those decisions ruin your life. Instead, you created your gang of misfits. Help kids when they're in trouble, and you're taking your business to another level."

He didn't speak, just studied her intently, a crinkle between his thick brows.

"You deserve to be happy, Kareem," she said. "You didn't kill that guy; Tim did."

"But I should've done something. I should have protected myself." Anguish filled his voice. "Not let Tim take the fall."

"Not taking a life, even after what he did, doesn't mean you're weak. Tim saved your life and sacrificed so that you could live. You don't have to punish yourself or mourn the life you lost."

Patrice stepped forward, pressing her soft body against his firm one. "Controlling everything isn't living." Her fingers flexed along the back of his head; her thumbs caressed his cheeks. "Embrace life, Kareem. Embrace me." Her voice cracked.

Her soul cracked. She loved him. Hurt for him. Kareem held her heart in his hands. Hands that could change a man's outlook with a set of shears. Hands that didn't know how to be loving, affectionate, or tender. Hands that didn't frighten her at all.

She rose to her toes and pressed her lips against his. Like a statue, he didn't move. Her heart hammered, and her nerves stretched thin. Kareem's arms inched their way around her waist. Patrice slid her tongue across his lower lip.

"Kiss me," she whispered. Her eyes opened, met his unsure gaze. "Kiss me, Kareem."

His tongue made a slow sweep over his lips. Dark eyes, alive and burning with desire, lowered to her lips. Gradually, he tilted his head and pressed his lips against hers. Kareem's tongue darted out, playing against hers in clumsy, unsure strokes that slowly turned into deep, confident sweeps. Patrice tasted the hint of cinnamon from the gum he preferred and inhaled the rich scent of shea butter.

Kareem's hands splayed against her back, massaging her pliable muscles. There was no rush, no urgency. Just a tentative exploration. An acceptance of something far deeper than just a kiss. She wanted the moment to last forever. To enjoy the firmness of his chest against her breasts and the strength of his legs brushing hers. Desire slowly rose, starting as a slow, slippery ache between her legs and growing to a roaring fire in her abdomen and chest.

She ran her hands down his arms to clasp his hands in hers, and pulled him backwards toward the bed.

"Make love to me, Kareem," she said against his lips.

She sat on the bed and slid backwards. Kareem watched her for a second, then crawled over her, blocking everything but his deep penetrating stare. Slowly, they undressed each other. Each inch of skin she revealed, Kareem kissed, tasting her body, unhurried and reverent in a way she'd never seen before. Long, thick fingers massaged her breasts, and full, warm lips kissed the flesh before pulling the pert tips into the deep wonder of his mouth. His hands skimmed across the skin on her thighs to play in the slippery wetness between them. Flashes of desire flickered from the tips of her breasts to the ends of her toes.

Leisurely, Kareem spread her legs wide and pushed her knees upward. He eased into her, thick and hard, stretching her muscles in a delicious way. His eyes never left hers. Sliding her fingers through the springy softness of his dreads, she cupped the back of his head and pulled him down. There was a slight tension in his neck, before he relaxed. There was no hesitation with this kiss. Just sure, bold strokes of the tongue that matched the strokes of his hips.

Kareem moaned, not a rough, deep groan, but a low, awed sound that seemed pulled from deep within. It radiated through her, bringing life and love deep into Patrice's soul. Her legs clasped his waist, and drew him closer, deeper.

Her eyes flew open as the pound of the orgasm exploded. "Kareem!" she cried against his lips.

His head flew back, his body flexed, and he jerked deep inside of her with his own orgasm. Kareem lowered his forehead to hers, his eyes narrow slits that bore into hers. The corner of his mouth raised, a simple smile that made her heart flip.

"I'm giving you more, Neecie," he said between heavy breaths. Then slanted his head and kissed her again.

CHAPTER 25

The next morning, Patrice smiled, stretched, and reached for Kareem on the other side of the bed. Emptiness met her hand. Disappointment chased away the smile.

"I'm right here," Kareem said and the bed dipped behind her. His warm hand clasped her shoulder and pulled her onto her back.

Kareem's dreads hung around his face, and his black wife beater clung to the thick muscles of his chest.

Patrice's grinned and she ran her hand across his thigh. "But you aren't lying beside me."

Kareem twisted one of her loose kinks around his finger. "I'm not used to sleeping beside someone."

"There are plenty of perks to waking up next to someone."

"I bet there are." He unwound her hair from his finger then tapped her chin. "I'm going to Columbia today to check on the shop. I'll probably stay overnight and check in on my parents. Want to ride?"

Patrice nodded, then she remembered the date. "I wish, but I can't. The fashion show I'm supposed to work for Lorelei is tomorrow night. How long will you be gone?"

He rose from the bed. "Just a night or two."

"Are you sure you don't want to come to the show?"

He cringed but softened the look with an upturned corner of his mouth. "I'll give you my secrets, but don't ask me to go to a fashion show."

Patrice giggled and tried, unsuccessfully, to picture Kareem sitting along the side of a runway admiring clothes. "I think we'll agree on that." Patrice slid up in bed and leaned against the headboard. "Did you really want me to go?"

He shrugged and pulled some of his things together. "It would've been cool. But if you stay, I don't have to worry about your toeprints on my windshield."

She tossed her pillow at him, and he grabbed it in mid-air. Kareem chuckled, and the easy, relaxed sound sent happy caresses down her spine. She felt the shift in their relationship. A subtle shift, but enough for her to notice he felt something more than lust. A week ago she would have considered herself crazy for believing Kareem was falling in love with her, but today she felt confident in that very thing.

Kareem grabbed his overnight bag and dropped it on the end of the bed. "Maybe I'll bring my bike back and take you for a ride." He got a few items out of the drawer and dropped them along with his sketch pad next to the bag.

"I'd love that. I've never ridden a bike before."

"Then we'll have to fix that." He strolled over to the bathroom door. "I'm going to take a quick shower."

"Sounds good."

Kareem smiled at her and went into the bathroom. A giddy buzzing invaded her insides. Tossing back the sheet, Patrice hopped out of bed and put on the pajamas tossed on the floor from the night before. She stretched her hands over her head. When she dropped her hands, her eyes landed on the sketch pad.

The shower came on, and she glanced at the door. Patrice tiptoed to the foot of the bed and ran her finger across the notebook's worn leather. Her foot twisted against the carpet and anticipation zipped through her in short quick bursts. What did he draw all the time that was so important but still made him go out of his way to close the book whenever someone was around?

Patrice spun away from the bed. Nope, she would not invade his privacy. He'd opened up to her, and if he wanted her to know what he drew then he would show her.

What if he drew you?

She swiveled back toward the bed and flipped open the front cover.

Her heart disintegrated. Pictures of Sandra filled the first page. Sketches of her in suits and dresses. In the center a picture of her with tears in her eyes. Another with her giving a flirty look from beneath lowered lashes.

The bathroom door opened. She snatched her hand away and twisted her fingers in the back of the pajama top. Facing Kareem, his gaze zoomed from her to the notebook. He still wore pajama bottoms but had lost the shirt. Kareem stalked across the room to stand next to her. Dark eyes left her face to focus on the open sketchbook. His lips tightened and thick brows drew together.

"Do you love her?" she blurted out, then cringed. *Stupid! Making demands after you're caught snooping.*

"At one time I thought I could, but I don't."

She licked dry lips and pushed the hair behind her ears. "But you drew her."

"Once," he said. "Look at the other pages."

With trembling fingers she flipped the pages. Pictures of his shop, the guys, his family, and his bike. She smiled at a beautiful sketch of Janiyah and her husband Fredrick. She flipped again and sucked in a breath. A picture of her laughing behind her station at Fresh Cutz covered an entire page. She flipped again.

Another with her hair twisted and curly, piled on her head like a crown, and a sparkle in her eye that she'd never seen before. The next page was a collage of her eyes, lips, wrists, and tattooed foot. All of the pages after were of her: at her parents' party, in the rose garden, in the lounge, in bed sleeping.

Kareem placed his hands on her shoulders and drew her back against his chest. "I drew Sandra once because I thought I was falling for her. I hate myself for a lot of things, including wanting my brother's woman at one time. But I don't hate myself for wanting you. You're all of the good things I never thought I deserved."

He turned her to face him. His face was hard lines and seriousness. "Last night was my attempt to try and make this thing between us real. I want you, Neecie. I don't deserve you, but I don't want to lose you."

Patrice wrapped her arms around his neck, even more confident in the hope that he loved her as well. "First, stop saying you don't deserve me. Because I can't think of anyone who deserves to be happy—" She kissed the corner of his mouth. "Who deserves someone who'll love him and accept him for all of his past mistakes more than you. There's no need to continue to punish yourself."

One side of his sexy mouth lifted in a half grin and his hand brushed up and down her back. "So we're in this."

She lifted up on her toes and his strong arms pulled her against his firm body. Desire slid down her spine, and his answering response rose against her stomach.

Patrice kissed him and whispered, "I'm all in."

CHAPTER 26

Patrice reached for a cupcake, but a cool hand on her forearm stopped her. She turned away from snack table set up for the participants in Lorelei's fashion show and met the reproachful stare of her mother.

The show was over, and Patrice had enjoyed herself, despite Lorelei's finger snapping at everyone. Now people hung out backstage chatting and making plans for after parties. Patrice just wanted to go home, kick off her shoes, and relax.

"The ones from Sweets Bakery are much better," Janice said.

Patrice understood the real meaning: don't eat the cupcake. She gave Janice a tight smile. "These are the ones that are here, Mother."

Janice pulled Patrice away from the snack table and out of earshot. "I just don't want you to regret it later." Janice's voice was filled with concern.

"Doubtful, but if I were to regret it you don't have to worry I'd hurt myself."

"I didn't worry before and you did hurt yourself."

Patrice froze mid spin toward the snack table. She met her mother's pinched stare. "Mother, I'm okay."

Janice ran a slim hand across the chignon at the back of her head. "Patrice, I'm only trying to help. I ignored the signs before, and I don't want to do the same now. Is Kareem aware of your past ... circumstance?"

Patrice's heart skipped in her chest. "No, and I don't want him to know. He has enough troubles without worrying about something that's no longer an issue."

Janice's disbelief was painted over her face. "If you're going to marry the man, he should know. What if you relapse—"

"I'm not going to relapse!"

Janice snapped her lips shut, and Patrice felt guilty for raising her voice. "I'm sorry, Mother. I'm not that person anymore. He never met the weaker version of me, and I don't want him to. Can we just leave it at that?"

Janice's head did a curt nod. Patrice didn't know what else there was to say. Kareem had enough to deal with and didn't need her tossing her old burdens at his feet.

"You did a great job tonight," Janice said, in a pleased as punch voice. "I think you'd really have a shot working for Lorelei long-term."

"Lorelei snaps her fingers at her employees and calls them fluffy. That doesn't make working for her an appealing long-term plan."

"But it is a great starting point. There are so many opportunities she would open up for you."

Beth breezed over looking like an angel in an A-line white dress that gracefully draped to her slim figure. She slipped her arm through Patrice's. "Excuse me, Mother, but I need to borrow Neecie for a second."

Janice's arched brows formed a line over her eyes. "Please call her Patrice, Beth."

"Of course, Mother." Janice waved a hand, and Beth quickly whisked Patrice away.

"What did you need to borrow me for?"

"To keep you from blowing up and embarrassing you and our mother," Beth said with a smile.

"That obvious?"

"To me, yes." Beth pulled on Patrice's arm. "What was the problem?"

"Nothing, really," Patrice said, tugging on one of the curls that escaped the ponytail she'd tried to tame her hair with. "She's worried I'll overeat and purge later."

Beth's face turned somber. "None of us want that to happen."

"Neither do I."

Beth placed her hands over Patrice's, which were pulling at the waistband of her houndstooth skirt. "Don't let Mother get to you. She's worried about you."

"I know, and I'll apologize later."

Beth's radiant smile was full of understanding. "Just give her time. She'll realize you're not the person you were before you left. She ignored the signs before; of course she'll be extra diligent now."

"When did you become so understanding? I'm supposed to be the big sister giving advice."

Beth let out a light laugh and leaned back. "Sisterly advice can come from younger siblings as well." Beth's smile slowly faded, and she became serious. "Which is why I want to talk with you about Kareem."

"Beth, let's not go there. Kareem and I are good."

"I know you say that, but Chad is worried. He thinks Kareem treats you like a mistress, not a fiancée."

"It's not like that."

"I know you love him," Beth said in a pensive voice. "And I can tell he cares, but I still worry."

"I thought you liked him."

"I do, but remember what I said. He's a Johnny, not a husband." Beth clasped Patrice's hands when Patrice opened her mouth to argue. "Men like that don't change. They're like feral cats. You can feed them, and they'll hang around the house for a while, but eventually they roam again. He's been through things, and even if he wants to settle down and be a good husband, can he really do that? For ten, twenty, fifty years?"

Patrice wanted to argue he could, but his confessions about what happened in prison, his thoughts on intimacy and love, blocked the words.

One of their mother's longtime associates, Delores Humbridge, who also helped plan the event, walked over. "Hello, girls!" Delores's nasal-infused giggle chased her words. She turned wide eyes on Patrice. "I hear you're behind that new gentlemen's lounge."

Patrice nodded, pleased to hear word about the lounge was getting around. "My fiancé is opening the place. I'm working with him."

Delores's face twisted until she resembled a pug. "I heard you'll offer goods besides haircuts."

Something about her tone set Patrice on alert. "What goods are you referring to?"

"Pretty girls, willing to please rich men for a price."

Patrice's entire body flinched, and her mouth fell open. Delores couldn't be serious. "I can assure you that is not the case. We're opening a high-end barber shop and cigar lounge, nothing more."

"Well," Delores said, still looking like an angry pug. "I truly hope Judge Baldwin's daughter wouldn't be involved in something that sordid."

"Where did you hear this?" Patrice asked.

"I don't remember offhand. Someplace. Hearing the opposite from you makes me feel somewhat better. Let's hope you're correct."

"I am correct. I know what my fiancé and I are opening, and it's not a fancy escort service."

The sour look on Delores's face finally relaxed into the semblance of a smile. "Good. If that's the case, I won't mind if my Melvin stops by." She waved a hand. "Have a good evening, girls."

Patrice spun to Beth, her body shaking with suppressed anger. "Can you believe that? Have you heard anything so crazy?"

"Don't worry. I'll get Lad to ask around and see if he's heard something similar. We'll clear everything up."

Patrice nodded and stared across the room to where Delores now spoke with her mother and Lorelei. She had to find out the source of that particular rumor and squash it. She refused to let lies ruin Kareem's dream.

●　●　●

Patrice grinned at the checker board and slapped her hands together. "King me!"

Roland lifted his eyes heavenward, and the rest of her family sprawled around the Baldwin sitting room laughed.

"I never could beat you in checkers," he said, shaking his head and grinning.

Patrice reached over and pinched his cheek the same way she'd done after beating him when they were younger. "And you never will."

Chad strolled over from the fireplace to stare down at the checker board on the table between Patrice and Roland. He raised a brow then shrugged.

"You might as well quit now, Roland," Chad said.

Beth hopped up from the sofa and skipped over. She wrapped an arm around Patrice's shoulder. "I love it when a man admits defeat."

"Hey!" Lad said, sitting in one of the chairs framing the fireplace. Milton occupied the other, while Janice and Melena talked on the sofa.

Beth blew him a kiss. "All in good fun, sweetie."

Patrice raised one shoulder and leaned across the table toward Roland. "No quitting. I want to beat you fair and square."

"I always loved your bloodthirsty competitiveness," he said lightly, but the spark in his eye sent a wave of unease through Patrice.

Patrice quickly leaned back. "Flattery won't make me go easy on you."

He winked. "I never expected you to."

Beth squeezed Patrice's shoulder. "Go on, Neecie, beat him good."

Roland studied the board to make a move, but no matter what move he made she had him beat, so his attempt to avoid losing didn't concern her. What did concern her was telling Kareem about the rumors when he returned. Her mother's impromptu dinner party had briefly taken her mind off of things.

"I don't plan to lose so easily," Roland said. His fingers hovered over one red checker piece, then another.

Patrice and Beth shared a look. Beth slid a finger from one side of her neck to the other, and Patrice giggled. She was definitely killing Roland on the checker board.

Roland looked up at them. "What's so funny?"

Patrice waved her fingers over the board. "The way you're procrastinating. No matter the move I'm going to take your piece."

"Fine." He slid a red piece in front of one of the three other kings Patrice had on the board. "Just make it quick."

Beth clapped as Patrice triple jumped him and won the game. Chad gave Roland a pat on the back but looked at the board like it was roadkill. Patrice got up and high fived Beth. They started their victory dance, a jerky version of the bump, when Kareem came to the door of the family room. He dropped his bag at the door and focused on her. The corners of his lips raised and revealed a row of white teeth.

Patrice's breath stuttered. "You're back."

He lifted a shoulder. "Just like I promised."

She rushed across the room but halted right before she would have thrown her arms around him. Kareem placed a hand on her waist and pulled her into him. The outside cold clung to his clothes, but the heat of his body beneath made her fingers yearn to run beneath his shirt.

"I missed you," he said loud enough only for her.

If he would have said he loved her she doubted her heart would beat harder. He lowered his head and kissed her. Not slow and deep like she wanted, and not quick and hard for show. But a gentle press of the lips and quick flick of the tongue, which sent a dart of need straight to the rising bud between her legs.

She licked her lower lip and pulled it between her teeth, savoring the taste of him. "I missed you, too."

Wrapping an arm around her shoulder, Kareem came further into the room. "What's up, everyone?"

The chorus of hellos and welcomes varied from nice and polite from her father and Beth to nonexistent or cool from Chad and her mother. None were warm, nor enthusiastic.

He lowered his lips to her ear. "I guess you're the only one who missed me."

His breath caressed her ear, and her body shivered. "I'm the only one who matters.

Roland rose from the table. "How was your trip home?"

"Decent. I dropped in on my folks and checked in on my shop."

Patrice looked up at him. "How are things?"

"Good," he said. "Lee's taking care of things."

"I'm glad to hear it," she said.

Kareem looked around the room. "Looks like I missed the party invitation."

Milton sat forward. "Not a party, but you did miss dinner. I'm sure Fran will prepare something for you. In the meantime, sit down and enjoy some cider."

Kareem raised a brow and looked at Patrice. "Cider?"

She grinned and playfully punched him in the chest. "Yes, warm apple cider and you're going to love it."

"I'm sure I will." His answering chuckle warmed her better than any fire.

Lifting up on her toes she brushed her lips across his. His eyes widened before they narrowed, and he lowered his head to kiss her again. Slow, sweet desire spread through her body.

"Before you two start making out right here," Beth's voice broke in, "let's see if Kareem fares any better against you in checkers than Roland."

Reluctantly, Patrice broke eye contact with Kareem to look into her sister's smiling face.

"You're good at checkers, huh?" Kareem asked.

Roland picked up one of the checker pieces, tossed it into the air, and easily caught it. "She beat the crap out of me."

Patrice held up a hand to stop them. "As much as I'd love to spank Kareem—"

Kareem nipped at her ear. "I bet you would."

She sucked in a breath. "I really need to talk to him about something."

Beth's lip twisted. "Sure you do," she said, then grinned. "You two can wait until later to *catch up.*"

Janice cleared her throat. "Beth, please."

"Well it's true," Beth said.

Kareem chuckled again. She could get used to listening to his deep, sexy laugh. "We'll only be gone for a minute."

She hurried and pulled Kareem from the room. Once they were in the hall, Kareem leaned against the wall and pulled her against him. The weight of his hands at the top of her behind made her think of the way he palmed her bottom whenever they made love.

"What do you need to talk to me about? Or were you looking for a reason to deliver on that look in your eye?"

"That look is because you actually seemed happy to see me."

"I am happy to see you. Didn't you say I deserve to be happy?"

She pulled one of his dreads between her fingers. He didn't have them pulled back, and she loved when they were loose. "I did."

"Then let me be happy, woman."

She grinned and wrapped her arms around his neck. "Fine, but that's not why I called you out here. I heard a rumor after the show the other night. I don't know where it started, or if it's just because people have the wrong idea, but I thought you should know."

His body tightened next to hers. "What's going on?"

"Nothing really, it's stupid. One of the women thought we were opening a high-end escort service."

He straightened suddenly, and she staggered back. "What?"

"I straightened her out, and she believed me when I explained we're opening a high-end barber shop, not escort service."

"Where in the hell did that come from?"

"I have no idea. We'll just have to work extra hard to make sure people understand what we're doing. No pretty girls half-dressed or anything like that."

Kareem rubbed the scar above his lip. "They won't be half-dressed."

"Say what?" Patrice stepped back and placed a hand on her hip. "You plan to hire pretty women?"

"Of course I'm going to hire good-looking women. You saw for yourself how much a man likes having a good-looking woman cutting their hair."

"Just because the men at Fresh Cutz liked to flirt with me doesn't make it okay to hire nothing but pretty women."

Kareem scoffed. "I didn't say that's all I'm hiring. I'll hire men, too." He grinned.

"You think this is funny? Kareem, I think you should only hire men. At least until we're sure the rumors have stopped."

Roland strolled out of the study. His gaze jumped from Patrice with her hand on her hip to Kareem and back. "Is everything okay?"

Patrice crossed her arms. "Yes."

Kareem looked to Roland. "She doesn't think I should hire good-looking women for the gentlemen's lounge."

"That doesn't make sense. Men will expect beautiful women."

Patrice pinched her nose and fought not to scream. "You say that because you're a man."

"No," Roland said. "I say that because it makes good business sense. The clientele he's going for are used to beautiful women. Having them in the lounge will only increase the draw."

"But people may get the wrong idea," Patrice said.

"What wrong idea?" Roland asked.

"That we're a high-end escort service," Kareem said.

Roland frowned. "Doubtful."

Kareem met Patrice's stare. "If it makes you feel better, I'll make it very clear the women aren't supposed to go out with the clients."

Roland groaned and furled his brow. "That won't stop the clients from hitting on the women."

"Flirting doesn't hurt business," Kareem said. "But I won't condone anything more between the employees and the clients." He took Patrice's hand in his and tugged her into his space. "You have to admit that it makes sense, Neecie. You can't tell me your pretty face in my shop didn't keep your chair full?"

She wished she could argue but understood some of the guys came in just to see her. "Are we talking stick-figure model types?"

Kareem cocked a brow. "When have I ever been into stick figure model types? It'll be good-looking women of all types. And they aren't walking around in bikinis or anything. I want a classy place, not something trashy."

"Fine, but we'll still have to stop the rumors that this is an escort service."

"Don't worry," Roland said. "If I hear anything like that I'll correct the person."

Kareem lifted his chin and stared at Roland. "I appreciate that, Roland, but it doesn't change the partnership request."

Roland nodded and held out his hands. "Patrice made that clear. I'm only offering to help as a friend. But I hope that once you get to know me better, we can bring the conversation up again. I like what you're doing and would love to be a part."

Roland held out his hand to Kareem. Patrice held her breath. Kareem regarded Roland for several seconds before taking his hand. "We'll see."

CHAPTER 27

Six weeks later, Patrice smiled at the latest arrival for the soft opening of Henderson's Gentlemen's Lounge. To her delight, she met the eyes of one of her father's oldest friends, and local magistrate judge, Walter Jackson.

"Welcome, Mr. Jackson. I'm so glad you decided to come today."

Mr. Jackson handed over the black and gold invitation the new—young and attractive—receptionist Kareem hired to help with the opening had created. The invites had only gone to an exclusive list of people recommended by her father and Roland.

"I had to check this place out myself." Mr. Jackson glanced around. "Nice place."

"Thank you." Patrice checked her tablet to see if Mr. Jackson had requested a complementary haircut as part of his RSVP. To both her and Kareem's surprise, most people who said they would come also wanted to experience the service. They were filled for the entire evening.

"We're on schedule for your haircut in twenty minutes. Please feel free to have a drink at the bar."

Mr. Jackson nodded and thanked her before strolling in that direction. Patrice watched as he appreciatively checked out the place, and her chest swelled with pride.

The lounge didn't officially open until next week, but today's trial run proved they were ready. Light wood floors complemented the dark leather seats around black tables. A black granite bar with several flat screen televisions lined the left side of the main area. The bartender mixed drinks for the men waiting to receive complementary haircuts at the stations in the back.

Kareem had just left to show off the cigar bar and meeting spaces just past the sectioned off hair cutting stations.

The door opened again, and a burst of cold air flew up the skirt of Patrice's black cocktail dress. Roland and Felicia entered along with a tall man.

"You made it," she said.

Roland gave her a quick hug. "There was no way I would miss this." He turned to the people with him. "Patrice Baldwin, I'd like you to meet Felicia's cousin, Paul Tribble."

Patrice smiled at the guy and immediately recognized him as the center for the city's professional basketball team.

"Paul doesn't have an invitation, but we were having lunch yesterday when I mentioned this place and he asked to come," Roland said. "I let him know he could get a haircut and see how he likes it."

Patrice checked the full schedule. Fitting Paul in would be difficult and inconvenient. She pushed aside her annoyance. The recommendation of a professional basketball player would go a long way to boost the business.

"We'll work out something." She held out her hand and craned her neck to meet the tall guy's gaze. "Feel free to make yourself comfortable at the bar, or in the cigar lounge in the back while I get you set up, okay?"

A suggestive stare accompanied Paul's friendly grin. He ran a large hand over the scruffy hairs on his chin. "I'd love to try things out, but only if you're the one giving the haircut." He spoke directly to her cleavage.

Patrice stepped back, though the gigantic ballplayer could still easily look down the front of her dress. He met her eye and cocked a brow while rubbing his hands together. Patrice stopped just short of scowling. Good customer service, even to womanizers like him, were the key to any successful enterprise.

"I'll see what I can do," she said.

Paul's leer ran over her body and paused at her breasts and butt on the way down and up. "Perfect."

"Roland," she said. "Why don't you show Paul the cigar lounge while I add him to the list?"

"Will do," Roland said. Patrice spun away, but Roland slid an arm around her shoulders and squeezed. "I know it's a pain adding him, but thanks."

"If I cut his hair we can make this work. Don't worry, I appreciate your help." She pulled away from Roland and glanced at Paul, who licked his lips while his eyes were trained on her rear. Patrice's skin crawled. "As long as he keeps his hands to himself."

Roland chuckled. "Don't worry, he's harmless. If he likes the place, he'll send his teammates here."

She forced back her unease. A half-hour of discomfort for a potentially great endorsement.

Roland led Felicia and Paul down the hall toward the cigar lounge. Patrice waved over the receptionist and asked her to handle greeting the guests.

Patrice checked the progress with the other barbers and finagled her way into slipping in Paul's haircut between two other appointments. She found Paul relaxing in one of the Italian leather chairs in the cigar lounge talking to Kareem.

Patrice strolled over and gave him a warm but forced smile. "Excuse me, but it's time for your haircut, Paul."

Paul's tongue did another *I'm hungry* sweep of his lips. Patrice considered asking if he wanted to borrow her ChapStick. Anything to keep him from looking at her like she was a porterhouse steak. "From you of course?"

Her tight smile rose. "Of course."

Kareem frowned and stood with Paul. "You're cutting hair?"

Paul's greedy stare zeroed in on Patrice's cleavage again. "At my request. I couldn't let the hottest woman in the place not lay her hands on my head." He winked at Kareem. "If you know what I'm saying."

Kareem's body turned to granite, and his signature scowl, which she hadn't seen in weeks, clouded his face.

Patrice placed her hand on his muscled arm. "I don't mind."

Kareem looked between her and Paul. The scowl disappeared, but his easy smile didn't return.

Kareem wrapped an arm around her waist and pulled her in close. "I owe you," he whispered in her ear.

She grinned. "Yes, you do." He gave her a squeeze, then she turned back to Paul. "Ready?"

"More than ready," he said.

Kareem took his time releasing her, and she led Paul to one of the barber stations. Separated from the cigar lounge and the bar area in the front, the barber area had more of a relaxed feel, with its dark brown leather seats, black porcelain wash bowls with cream, and gold accents. Another sixty-inch television was set in the wall across from the mirrors.

Paul sat in the chair and ran his hands over the leather armrests. "So, you and Kareem. You two together?"

"More than together, we're engaged." She snapped a robe open and placed it around his neck.

"I got you," he said, but he didn't really sound like he "got" her. Thankfully, Paul didn't talk much while she washed and cut his hair. His eyes talked enough, lingering on any inch of skin exposed by her clothes.

Once she finished, he ran a hand over his shaved cheek and closely cropped hair. "You did a good job." He met her eye in the mirror.

Patrice rinsed off the comb and brush she'd used and smiled back. "Thank you."

She finished cleaning her supplies. When she turned around she nearly bumped into Paul.

"Oh, excuse me," she said, though he'd invaded her space.

"No need. So how much for the extra service?" Paul said, rubbing his hands and licking his lips.

"What extra service?"

He raised a brow then leaned in close. His expensive cologne made her stomach roll. "Don't be cute. I know what you're really offering."

Patrice's hand balled into a fist on her hip. "What am I supposedly offering?"

"I get you're with Kareem, but I assumed all of his ladies were available for the right price. If not, that's cool, just tell me how I make arrangements with that Asian cutie cutting hair over there." He pointed to Candace with a hungry gleam in his eye.

"I don't know where you got that idea, but that type of service isn't available here."

"That's not what I was told."

"Please tell me what idiot gave you that impression."

Paul scoffed. "The idiot is your fiancé. He mentioned it while we smoked cigars. If you're not one of the women, I'll get with him to set something up with me and the honey over there."

Paul did one last leer of her cleavage then casually strolled away. Patrice threw down the towel she held and hurried after him. Paul stood with Kareem and a few other guys at the bar. Paul pulled Kareem to the side. He leaned in and pointed toward the back of the place. Kareem nodded then smiled. They clasped hands and shook, before Paul smirked at her and left.

What the hell was that!

She wanted to snatch the smile right off Kareem's face. There was no way he would have agreed to try and set something up between Paul and Candace. But the easy way he'd smiled and shook Paul's hand sent an uneasy shiver down her spine.

Patrice crossed the room to him. Kareem smiled when he caught her eye, and despite her discomfort his smile scattered her insides and made her heart flip.

"We need to talk," she said when she reached him.

"Now?" he asked, glancing around. "We're almost done here then we've got the party at your parents'. We can talk on the way home."

"No, we need to talk now." She snapped the last word.

His smile turned into a hard-pressed line of his lips. Months ago she would have backed down at the look, but not today.

"Let's talk."

He placed a hand on her lower back and gently pushed her toward the back. They didn't talk on the way down the hall to his office.

"What wrong with you?" Kareem asked when they passed the cigar lounge and stood outside of his office.

Patrice whipped around to face him. "Paul asked me about *additional* services."

"What services?"

"He said you informed him he could hook up with the women working here. Then he went over to you and asked about being set up with Candace."

A murderous look clouded his expression. "I would never tell him something like that."

"What did he say about Candace?"

"That he wanted her to cut his hair next time."

"That's it?"

His gaze flicked away and back. "That's all."

"I don't believe you. Kareem, please tell me that this isn't true."

His dark eyes blazed with disbelief. "How could you even think I'd do that? I've never met Paul before today, and I wouldn't use my people. Not after what happened to me."

"Then who would?"

Kareem's eyes narrowed, and he crossed thick arms over his chest. "Roland brought him, maybe he told him."

"Roland wouldn't dare."

"Yes, the hell he would. He's trying to get back into your pants, Neecie. And this bullshit is letting him."

"He is not. Roland knows we're only friends."

"Then why sabotage my business?" he asked.

"He's not sabotaging you." She ran a hand through her hair, straightened for the soft opening. "Based on what Paul said you're sabotaging yourself."

"I can't believe you would say that." Kareem pushed her aside and opened the door to his office. He took two steps in and froze. "What the hell is this?"

Patrice rushed in behind him. Roland and Felicia were wrapped in an embrace on Kareem's desk. They broke apart. Roland shielded Felicia's bared breasts and hastily zipped his pants. "I'm sorry, Kareem. We needed a second."

"Get the hell out of my office." Kareem didn't yell, but his rage vibrated with every word.

Felicia jumped off the desk and ran out of the room. Roland avoided eye contact and followed.

Patrice pointed after them. "Does that look like a man who's trying to get back in my pants?"

Kareem slammed the door after them. "It looks like a man who doesn't know his boundaries when it comes to women." He glared at her. "Especially women that belong to me."

"I don't belong to you."

Kareem knocked a stack of papers off his desk. He spun toward her, his eyes flat and hard. "And you don't trust me, either."

The hurt in his voice made Patrice flinch. "I do trust you."

"I didn't tell Paul he could sleep with the women working here."

"Then who did?"

He slammed his hand on the desk with enough force to shake everything on the surface. Patrice backed into the wall. Kareem stepped toward her, and she shrank away.

Kareem's body stiffened, his lips pressed tightly together. Slowly, he took two steps back. "You think I'd hurt you?"

Patrice shook her head but didn't meet his eye. "No, I know you wouldn't."

"But I scared you." He scoffed and ran a hand over his brow. "This is crazy. If you could even think I'd hurt you, or that I'd do what Paul accused me of, you don't know me at all." He dropped his hands. Cold, flat eyes stared at her. "Thank you for letting me know where we really stand."

Kareem jerked the door opened. Patrice tried to grab his arm, but he pulled out of her reach and marched out the door.

CHAPTER 28

The ride back to the Baldwin home in a car with Neecie, Beth, and Lad didn't do a thing to improve Kareem's sour mood or give time to reduce the pain of discovering the first person he'd decided to trust completely could so easily turn her back on him. He answered questions thrown his way during the car ride but didn't share in the joy over the success of the soft opening. Kareem clenched his teeth. He should be celebrating a major milestone, not feeling as if someone had squeezed out his insides like toothpaste in a cheap tube.

Several cars lined the driveway of the Baldwin residence. Milton and Janice had insisted on holding a small party to further celebrate and promote the soft opening of Henderson's Gentlemen's Lounge. Milton more than Janice. Kareem's appreciation was the only reason he'd come back. Otherwise, he would have said goodbye to Neecie right after the opening and found somewhere else to go.

The car stopped, and Kareem jumped out before the wheels finished turning.

"Kareem, wait," Neecie's voice came from behind, wavering as she ran. Her hand grabbed his elbow. Kareem stopped and faced her but didn't look at her. "Can we talk about what happened?"

"There's nothing to talk about." Her mouth fell open, and Kareem turned back to the house.

He didn't want to *talk* and hear some excuse about why she would believe what Paul said. Her lack of faith hardened his heart against any guilt for brushing her off.

"I had to bring it up," she continued, following him. "He said you told him that. What was I supposed to do?"

He spun so fast she stumbled back. "You should have called him on the lie. You should have known I would never say or do something like that. You should have had my back."

Beth and Lad walked up. Beth came up and placed a protective hand on Neecie's arm. "Hey, what's going on?"

Kareem took a step back. "Nothing." He narrowed his eyes at Neecie, blocking the discomfort that came from the anguish in her eyes. She needed to feel anguish. Her anguish couldn't possibly hurt as much as his pain after realizing she could doubt him so easily. "Nothing at all."

Kareem slowly turned away and made his way into the house. The sounds of music, laughter, and conversation greeted him along with Fran holding a tray with steaming mugs.

"Hot chocolate?" Rush asked in her normal disdainful tone.

"Only if you put Kahlua in it," he bit out. Ignoring her raised eyebrows, he marched past her further into the house. He passed the full seating area and dining room and went straight for the stairs to the wine cellar.

Footsteps chased him. "Kareem, a second."

Kareem bristled at the sound of Roland's voice. He faced the guy and clenched his teeth. Roland took a few hesitant steps forward. Good, because Kareem wasn't sure if he would be able to keep from decking the guy if he approached with his normal smug attitude.

"What."

"I want to apologize about what you saw earlier. Felicia is always telling me to be spontaneous." Roland shrugged and rubbed the back of his head. "I thought I'd take a lesson from you."

Kareem scowled. "What?"

"You know, the way you dragged Patrice off at her parents' party. That seemed to work with her, so I thought I'd try something similar with Felicia. After losing Patrice, I didn't want to mess things up."

"Next time find another office." Kareem didn't care about Roland's copycat attempt at being sexy.

"Wait a second."

Kareem suppressed a sigh and faced Roland again. "What." The word cracked like a whip.

"I'm glad you've made Patrice happy. Not once has she ... you know, since she's been back."

Kareem didn't know, and he didn't like that. "What are you talking about?"

Roland's eyebrows rose. Remorse transformed into a shifty, calculated gleam. "You don't know? I thought she would have told you the reason she left."

Roland's reminder that the woman he trusted hadn't trusted him with that bit of information rubbed Kareem's insides like glass-covered sandpaper. "She didn't."

"Oh, well, you have a right to know." The smug look returned to Roland's face. "She was bulimic. Threw up after every meal. I knew, and didn't say anything. Not saying, and losing her, is one of the biggest regrets in my life."

Kareem's shock rocked him. Neecie, bulimic? He couldn't picture that. She was so confident, so sure of herself. What could possibly lead her to do that? The questions popped in his brain, giving him a headache. The biggest: why hadn't she trusted him with that? Further proof she hadn't felt for him what he'd opened himself up to for her.

He didn't give Roland's self-satisfied self the benefit of a response. Kareem swiveled around and stomped the rest of the way to the wine cellar.

Joshua's voice greeted him. "Do you think we'll get away with it?"

Kareem stopped at the top of the stairs. What the hell was the kid up to?

"Of course we will. This is crazy easy." Kareem recognized the voice of the blond kid he'd met at Milton and Janice's anniversary party. "All we've got to do is meet them in the Panera Bread parking lot, and when they show us the tablet, take it, jump in the car, and haul ass."

"Yeah, but we can get tablets anywhere," Joshua said without any enthusiasm.

"True, but those would cost. If we take one it's free. Then we turn around and sell it. It's perfect."

"I don't know about that." Joshua had enough sense to say that.

Kareem had never heard of a stupider idea.

"Don't be scared," the other kid said. "We start with tablets then move on to other stuff. Besides, I'm bored as hell. This will be more fun that hanging out at your grandparents' party."

Kareem heard enough. He re-opened the door and slammed it before stomping down the stairs. Both boys stood straight and watched him warily as he entered the wine cellar. The smell of marijuana hung in the air. Kareem eyed them. Young and dumb—that's how they looked with their bloodshot eyes and rumpled country club attire.

"What are you two doing down here?" Kareem strolled over to one of the rows of wine and looked at the labels. Expensive and in French. Of course they'd have complicated wine.

"Just talking." Joshua's voice was filled with guilt.

"Talking, huh?" Kareem turned and leaned against one of the shelves. Joshua broke eye contact, but the other kid met his stare head on. "What you talking about?"

"Nothing," Blondie said.

"Doesn't sound like nothing."

Josh's eyes jumped to his. "Were you listening in?"

"Depends, did I hear you planning to do something stupid, or are you going back upstairs to the party?"

After exchanging glances with Blondie, Joshua turned back to Kareem. "We're going upstairs."

"Good." Kareem turned back to the bottles in the shelves. Their footsteps shuffled up the stairs before the door closed behind them.

"Dumb kids," he mumbled. He'd been that dumb once. Bored at parties and looking for an outlet. Anything seemed better than hanging out listening to his parents tell jokes that weren't funny while showing him off as if he were the prodigal son. Even if he would've been overheard, Kareem still would have snuck out and snatched a tablet from an unsuspecting person in the parking lot just for fun.

Kareem's hand squeezed the bottle. He looked at the stairs, and an unsettled feeling washed over him. He shouldn't care. Shouldn't get involved in a family that obviously didn't want him. If Joshua went through with it and ended up in jail it was his own fault.

A vision of Cide, or someone like him, grinning when Joshua and his friend were thrown into his cell flashed in Kareem's mind. Kareem dropped the bottle. Ignoring the sound of broken glass, he sprinted up the stairs. He hurried down the hall and rushed into the crowded sitting room. Scanning the room, his unease grew when he didn't see Joshua or Blondie.

"There you are," Neecie's voice said from the side. "Please, Kareem, can we talk about this?"

He turned to her. "Where's Joshua?"

She frowned and pointed over her shoulder. "He and his friend just left, but—"

"Damn!" He pushed past her and ran for the door. That boy was just dumb and bored enough to do something stupid.

• • •

Kareem would've liked to believe Joshua and his friend wouldn't try their little stunt in a shopping center close to the Baldwin residence. But considering their ridiculous plan, he headed to the closest Panera. He drove his motorcycle into the parking lot and immediately spotted the boy's Acura in one of the outer parking spaces. Nearby, Joshua and Blondie spoke to a man who had an arm wrapped around a woman. Two kids stood behind them.

Come on, Joshua, don't be that stupid!

The parking spaces near the ill-fated transaction were full, so Kareem swerved his bike into a space several spots over. He jumped off the bike just as the man handed over a tablet to Joshua. Josh and his friend exchanged glances before Blondie nodded.

Joshua was that stupid.

"Hey!" Kareem yelled and broke into a jog.

Joshua and Blondie took one look at Kareem, and Blondie took off running. The man held out his hand for the tablet, while the woman ushered the children closer to the mid-sized SUV. Kareem reached Joshua and snatched the tablet from him. He turned to apologize to the man, when Josh ran in the same direction as Blondie.

No the hell he didn't!

Kareem sprinted after the boy.

"Stop, thief!" the man yelled.

"Shit!" Kareem said, tossing the tablet in the general direction of the man and then ran after Joshua. He dodged between cars toward the back of the shopping center where both Joshua and Blondie had gone. Behind the building he found a row of hedges that separated the back lot from another, dumpsters next to the building but no stupid teenagers. Kareem scanned the area, ran to the other side of the building and back, checking behind each dumpster. The hedges shook. Kareem ran over, his hands itching to snatch up Joshua and knock some sense into him. He shoved the hedges aside and a cat jetted out past him.

Kareem punched the bushes and grunted. That damn kid. They would have to come back to the car, and when he did, Kareem would take immense pleasure in dragging the boy home by his expensive shoes.

He jogged back around the building to wait and stopped in his tracks. Blue lights flashed on the top of a cop car next to the man Joshua tried to rob and his family. They spoke to a police officer and pointed toward the building. The man spotted Kareem and grew frantic with his pointing.

Just fucking great. Now I have to deal with this.

Kareem crossed the parking lot, the tension in his shoulders growing tighter with every step.

"That's one of the guys that tried to rob me," the man said.

Kareem held up his hands. "I didn't try to rob you."

The officer placed his hand on his gun and faced Kareem. "Hands behind your head and face the vehicle."

"Are you serious?" Kareem said. "I didn't—"

The woman ran forward and wrapped her arms around her husband. "The two kids distracted us, and he ran over and snatched the tablet. Then the three of them ran behind the building."

"Why would I come back if I tried to rob you?" Kareem said.

"Against the vehicle," the officer said, stepping forward. He snapped open the clip on his gun holster.

Kareem put his hands behind his head. "Fine. But can I explain."

The cop jerked one of Kareem's arms behind his back. Pain shot up Kareem's arm.

"You can explain at the station," the cop said, his hard voice daring Kareem to continue his argument.

For the next few minutes the family cried about the attempted robbery before their children, while Kareem was handcuffed and put in the back of the cop car. With every throb of pain in his shoulders he wanted to scream. He never thought he'd find himself in the back of a police car ever again. Tonight was supposed to be the start of his success, his new life, not this.

Through the cracked front window he heard the officer tell the family, "I believe our guy has a record. I'll take him down to the station and book him, and put a patrol out for the two other perps. If you'll come down and complete your statements."

"Gladly," the man said, glaring into the car.

Kareem closed his eyes and shook his head. Fucked up wasn't a strong enough phrase to describe this situation.

CHAPTER 29

When the doorbell rang, Patrice abruptly turned away from the group of people she was barely listening to and hurried to the door. Kareem wasn't likely to ring the bell, but since he disappeared three hours ago she couldn't help but hope he'd come back. She couldn't blame him if he didn't. She never should have questioned him about Paul's accusations. Kareem wouldn't prostitute out the women working in his lounge.

Fran gave a reproachful look as Patrice reached the door and gently pushed Patrice to the side. As if it were crazy for her to relinquish her duties.

"Sorry," Patrice mumbled.

"Expecting someone?" Fran asked as she unlocked the door.

"Just hopeful," Patrice said.

Fran raised a brow but didn't say anything before opening the door. A tall thin man wearing a Charlotte Mecklenburg police uniform stood on the other side. Patrice's heart scrambled into her throat.

"Excuse me, but I need to speak with the police chief. I was told he's at this party," the officer said. "It's important."

Patrice's shoulders slumped. At least the officer wasn't here to say Kareem was hurt or in trouble.

"I'll get the chief," Patrice said. "If you'll follow me to my father's study, you two can speak in there."

The officer nodded his head. "Thank you."

She led him to the study, before interrupting the conversation the police chief was having with Chad. "Excuse me, but one of your officers is here to see you. I left him in my father's study. He said it's important."

The bushy white brows of Chief Parker met over his steel grey eyes. "Thank you."

After leaving the two of them together, Patrice went back to the front of the house. The party was going full swing, but she couldn't force another laugh or another conversation. No one seemed to care that a party in honor of Kareem was going without him. Her father may like Kareem somewhat, but the rest of her family along with their social circle couldn't care less about the man she loved.

The door to her father's study burst open. Chief Parker stared at her with serious eyes. "You may want to go into the study. I'll get the rest of your family."

The heart that scrambled up her throat earlier plummeted to her stomach with a sick thud. Kareem had been angry when he left, but she couldn't believe he would do something reckless.

The minutes oozed by slower than molasses in January as she waited for the rest of her family to join her in the study. The other officer waited with her, but his lips were sealed when she asked what was wrong, saying it was best for the chief to explain.

Her mother took one look at her and hurried over. "What's wrong, Patrice?"

"I have no idea," Patrice said. "Chief Parker asked me to wait in here."

Her father came in next, followed by Chad and Melinda and Beth and Lad. Roland pushed through the door as Chief Parker tried to close it.

"This was mainly for family," Chief Parker said.

Janice nodded and waved Roland over to their side. "Roland and Lad are family."

Resentment sizzled and popped in Patrice's midsection. No doubt her mother would fail to extend that same familiarity with Kareem.

Chief Parker nodded. "Fine. I'll get straight to the point. Officer Jones responded to an attempted robbery at the Panera Bread not too far from here. Two teenage boys and an adult male were implicated in the robbery."

Melinda gasped and Chad wrapped an arm around her shoulder. "What does this have to do with us?"

"One of the boys is your son Joshua." Chief Parker then looked to Patrice. "The man is Patrice's fiancé."

The room swayed, and Patrice sputtered. "You must be mistaken. Kareem wouldn't rob the Panera."

Officer Jones stepped forward. "They didn't rob the Panera. The boys responded to an online ad from a family who wanted to sell their tablet. When the family met, allegedly your fiancé jumped out of a car, snatched the tablet, and they all took off running."

A humorless laugh escaped Patrice. "This is ridiculous. Completely absurd. Why in the world would Kareem try to snatch a tablet and run?"

Chad crossed his arms. "And why would Joshua think to do something so ludicrous if your *fiancé* hadn't put the idea into his mind."

"Kareem wouldn't put Joshua up to this," Patrice said with her hands on her hips. "If anything he would try to talk him out of it."

Officer Jones cleared his throat. "Either way, we've got your fiancé in custody and are still looking for the two teens. When we ran the plates on the car and discovered who he was, I took it upon myself to come and alert the family first."

Because of who they were.

"How did you get Kareem?" Patrice asked.

"He returned to the scene, and that's where we apprehended him," Officer Jones said.

Patrice threw up her hands. "Do you hear how crazy this all sounds? There's no way he would return to the scene of a crime if he committed one."

Janice placed a hand in the middle of Patrice's back. "He's been out of the gang for a while dear. Maybe—"

"If you're about to imply he's rusty on his robbery skills then can it, Mother." Patrice jerked away from her mother's touch and looked back to the chief. "Have you questioned him? Found out what happened, gotten some type of explanation?"

Chad slapped his fist into his palm. "The only explanation is you brought a thug into the family who put Joshua and his friend at risk. I told you he was no good."

"I don't have time for this," Patrice said. "I'm going to the station, and I'm bailing Kareem out. You worry about finding Joshua and getting the real story about what happened."

She hurried to the door.

"Wait!" Roland called out. "I'll go with you."

"Roland, I've got this," she said.

"You're upset and shouldn't drive. Please, let me go with you."

Her father stepped forward and nodded his approval. "Let him drive, Patrice. It would make me feel better."

She clenched her teeth and sucked in a heavy breath. "Fine."

Roland placed a hand at her elbow and led her out of the house. The sound of her family's murmurs as they strategized a plan to find Joshua and cover the scandal of Kareem's arrest followed them before the door closed. This entire situation was a nightmare. She had no doubt Kareem wasn't involved, but she couldn't fathom Joshua agreeing to such a harebrained scheme. If this thing blew up—no, when it blew up—the backlash would hurt her father's career, and tarnish the Baldwin name. Combine that with Kareem's name tied to it, and the unexplained rumors of prostitution at his gentlemen's salon and things would be terrible.

She pressed a hand to her throbbing temple and tried to suppress the impending headache from all of the crap that happened today.

"Are you okay?" Roland asked as he maneuvered his car out of her parents' crowded drive. He reached over to gently pat her leg.

"I'm fine. I just want to get this entire situation straightened out." She shifted in the seat until he pulled his hand back.

"I can't believe Joshua would do something like this on his own," Roland said.

"I'd bet money it wasn't his idea."

"Then whose idea was it?"

She cut her eyes his way. "You can't possibly believe it was Kareem's idea?"

Roland shrugged but didn't take his eyes off the road. "I don't know, Patrice. I like Kareem because you love him. But after the things I heard tonight ... I just don't know if he's good for you."

"Oh please, not you too."

"I thought the prostitution rumors were something that would blow over, but they came up again tonight." Roland glanced at her quickly. "Then there's this robbery with Joshua. I know you want things to work out with him, but some people don't change. He was once in a gang. He's used to easy money and hurting people. Patrice, what if he just looked at you as his ticket to deeper pockets?"

"It's not like that."

"Then what is it like? Because he doesn't treat you like a fiancée," Roland said in a snappy voice. "I'm sorry. I didn't think it was my place to say anything. Not after I ignored your problems when we were together."

"You know what, forget it. Let's stop this conversation right now. I don't believe the rumors about the business, and I don't believe he's actually involved in this robbery."

"But—"

"No buts, Roland. I don't want to talk about it." She punched the armrest.

He gripped the steering wheel. "Fine. I won't say anything else."

"Thank you."

They were silent for the rest of the trip to the police station. She ran into the stone and brick building to the information desk.

"I'm here to bail out Kareem Henderson," she said to the officer behind the desk.

"Just a moment." The man said, then punched in something on the computer on his desk. "Attempted robbery. Give me a minute." He said and got up. Several minutes later he came back. "Looks like someone beat you to it. He's on the way out now."

Patrice frowned. "Who?"

The officer shrugged then answered the phone ringing on his desk. Patrice glanced around the crowded lobby. Her gaze landed on Sandra. Patrice sucked in a breath.

He called Sandra instead of me.

"What's wrong?" Roland asked.

"A lot," she said.

Another officer led Kareem out, and Sandra ran over to hug him. A sharp, jagged pain sliced through Patrice's heart.

Patrice stomped over to the two. "You called her. Instead of reaching out to me, you call your *brother's* fiancée. I thought you weren't in love with her."

Sandra's eyes widened, and she held up both hands. "I'm going to walk away and let you two handle this."

Kareem glared at Patrice. "That's the first thing you're going to say."

"What the hell else am I supposed to say, Kareem? You stormed out of the house, an officer comes and accuses you of helping Joshua with a robbery, and instead of reaching out to me you call Sandra?"

His eyes narrowed to slits. "For your information, I called David, who then let me know Sandra was in Charlotte for her job. Thank you for once again proving how little you trust me."

"I ... I thought ..." she stammered.

"Yeah, I know what you thought. Just like you thought the worst of me earlier. Just like you and your family probably believe I would convince your teenage nephew to participate in the dumbest robbery scheme ever."

"No, I don't believe that."

Kareem looked over her shoulder, and his jaw hardened. "Just like you thought it was okay to come bail me out with him by your side."

Patrice ran her hands over her face. Her heart twisted into a figure eight knot, and she didn't know where to start to untangle things.

"Kareem, I'm sorry." She dropped her hands. The hard, flat look of his dark eyes tightened the knot in her chest. "I was worried, and when I saw her I got jealous. I know earlier tonight was ... royally screwed up, but if we just stop and talk about things—"

"Why didn't you tell me about the bulimia?"

Patrice's mouth fell open. Her skin tightened, and the air in the room burned in her chest. "You know about that?"

Some life returned to his eyes in the form of pain and betrayal, both of which cut her deeply. "Yes. The problem is, why didn't I hear about it from you?" He took a step forward, his body vibrating with anger. "Why didn't the woman I trusted with my secrets not care enough to trust me with hers?"

Patrice licked her lips and tried to think of a good enough reason, but they all rang hollow. "I was embarrassed," she whispered.

An angry, bitter smile twisted his lips. "You were embarrassed. Yeah. That's cute." He took a step back and shook his head. "I'm done talking. Let's cut our losses and move on."

"No." Her voice trembled. Patrice reached out to put her hand on his arm.

Kareem pulled back. "Yes. I'm tired of playing your thug boyfriend. You've got the perfect guy for you right over there. One you can trust, because obviously you don't trust me."

He brushed past her and strode over to Sandra. Sandra gave Patrice a wary look, but Kareem shook his head and headed for the door. Sandra followed, but threw a glance over her shoulder. Patrice's heart shattered. He'd walked out of her life, and she had no one to blame but herself.

CHAPTER 30

"So, you want to tell me what that entire scene was about?" Sandra glanced at him from the corner of her eye.

Kareem twisted in the passenger seat of her small SUV and stared out the window. "No."

"Well, I think you need to tell me something. I thought things were going pretty good with you up here with her so much. You told your mom you like her. Now I'm bailing you out of jail, and she's spouting off you're in love with me. Sorry, Kareem, but you need to explain."

Kareem ran a hand over his face. Irritation tightened his skin and made him want to scream. Today had turned into a colossal mistake of epic proportions.

"For you to call David must mean things got bad," Sandra said in a softer, less scolding tone.

"I called David because there was no way I would ask my parents to bail me out of jail again, and Aaron is out of town."

"Fine, David was your last resort, but you still owe some type of explanation. Come on, Kareem, talk to me."

He let out a loud sigh and leaned his head back on the seat. "I thought things were good with Neecie, but they aren't."

Several seconds passed. He hoped she let the subject drop.

"Aren't how?"

"I trusted her with things I haven't trusted with anyone else," he said. "Things I don't even like to think about I shared with her. And instead of trusting me in return, she automatically doubted me."

"Doubted you how?"

His neck tightened. Sandra was worse than the cop who'd interrogated him. "Someone accused me of something." He glanced at Sandra, noticed the twist of her lip and decided he might as well tell the rest of the story. "I'm up here opening my gentlemen's lounge." Sandra nodded. "Tonight was the soft opening and a player from the basketball team told Neecie I said he and other patrons could pay to sleep with my female employees."

Sandra sucked in a breath. "That's unbelievable."

"That's what I expected Neecie to say."

"Did she believe him?"

"She came and asked me about it. She didn't come right out and say she believed him, but the pissed off way she came at me said all I needed to know. She wasn't completely sure."

Sandra lifted a shoulder, and her hands slid back and forth on the leather wheel. "You're still discovering things about each other. It's only natural that she would ask you about something that important."

"But she should have known I would never take advantage or use my employees like that. She worked for me for a year, and I told her about what happened in jail. I shouldn't have trusted her."

Sandra's upper teeth toyed with her lower lip. "What happened in jail?" she asked softly.

"I don't want to talk about it." He wouldn't tell another person about what happened. "But that's not all. She kept things from me. Important things. I don't know if I can trust her."

"Okay." Sandra shook her head. "Look, I'm not excusing her. I know better than anyone that without trust a relationship can't work. But are you sure you two can't talk things out?"

"For what? Even if we were to work things out there's still the issue of her family. They come with more drama than I want to deal with. I chased her sorry-ass nephew to Panera to try and stop him from stealing a *tablet* from a guy advertising on the Internet. I'm the one who ends up accused of being a part of the crime."

"Why didn't you call Neecie and explain?"

"The Baldwin family screwed me over twice today. I didn't want to call and give them another chance to screw me over again." He let out a humorless laugh. "But she showed up and I got it anyway."

"I still don't know why she's so upset about me. She said you loved me. Kareem ..."

He groaned and pinched the bridge of his nose. "Don't worry. We both know that for a brief period of time, I thought ..." Kareem dropped his hand. "I considered what would have happened if you and David hadn't reconnected at that party. If maybe our first date would have turned to something more. But that was for a brief period. I'm happy for you and David." He pointed to her stomach. "Happy about the baby."

He meant the words. All the spinning emotions in his brain tonight and none included leftover longing or jealousy where David and Sandra were concerned. Just a bunch of damn hurt and discomfort over Neecie.

"So you aren't in love with me."

"No. I love Neecie." *Damn! Where the hell had that come from?* The words just spilled out. Pain followed them. Rip out your intestines and tie them like shoelaces pain. Pain around his heart, deep in his gut, pounding through his brain. He loved a woman he couldn't trust, a woman too far out of his league even if he could trust her.

"Oh, Kareem," Sandra said all soft and sappy.

"Stop. This thing I started with Neecie is done. We both knew it wouldn't last. I don't belong in her world. Her family barely tolerates me and is happy to point out that she deserves better. And after tonight, I can't trust any of them."

"But you love her. Kareem, that means something."

"It means I'm bad about choosing the women I care about." He gave her a meaningful look.

Sandra's brows knit together. "I understand you're mad, and maybe you and Neecie aren't destined to be together. But if you love her, and if you thought she was worthy enough to tell something you won't even talk to your family about, that's important. You deserve to be happy, Kareem. Don't throw happiness away at the first sign of trouble."

Kareem stared out of the window. Everyone told him he deserved to be happy, but whenever he thought he found something that made him happy things blew up in his face. The thought of being without Neecie filled him with regret, but regret was better than a lifetime of trying to prove to everyone, including himself, they belonged together.

• • •

All of the cars from the party were absent when Patrice and Roland arrived back at her parents' home. Her body felt heavy, weighted down with the knowledge things were over between her and Kareem. He'd trusted her, and she'd accused him of terrible things.

Roland came to her side and slid his arm around her shoulder. "Are you going to be okay?"

She was too tired to care about moving away. "I'll be fine."

"Despite what I said earlier, I'm not happy to see you and him split. Not if you're hurting."

Roland's words of comfort only grated her nerves. "Thanks, but I'll be fine." She picked up her pace toward the front door and eventually his arm fell away.

The people were gone, and the music had stopped. Fran along with several other staff members went through the house cleaning things up.

"Where are my parents?" she asked.

"In the study," Fran answered.

Patrice felt Fran's questioning gaze as she walked to the study. By now Fran would have heard the rumors. Patrice didn't doubt Fran believed Kareem guilty as much as the rest of the family. She entered the study to a deafening quiet. Her father sat behind his desk, his face pensive as he rubbed his chin. Her mother sat on the sofa comforting Melinda who cried silently, while Chad paced back and forth. They all looked up when she entered.

"Well," Chad said in a clipped voice. He stalked across the room to here. "Where is he?"

Patrice tightly crossed her arms over her chest. "He's not with me. His sister-in-law bailed him out."

"So he ran?" Chad said disgustedly.

"He didn't run," Patrice countered.

Roland stepped forward. "Do you blame him for running? Of course he's afraid of facing the family after what he did."

Patrice spun to face Roland. "He didn't do anything. We don't know the circumstances behind what happened tonight."

"I think we know enough," Roland said, looking to Chad.

She narrowed her eyes. "Back off, Roland."

Roland appeared startled by that. Good, he needed to be startled.

The study door burst open, and Joshua strolled in, his shirt untucked. His wide eyes scanned the room.

Melinda sprang from the couch, knocking Janice backwards. "Joshua!" She ran over and wrapped him in an embrace.

Chad hurried over and pulled her off the boy. "Where have you been?"

"I just went out," he said to his feet. "The party over already?"

Milton stomped around his desk. "That innocent act won't work on us. The police have already been here."

Joshua's eyes jumped up to his grandfather. "I came here because I thought I'd avoid them."

Chad scoffed. "So you're admitting to taking part in that robbery."

Joshua lowered his head. "I did."

Milton shook his head. "What were you thinking doing something so stupid?"

Joshua shrugged. "I don't know. It sounded like a cool idea."

Chad spun toward Patrice. "You see what your thug of a fiancé did? He convinced my son stealing was cool."

Joshua's head snapped up. "What? I don't need Kareem to convince me of anything. He screwed up the entire deal anyway. Showing up acting like the law or something."

Patrice stepped forward. "What really happened?"

"Nothing. Things would have gone fine if he hadn't butted in, trying to stop the entire thing. So we ran," Joshua said.

"You ran!" Patrice yelled. "Kareem was arrested. The people you tried to rob accused him of being a part of the robbery."

"What!" Joshua shook his head. "He should've just stayed at the party."

Chad grabbed Joshua's arm. "I want to know why you did it in the first place. Was it because of something he said? Did he make you think being a *thug* was cool?"

"No. He wouldn't even talk to me about his life in jail or the things he did while in the Runners." Joshua sounded disappointed. "I thought he was kind of lame for not sharing. It was John's idea to rob that guy."

Janice stepped up. "Joshua, why would you agree to something so stupid?"

Again, Joshua shrugged. "I don't know."

Chad shook his head. "It wasn't cool. If it weren't for the police chief insisting this be handled quietly, your antics would be all over the news. You've threatened your grandfather's career, my credibility, and hurt your plans for the future."

Joshua's brows drew together. "It's no big deal. We'll cover things up."

Chad pushed Joshua back, making the teen stumble. "First, we're calling our lawyer. Second, we're going to the police station to clear Kareem's name. After that, I'll deal with you personally."

Patrice relaxed. "Thank you, Chad."

Chad glared at her. "I don't like him, but I won't let him ... you, suffer for Joshua's idiotic mistake." He pulled out his cell phone and dialed.

Joshua looked her way. "I'm sorry, Aunt Neecie."

The use of the nickname only brought pain to her heart. She and Kareem were really over.

"Don't do anything like this again," she said. Her eyes burned with tears, and she rushed out of the study. The thought of going to the room she'd shared with Kareem only intensified the pain in her chest. Instead she walked through the family room to the terrace.

"Tonight's been crazy." Roland's voice came from behind.

She closed her eyes and took a deep breath. She didn't want to deal with him right now. "It was."

"No one will blame you for believing Kareem was involved in the robbery."

"I didn't believe he was."

"Still, the guy isn't perfect. There's still the situation with the prostitution in the lounge."

Patrice spun to face him. "I don't believe he said that either. Kareem would never take advantage of the women who work for him. Someone else spread the rumors."

"You can't honestly believe that."

"I do. In fact, Kareem thinks you're behind it."

Roland scoffed and looked away. He quickly licked his lips and stared up at the stars. "That's preposterous."

Patrice's eyes narrowed, realization hitting hard. "You did do it."

"Don't be crazy, Patrice." He licked his lips again and avoided eye contact. His tell.

"I can't believe you'd betray me like that, Roland. I trusted you, and you lied about Kareem and tried to sabotage his business."

Roland finally looked at her. Anger in his eyes. "What did you expect me to do, Patrice? You come home after five years engaged to a former gang member. You deserve so much more than that."

"That's not for you to decide."

"I care about you and don't want to see you hurt." He took her hand in his. "Patrice, I still love you. I never got over you. I want us to have another chance. This time I'll do better."

She snatched her hand away. "I'd never be with you again. Not after this. I was willing to forgive you for ignoring my obvious pain when we were younger, but this is outright deceit. I could never trust you."

"But you can trust that thug?"

"Kareem isn't a thug. He cares about his employees, his family, me. No, he's not suave and polished, but he also isn't fake. Which is more than I can say for you. Get out, Roland, and don't bother calling me again."

Roland's lips pressed into a thin line. He lifted his chin and sneered down his nose at her. "Fine, go with your hoodlum if you want. After tonight he's through anyway. Between the rumors and the arrest no one who's anyone will go to his lounge. You could do better."

"You wouldn't be better. And despite your influence, Kareem isn't through. He's more of a man than you'll ever be, and because of that, he will succeed."

Roland sucked his teeth and spun on his heels. His exit left her with another regret: putting her trust in the wrong person.

CHAPTER 31

Kareem stepped out of the cab and stared at the front of the Baldwin mansion. He sucked cold winter air in through his nose and let it out in a long exhale. Get in and out of the house with minimal interaction with the family. That was the plan. Arriving at five a.m. on Sunday morning should assure him of that. If Fran would let him grab his things and go without sounding the alarm that the evil former fiancé was there, he'd be out of the house and on the way to Columbia before the family realized he'd been there.

With determined steps, he strode to the front door and used the key Neecie made for him rather than ring the bell. The foyer was quiet; no trace of the party from the night before remained. He quickly crossed the room to the stairs.

"Kareem, wait," Chad's voice said from behind.

Damn! His foot was barely touching the second stair. Pressing his lips together he turned to face Chad, fully expecting the man to tell him again about how no good he was for Neecie.

"I'm just getting my stuff and getting out of here," Kareem said.

Chad came further out of the study and crossed the hall to the end of the stairs. The white button-up shirt he'd worn the night before beneath his suit was wrinkled and untucked. His pants had lost the crisp edge, and a shadow of a beard darkened his cheeks.

"There's no need for you to run away," Chad said. "Joshua confessed what happened last night. To us and to the police. Your name is cleared."

Kareem nodded stiffly. Internally he breathed a sigh of relief. "That's good to know."

"I want to say—" Chad stopped and ran a hand over his scruffy chin. He raised eyes lined with fatigue to Kareem's. "I want to thank you for trying to stop him. You were paying more attention to my son than I. If you hadn't shown up things could have gotten worse. If not last night then in the future. Thank you."

"How much trouble is he in?" Kareem asked.

"A lot, but that's why I pay my lawyer a ton of money. We'll get him out of as much trouble as we can."

Chad's weary expression and defeated tone tugged at Kareem's old guilt. Had his father felt just as worn down and beaten having to bail Kareem out of his troubles?

"I should have said something sooner." Kareem leaned against the bannister. "I saw the signs, but thought it best to stay out of your business."

Chad's mouth lifted in a tired grin. "I can't blame you. I did nothing to make you feel welcome in this family. I understand why you chose to stay quiet. The fact that you stepped in when things were getting out of hand speaks more for your character than mine." He stepped up and held out his hand. "You're a better man than I accused you of being."

Kareem took his hand, shook it, then dropped it quickly. Chad's acceptance was too little too late. If Joshua hadn't confessed, no one would believe he hadn't been a part of the robbery. He didn't fit in this family, and never would.

"I appreciate that." Kareem turned to go upstairs.

"Are you still leaving?" Chad asked.

Kareem faced Chad. "Yes. My deal with Neecie is up."

"Deal?"

"She asked me to come as her fake fiancé to keep you and the rest of the family off her back. In return, she helped me open my lounge. Now that things have turned out the way they have, I think it's best to move on."

"I don't understand."

"Why not? Isn't it what you accused us of from the start?"

Chad nodded. "True, but she loves you now. And I believe you care for her."

"You said I treated her like a whore."

"I never should have said that. I thought Roland was better for her, but learning he spread the rumors about you proved yet again I'm not a good judge of character."

Kareem's eyes narrowed. "He confessed to that?"

"Yes, last night."

Kareem scoffed, and he yearned for five minutes alone with that prick. "He better hope I never see him."

"Doubtful you will. If you and Patrice choose to stay together, and I hope you do, you won't have to worry about seeing him because of us."

Kareem nodded, then turned and walked up the stairs, no longer interested in Chad's weak attempt to mend fences. That fence was broken and run over with a tractor from hell. Roland's confession did little to make him feel better. He'd known all along Roland was behind the rumors. All to get closer to Neecie.

He braced himself to enter the bedroom and see her. Thoughts of the nights they'd spent making love in that room sent warmth straight to his heart. Seeing her in bed would only make walking away harder. He still wanted her. That was some shit that wouldn't just go away. But they didn't belong together.

He opened the door and instantly looked to the empty bed. No sooner had relief that he might not face her swept through his chest did the door to the bathroom open. She flipped off the light and came into the room. Two steps in, she noticed him and froze. Her hand came up to the smooth cinnamon skin exposed above the neckline of the white tank top she wore. A pair of red pajama pants hugged her curves so well his hand flexed with the need to slide down the back and cup her luscious backside.

"You came back," she said in a quiet voice that didn't hide her hope.

"Only to get my things." His throat seemed tight, constricting to hold back words he couldn't say. *I still want you. Let's make this work. I want to trust you again.*

"Oh ... I thought you were staying." She crossed her hands beneath her breasts. Her foot twisted on the floor.

The cute action sent desire thrumming through his body. "Our deal is up. The lounge will open next week. Your family is off your back. There's no need to pretend anymore."

She swallowed hard, her chin rose, and fire flashed in her eyes. "Pretend. We were pretending?"

"Yes. Pretending we could make this thing real between us."

Her eyes shone, maybe with tears, but she spun away and stalked to the balcony. A vision of her straddling him in the afternoon sunlight flashed in his brain. He cleared his throat to mask the groan rising.

"You said you wanted to try."

"That was when I thought I could trust you." Her shoulders flinched with his direct words. But they both needed to hear it. "Yesterday proved I can't."

"I never believed you robbed those people." She spun and faced him. Trust was written all over her face.

"But you accused me of calling Sandra for the wrong reasons."

"Why didn't you call me?"

"Because earlier in the day you actually believed I would prostitute out my employees."

She closed her eyes and groaned. "I didn't believe it, not really."

"It didn't seem like a *not really* accusation in your voice."

"I know. Paul threw me off when he accused you. Kareem, I'm sorry."

"Okay, then why didn't you tell me the truth about the bulimia?"

Neecie swallowed hard. "I didn't want you to think I was weak."

"Why would I think that?"

"Because you've been through so much and survived. Here I am, the rich kid so pressured by her life she decided to throw up after every meal."

He stalked forward. "You don't think I would've understood?" He slapped his chest with his palm. "The rich kid who joined a gang because he was bored. I wouldn't have thought you were weak, Neecie. I would have realized you had your own flaws, but you overcame them. I see your strength."

"We made our mistakes. But that doesn't mean we can't try to move forward."

Kareem's heart raced in his chest and sweat trickled down his back. He fought back the need to reach out for her. She said she had his back, and he'd believed her. But history taught him people didn't change. Trusting her would only hurt him in the long run. "I meant it when I said things were over. We had our fun. Let's not get sappy about ending this."

Her wide eyes blinked several times. Neecie looked at him, then the floor and the door. Crossing her arms, she took a deep breath then finally met his gaze again. "If that's how you feel." She used her thumb to wipe her eye. "Then maybe this is for the best." She stalked past him. The scent of her perfume sent another shot of need through him. Kareem's hand shot out to take her arm, and his thumb slid over her soft skin.

Her large, loving eyes stared up at him, hopeful and wary at the same time. He pulled her closer, until her breasts brushed his chest. Her body trembled.

He lowered his head to kiss her, but she turned away. "Don't. If we're really over ... just don't. I'm not Misty or one of the freaks from the Runners. I won't be your off and on lover after we break up. I deserve more than that."

Kareem's hand dropped away, and he took a step back. He hadn't thought, only gone for what he wanted. Which would take him down the road he'd already traveled. Wanting Neecie wasn't the same as trusting her.

"I won't take long," he said in a rough voice.

"Good," she replied then strode out the door.

CHAPTER 32

Kareem leaned against the wall outside of the club in the seedy part of Columbia and took a drag from his cigar. After being there for thirty minutes he was ready to go. The music grew louder as the door opened to let in more partygoers. His cell phone vibrated in his pocket. Pulling it out he saw his friend Omar's number on screen. Probably looking for him in the crowd of people inside.

"Yeah?" Kareem answered.

"Where you at?" Omar yelled over the pounding music. "Misty is in here, and she's looking for you."

Kareem cringed. Misty was the reason he'd hurried out of the club after spotting her inside. He'd come out with Omar for the sole purpose of forcing himself to forget about Neecie and find another woman to distract him. But the thought of touching anyone other than her turned his stomach.

"I'm outside smoking. I'll be back in in a minute." He ended the call and slid the phone back into his pocket.

If he went back inside he knew what would happen. Misty would ask where he'd been, then suggest they go back to his place, and they'd spend the night having the rough and wild sex that cemented their previous relationship. This used to be his life, the way he occupied every weekend since getting out of jail, back when he didn't think he'd had a chance at or deserved a happy life.

He pushed away from the wall and stubbed out the cigar on the heel of his shoe. Instead of enjoying himself the thought of what would happen if he went back in churned his gut. Forcing himself to go back to his old life felt like punishment. Exactly what Neecie accused him of doing. Punishing himself for participating in the carjacking, going to jail, wanting to kill Cide. He didn't want to punish himself anymore.

Pulling out his cell phone, he didn't stop to think before calling David. He walked away from the club toward his motorcycle.

David answered on the forth ring. "What the hell, Kareem? It's after midnight."

"It's still early. Look, I'm calling a family meeting."

"What?" Some of the grogginess left David's voice.

"My house in thirty minutes."

The sound of Sandra's voice in the background drifted through the phone. "Hold up. Tonight? What brought this on?"

"I need to talk," Kareem said. He hung up on David then dialed Aaron's number.

"Yo, Kareem, what's up?" Aaron said, a lot more chipper than David.

"Where are you?"

"I got back in this afternoon. Now I'm up playing Madden online with some guy out of Nevada who's kicking my ass." In the background the sounds of the video game played.

"I'm calling a family meeting. My place in thirty."

"Whoa, seriously?" Aaron sounded distracted. "Shit, Kareem you caused me to throw an interception."

"Forget that. I need to talk." He hung up from Aaron.

When he got into his car, he put the phone in the cup holder. Then picked it up again and called Fredrick. Hell, if he was going to get advice on relationships, he might as well call his newest brother too.

• • •

Thirty minutes later, his brothers arrived—David in pajama pants and a t-shirt beneath his tan leather coat, Aaron dressed in wrinkled jeans and a button-up, his wireless headphone around his neck, and Fredrick in a pair of khakis and a sweater. Except for Aaron, they looked tired and confused by the late night interruption.

"Follow me," Kareem said and walked toward the kitchen. He grabbed a bottle of Crown Royal off the counter and four mismatched shot glasses from the cabinet. He firmly set the bottle in the middle of the kitchen table, followed by the shot glasses. Aaron, David, and Fredrick all exchanged looks.

"Sit," Kareem said. He pulled out one of the four chairs at the table and dropped into one.

David took a step forward. "Look, Kareem, you said you needed to talk and called all of us over here in the middle of the night. What's going on?"

Kareem popped the top of the bottle and poured a shot into each glass. "Sit down. I do need to talk, but I'm going to need a drink before I do that."

Again, the three guys exchanged looks before Aaron slid out a chair and plopped down next to Kareem. Fredrick took the seat opposite Kareem, and David sat to his left. Kareem slid the full glasses to each of them.

"Drink." He lifted his glass and held it out. Slowly, his brothers lifted theirs and clinked their glasses with his. Kareem downed his shot. "I need to tell you what happened in prison."

Fredrick coughed in the middle of his shot. David slowly lowered his back to the table. Aaron gulped the shot and slammed the glass on the table.

"We're ready to listen," Aaron said.

Kareem nodded, filled his glass again, and told them what he'd told Neecie. When he got to what happened with Cide his brothers each took another shot.

David cleared his throat after Kareem finished. "You didn't lie about needing to drink to tell us."

"I didn't tell you because I want any sympathy. I just needed you all to hear the entire story before I go on." He twirled the shot glass between his hands. "For years I carried that entire situation around with me. The guilt I mean. I wanted Cide dead, but instead I let Tim do it and take the blame. He told me to live, that I didn't deserve to let my mistakes ruin my life. I didn't think I had. I opened my business, tried not to disappoint my family again."

David sat forward. "Talking to us and letting us know what was going on, or allowing us to help, isn't disappointing."

"I get that," Kareem said. "But I thought I had to do things on my own to prove myself. I didn't understand why everyone said I deserved to be happy when I wasn't. I was angry at myself, the situation I put myself in, what happened to me. I didn't think I deserved to be happy."

Aaron poured another shot, but didn't drink it. "Now you think differently?"

Kareem glanced at his brother and nodded. "I do. That time with Neecie, even though it wasn't supposed to be real—"

Fredrick held up a hand. "Wait, I thought you two were real?"

Kareem shrugged. "Nah, it was just a front." He briefly went into their arrangement.

After Kareem finished, Fredrick nodded and watched Kareem over the rim of his glasses. "But you fell in love."

Kareem shifted in his seat, not ready to admit to the emotion he couldn't believe had taken over his heart. "I won't say all that. I like her. A lot. I still want her, but I don't know if I can trust her."

"Why not?" Aaron asked.

He told them about the soft opening and the fiasco of the rest of the night. Then about her keeping the bulimia a secret. "I mean, I told her everything, and she held back. And she doubted me so easily."

David slid the bottle across the table to refill his shot glass then passed the bottle over to Kareem. "But you admit that by the time you got to her parents' house she seemed to have realized her mistake."

"Before that really," Kareem said. "When we were talking. But I was so pissed that she'd even considered it."

"Look at it from her end. A celebrity comes in and tells her some crap like that. Of course she's going to ask you about it."

"It's more than that. The whole thing with her ex and her family."

Fredrick laughed. "Ex-boyfriends and family come with the package, man. You have to deal with all of that if the woman is worth it."

Aaron looked at Fredrick, his best friend since grade school. "So you're dealing with us because of Janiyah."

Fredrick held up the shot glass. "Family meetings in the middle of the night where I get buzzed with her brothers. Yes, all for Janiyah."

Aaron refilled Fredrick's glass. "That's because you're a lightweight."

"Men who don't drink typically are," Fredrick said. He'd only had two shots before sliding his glass away. "Kareem, you've got to learn to work through all of the differences to make a relationship work. The good, the bad, the moments of distrust, the moments of uncertainty, they're what make you stronger. So she kept back some of her issues, but I don't think it was malicious. Maybe she was just as afraid to reveal her problems as you were. And after digesting everything you told her, she might not have wanted to up the ante by throwing in an eating disorder."

David leaned back in his chair. "Think about this, Kareem. I went ten years without the woman I wanted, and my screw up was a lot worse than what either of you did. Don't let time pass when you can fix things. I say go after your woman."

Fredrick nodded. "I pushed Janiyah away for too long. Relationships are hard; you have to continue to work. We aren't perfect together all day, but every day I'm with her is. If you feel that way about Patrice you've got to go for it."

Kareem spun the empty glass then looked at Aaron who shrugged. "Hey, I've never pined for a woman," Aaron said. "But when I want a particular woman I don't let the opportunity pass. If you want Neecie, go get her."

Kareem thought about going the next ten years without Neecie, or even longer the way Fredrick had with Janiyah. The idea of possibly seeing her and not having her made him uncomfortable, and the idea of never seeing her again seemed unreasonable. He wanted her. He did deserve to be happy. He wanted to be happy with her. He loved her.

"Nothing I said tonight leaves this room. Understand?" He gave each man a hard stare and didn't look away until they nodded their agreement.

"And as for the lounge," David said. "I know Lucas Perry, the star running back for the Carolina Panthers. He's got more pull in the city than Paul, and if he likes your place, you're set."

Kareem raised a brow. "How do you know him?"

David gave a cocky grin. "I sold him a car once. We hit it off, and I hit him up whenever I'm in Charlotte."

"And I know several successful accountants in the area," Fredrick said. "Many work at some of the larger firms. I'll put in a word for you."

Aaron tapped his glass on the table. "Believe it or not, I hang out with the son of Raul Miles, the COO of Omeris Bank. I'll tell him to check out your place."

Kareem stared at them, stunned. "I had no idea you all had hook ups."

David shrugged. "You never asked. I know we've had our differences, but you're our brother and we love you. We're your family, and we'll do whatever it takes to support you, Kareem."

Words stuck in Kareem's throat. Never had he imagined having such strong support from his brothers. He looked at each man at the table and felt a bond stronger than anything he once thought he would only get from the Runners. Everything he needed was right here in front of him. Everything except Neecie.

"Then maybe you three can help me with one more thing." He tugged on the edge of his black t-shirt. "There's something else I need to change before getting Neecie back."

CHAPTER 33

Patrice zipped closed the suitcase on the bed. She let out a sigh and looked around the room. She was struck, as she had been for the last few weeks, by how empty the space seemed without Kareem there with her.

She shook her head with the hopes of driving away another round of the *If only I'd done this* thoughts that had paraded through her brain ever since he walked away. What could have been different didn't matter. He was gone. She wouldn't pine away over what went wrong.

"All packed I see." Janice's voice came from the door.

Patrice turned toward her mother who leaned against the doorframe, a slight frown on her beautiful face.

"At least this time I actually get to see you pack up and leave," Janice said.

A twinge of guilt tugged at Patrice's insides. She didn't regret leaving her family years ago, but she was sorry she hadn't explained to her parents why.

"I'm not going far," Patrice said and tugged the suitcase off the bed onto the floor. She'd signed a lease on an apartment in Concord on the northern end of the city. Going back to Columbia was out of the question, so she'd begrudgingly accepted a position with Lorelei's modeling agency—after putting her foot down about not accepting any flack about her weight.

"Do you need help taking the rest of your things?" Janice asked.

"No, I only had a few items of clothes, and Fran arranged to have movers bring over the bed later. Thanks again for letting me have it."

Janice shrugged. "I wish you'd let us get the rest of your furniture."

"I can handle it, Mother. But I do appreciate the offer."

Janice walked into the room and stared around as if she too realized it felt too empty. "Are you going to Kareem's opening?"

Patrice sucked in a breath through her nose and gripped the suitcase handle. Her father had reported Kareem was indeed back in town and working with his brothers on the delayed opening of his lounge. While she was glad the brothers had reconciled and Kareem hadn't let go of his dream, a part of her mourned the loss of not being there to celebrate with him.

"Is it today?"

"It is," Janice answered, her tone saying she was aware Patrice knew the lounge opened today.

"No. Now that we're over it's better to just limit contact." Better for her heart anyway.

Janice ran her hand over the footboard of the bed. "I gave him a hard time when he first arrived. We all did. I didn't like the way he looked at you. So intense, as if he couldn't believe he had you." Janice shrugged. "I thought that was because he couldn't believe he'd snuck his way into the family. By the time I realized it was because he loved you, it was too late."

Patrice's throat constricted. If only he had. "We weren't real. You imagined that." The pain of those words seared her heart.

"I'm not so sure." Janice pulled a white card out of her back pocket. She came around the bed and handed it to Patrice. "This came for you this morning."

Patrice took the note out of her mother's hand. On the front in bold black script were the words "You're Invited." Her heart jacked up on speed, not at the basics of an invitation inviting her to the grand opening of Kareem's lounge, but instead at the straight, tight handwriting on the left side of the card.

Neecie,

I hope want *need to see you. Please come to the opening.*

Kareem

She sucked in several quick breaths as her skin tightened. He wanted to see her, personally invited her. Hope that the invitation meant he wanted to try again sent trembles through her.

"Are you going?" Janice asked.

Patrice gripped the card and met her mother's hopeful eyes. She ran her tongue over dry lips and nodded. When Janice smiled, she couldn't help but grin back.

"Yes."

She quickly changed into a gold, knee-length skirt and black turtleneck. Her kinky curls were somewhat tamed into a puff at the top of her head. Her hands shook as she walked up the sidewalk to the front of Kareem's lounge. Pressing one trembling hand to her stomach, Patrice hoped to stop the butterflies from playing ping pong there.

Kareem could have invited her only because she'd helped so much. Maybe he still wanted them to be friends. Or he could think this was a good way to ask her to still cut hair for him. The personal invitation didn't mean he wanted her again. But her pounding heart wanted him to.

She crossed the threshold into the waiting area. The surprisingly full waiting area. Just as crowded as the night of the soft opening. Patrice quickly scanned the room for Kareem. There were several men at the bar talking, some sitting in the dark leather chairs watching the flat screen televisions. Conversation drifted down the hall from the meeting rooms and cigar room. Pride swelled in her chest. He'd done it.

"May I help you?" the receptionist at the desk to the right of the door asked.

Patrice snapped her attention back to the woman behind the desk and cleared her throat. "Yes, I'm here to see Kareem. My name is Patrice Baldwin."

The woman smiled. "He said if you came to lead you directly to him." The woman stood and pointed toward the bar. "He's actually over there now."

Patrice frowned; she hadn't seen him at the bar. She turned that way again and made eye contact with Kareem's dark stare. Her heart spun like a ballerina, and her jaw fell open. Kareem wore a white button-up shirt tucked into grey pants. The bright color brought out the richness of his skin. The dreads were gone, replaced with a stylish fade, thick and curly at the top and tapered to precision on the sides.

He strode her way, but she quickly hurried to meet him halfway. "What did you do to your hair?"

A sexy, sheepish grin came across his face, and he ran a hand over the back of his head. "I cut it."

"You cut it?" Her voice squeaked. Then she burst into tears.

"Whoa, wait, hold on, Neecie." His warm hands clasped her shoulders while she bawled as if someone had run over her pinky toe. "Why are you crying? It's my hair."

"Because I loved your hair," she said in a trembling voice. She wiped the tears from her eyes, but when she looked at him they flowed again. "I can't believe you cut it."

The corner of his mouth lifted. "I had to, Neecie. I started them for the wrong reason. You remember what I told you."

She wiped her eyes with the back of her hand again. "To fit into the gang."

He nodded, a sad look in his dark eyes. "It was time to let that guy go."

She sniffed and pressed the back of her hand to her nose. She glanced around the room. The conversations had quieted as several people watched her; the fool who burst into tears over a hair cut in a high-end barber shop.

"I guess I can understand that," she said. She opened her purse and searched for a tissue. A handkerchief appeared before her eyes.

With wide eyes she looked back at Kareem who held it out to her. "Here."

"Thank you." She took the white cloth and wiped her eyes.

"I need you to really understand," Kareem said. He put a hand on her waist and pulled her to the side. The strength and heat of his touch made her body shiver. "Understand why I had to do this." He pointed to his head.

"You're letting go of the past." Including the past he shared with her. The pain sent another bout of tears, but thankfully no sobs, streaming down her cheeks.

"I'm letting go of the guilt. It's time for me to finally come to terms with what happened. I didn't force Tim to stand up for me, but if he hadn't I wouldn't be here. I wouldn't be living my dream. I wouldn't have met you." He swallowed hard and shifted on his feet. "Loved you."

Patrice's jaw dropped again. "Loved me."

"Love you. Neecie, I'm sorry. I backed out of this relationship at the first sign of trouble. I understand why you questioned me, why you waited to tell me about your past. That night with Joshua was so crazy, I let my jealousy of you coming to check on me with Roland justify lashing out instead of listening."

She shook her head. "It was my fault. You trusted me, and I should have trusted you. I know, knew, you would never do something like that. I don't blame you for being angry."

"Being angry, and breaking up with you are two different things. Letting you go wasn't for the best. It was my overreaction to not knowing how this relationship stuff works. But it's time for me to live. I want to live with you. I want to be with you. The hair, the clothes," he tugged on his white shirt, "that was all for me. I had to come to terms with who I wanted to be before I stepped to you again. You deserve a man that isn't hung up on things that can't change."

Kareem's strong hand gripped her waist, and he pulled her close. The heat from his body, and the scent of his cologne turned her legs into water. "I'm not living for the past anymore. It's only about now, the future. Let's make this thing real. Not for a moment, not just in the bedroom, but for a lifetime. It may take that long for me to learn everything about compromise, and intimacy, but I'm willing to take as long as necessary to make you happy." He pressed her body against his hard body. "Do you love me too?"

She stared into his handsome face. So different without the dreads she'd loved, but sexy, open, alive.

"Yes, I love you too, Kareem. I don't want anyone else. Just you."

He grinned, lowered his head, and kissed her. Slow and easy, his tongue gliding across hers, and without hesitation. Heat spread to every corner of her body. Her arms wrapped around his neck and she leaned into him.

Someone clapped and whistled. She broke away and peered over Kareem's shoulders into the smiling face of his younger brother Aaron. David stood next to him grinning. The rest of the people in the place watched, smiling, some clapping. Many she recognized from her father's social club, a few others as football players.

"It's about time," David said. "He was miserable without you."

Aaron nodded. "Give him hell."

Kareem leaned down and kissed her cheek. When she looked at him the corner of his mouth quirked in the sexy grin she loved. "Welcome to my family, Neecie." He tightened his hold on her. "Welcome into my life. For real this time."

ABOUT THE AUTHOR

Synithia Williams has published over twenty-five novels since 2012. Her novel, A Malibu Kind of Romance was a 2017 RITA® finalist, she is a 2018 and 2019 African American Literary Award Show nominee in Romance. Her books were listed as Amazon Editor's "Best Book of the Month" in Romance. Reviews of Synithia's books can be found in Publisher's Weekly, Library Journal, Woman's Word, Kirkus and Entertainment Weekly. Synithia lives in Columbia, South Carolina with her husband and two kids. You can learn more about Synithia by visiting her website, www.synithiawilliams.com[1].

---

1. http://www.synithiawilliams.com

EXCERPT FROM FROM ONE NIGHT TO FOREVER

Aaron Henderson's stomach kept up the angry growl it had started twenty miles down the road as he walked across the packed parking lot of Momma's Kitchen. The hotel clerk had recommended the restaurant after Aaron had parked his big rig, Bertha, and checked in. The lively sounds of a band filtered from the restaurant's closed door. The name *Momma's Kitchen* in pink neon letters glowed from a sign over a front porch. When the clerk had mentioned the place, Aaron remembered his friend Reggie Holmes saying something about the restaurant and the good food.

Reggie was the reason Aaron was in Resilient, Tennessee. After two years of talking about merging their trucking companies, Aaron and his old college friend were actually taking the steps to do it. Both successful in their own right, the merger would make their company a leading contender for transportation in the Southeast.

Not bad for a college dropout. A grin spread across Aaron's lips. Many people had sneered and thought he was crazy when he'd sold all his belongings, cashed out the savings account his parents had set up for him, dropped out of Appalachian State, and bought Bertha ten years ago. Hell, he hadn't thought his spur-of-the-moment decision to drive big rigs and see the country would turn into running his own business, and four years ago when he'd hired his first driver he hadn't imagined he'd be on the verge of doubling the size of his company. Henderson and Holmes Trucking would one day be a powerhouse in the freight industry. He not only believed that; he was certain. Things always worked out for him.

A couple came through the front door, increasing the sound of the music and bringing out the savory smells of good food. Aaron's stomach growled in appreciation, and he jogged up the stairs and through the front door. He quickly scanned the busy seating area. Tables covered the black-and-white-checkered floor and were filled with couples, some families, and groups of guys. A young woman belted out Tina Turner's "What's Love Got to Do With It," accompanied by a band in the far right corner. A long wooden bar with silver and black stools ran along the left wall.

Aaron turned to the hostess standing behind a podium right near the door. "How long is the wait?"

The hostess smiled, emphasizing a pair of cute dimples. Her ponytail swung to the side as she checked the list. "Umm...about twenty minutes. Unless you want to sit at the bar."

She met his eye and the corner of her friendly smile went up a little more with interest. Aaron grinned and his eyes flicked down to the abundance of cleavage in the white button-up shirt straining to contain her blessings. Cute, definitely, with golden tan skin and shiny dark hair, but he guessed she was in her early twenties. Not too young for him, since he was only thirty, but the early twenties came with drama and he didn't need more drama.

"I'll wait at the bar, sweetie, thanks." He winked and the hostess licked her full lips.

Aaron chuckled to himself and rubbed the stubble on his chin. He strolled to the bar and grabbed an empty seat in the middle. The female bartender scrambled from the back holding a tray filled with glasses in her arms. She dropped the tray with a rattle on the shelf behind the bar, wiped her forehead with the back of her hand, and then waved his way.

"I'll be with you in just a second," she said and hurried to fill two of the new glasses with beer from the tap and gave them to two men sitting at the end. After chatting and laughing with them, she made her way down the bar to him.

"What can I get you?" She looked up from her notebook and her friendly smile tilted up with interest.

She was another cutie, more his age, and with enough curves to cushion a man for days. She wore the same tight white button-up and black pants as the hostess and other waitresses he'd spotted. No wonder Reggie told him to check out this place. The women were beautiful.

"I'll start with a Budweiser and a menu." He glanced at the name tag on her chest. "Monique."

"You got it, handsome." She winked and handed him a menu from beneath the bar, then sashayed over to fix his drink.

The woman on stage finished her song and the place erupted in cheers. The guy next to him whistled. "Another one, Kacey!"

The rest of the place joined in whistling and asking for more. Aaron raised a brow and watched as the performer waved a hand and shook her head.

"Come on, this is my night off." The smile on her face said she was loving the call for encores despite her words.

"One more. One more!" someone chanted.

"Fine, one more, then I'm going back to the bar. I'm supposed to be celebrating," she said with a laugh. "Not working."

The guy next to Aaron bumped him with his elbow. "She can celebrate with me, know what I'm saying?" The guy chuckled.

Aaron grinned and let out a light laugh. "I guess she's a local favorite."

"Oh, yes. Everyone loves Kacey. Good girl, but that doesn't mean I wouldn't mind being her surfboard for the night." He elbowed Aaron again. "Know what I'm saying?"

Aaron nodded. "Yeah, I get you."

The cute bartender came back with his beer. "Ready to order?"

Aaron barely glimpsed at the menu. "Just bring me the best thing in the place."

She flipped her waist-length hair over her shoulder and batted her long lashes. "I'm not on the menu."

Aha, so it was like that. Aaron checked her out again, appreciating the smooth brown skin and voluptuous curves. Her thick makeup wasn't his thing, nor the extra-long lashes, but that wasn't enough to make him not take interest.

You're here on business, not to get laid, he reminded himself. That could wait until he got things settled with the merger. But it didn't mean he couldn't lay the foundation for a future hookup with a little harmless flirting.

"That's too bad," he said with a smile. "I guess I'll have to compensate with a burger and fries."

She slid the notebook into the pocket of her apron and gave him another flirtatious look. "Coming right up." Her full hips swung suggestively as she sauntered over to put in his order. She gave another glance at him over her shoulder.

Business, man, business. He had enough female drama in his life right now. Too many glasses of champagne at his sister

Janiyah's wedding to his best friend, Fred, had contributed to Aaron making the monumental mistake of sleeping with Janiyah's best friend, Liz. The sex was good; the two—or three—hookups the organ below his belt agreed on later weren't bad, either. On the way up his oldest brother, Kareem, had called to say that Aaron's hookup with Liz had led Janiyah to believe Aaron and Liz were becoming serious.

At least the misinterpretation wasn't on Liz's end. They'd been on the same page with their friends-with-benefits relationship. He and Liz hadn't hooked up in the last three months. He hadn't been in town much, and she'd gotten back together with her ex-boyfriend, an architect she had an off-again, on-again relationship with.

The band revved up and the sounds of "Lady Marmalade" filled the place. The guy next to him drummed his hands on the bar. "I love it when she sings this," he said to Aaron.

Aaron nodded at the guy's enthusiasm. "Number-one fan" would be an understatement of the man's excitement. Aaron focused back on the woman who had the poor guy so enthralled.

His first thought was she was a little too skinny. He liked them like the bartender, but the songstress had perfect curves in just the right locations. Her face immediately drew him in. She wasn't classically beautiful—some would say her lips were too full or her cheeks too sharp—but that didn't prevent Aaron's heart from starting a crazy rhythm.

She swayed from side to side with the music. Her slim hips hypnotized him and the rest of the men in the crowd with their easy flow in dark jeans and tall black heels. A red tank top with a white heart with wings spread across her perfect rack, and dark straight hair brushed her russet brown shoulders. With each word and graceful movement she commanded the stage. Her voice belted out to perfection the suggestive lyrics with enough passion to have Aaron shifting in his seat.

Aaron tapped the guy next to him. "Hey, what's her name again?"

"Kacey," the guy said almost with idolization.

Kacey? He would've expected something more elaborate or flamboyant. Something more suited to the goddess onstage.

"Me and her used to hang out," the guy said. "I think I may try to rekindle that flame tonight. Know what I'm saying?" Another elbow to Aaron. "Show her why breaking up with me wasn't such a good idea."

Aaron shook his head. The guy's overuse of the elbow and "know what I'm saying" made Aaron think Kacey was smart for breaking things off.

Aaron picked up his beer without taking his attention off the woman onstage, the curvy bartender forgotten. Aaron brought the bottle to his lips and watched the seductive sway of Kacey's hips as she sang the Creole words every man wanted to hear from a beautiful woman. "Do you want to go to bed with me tonight?" Heat rose slowly up his body, an affirmative answer to her lyrical question.

No complications, remember?

Aaron pushed the thought aside. Talking to her a little wasn't the same as going home with her.

"Can I get you another drink?" Monique asked.

Aaron shook his head. "No, but you can send one over to her on my tab when she's done." He pointed to his stage goddess.

Monique cocked a brow and chuckled. "No offense, but you're the sixth person who's ordered my sister a drink tonight."

Aaron leaned on the bar. "Sister, huh? One of these guys in here special to her?"

Monique shook her head and leaned a hand on her hip. "Nope."

"And there are five guys ahead of me interested in getting her attention tonight?"

A smirk crossed Monique's features. "Yep."

Aaron raised a brow. "None of us stand a chance, huh?" He took another sip of the beer.

"She's the good sister. If you want some fun tonight, you might want to look elsewhere." Monique winked again, then went down the bar to tend to the other customers.

A smart man would follow the path of least resistance. One night stands and easy hookups were more his thing. Anything else lead to feelings, which lead to serious relationships followed soon after by the bad break up. Aaron was very familiar with bad breakups having been through one before. Bad because he'd chosen to walk away rather than accept at twenty-two he was ready for a long-term commitment. He'd broken up with Denise, the only woman he'd come close to loving, and lived his life since having fun and being free.

Aaron glanced back at the goddess onstage. Her gaze swept the room, caught his, jerked away, and then snuck back. An electric sizzle zoomed across his skin from the brief contact. Aaron smiled and brought the beer to his lips. One night of fun didn't mean a relationship. And he wasn't interested in the path of least resistance. He always preferred a challenge.

ALSO BY SYNITHIA WILLIAMS

HENDERSON FAMILY SERIES

Just My Type

Love's Replay

Making it Real

From One Night to Forever

CALDWELL FAMILY SERIES

Show Me How to Love

Love Me as I Am

Trust Me With Your Love

SOUTHERN LOVE SERIES

You Can't Plan Love

Worth the Wait

A Heart to Heal

HARLEQUIN KIMANI TITLES

A New York Kind of Love

Full Court Seduction

Overtime for Love

Guarding His Heart

His Pick for Passion

BOOKS AS NITA BROOKS

Redesigning Happiness

The Essence of Perfection